DEATH
OF AN
ANTIQUARIAN

DEATH
OF AN
ANTIQUARIAN

A MIA REID, ARCHAEOLOGIST, MYSTERY

ROSE KERR

To Gary, thanks for listening, plotting with me, and being there through it all.

Praise for Death of an Antiquarian

"With its well-drawn Canadian setting and fast-paced plot, *Death of an Antiquarian* is a must-read for cozy mystery fans. When an antiquarian and family friend dies under mysterious circumstances, archaeologist Dr. Mia Reid is compelled to dig into the gritty details of another murder, drawing the reader into the underworld of antique and artifact theft. I was invested from page one and can't wait to read the next installment!"—Kara Lacey, author of the Camera Club Mysteries

"*Death of an Antiquarian* kept me awake and turning pages. The characters are delightful, and the mystery is intriguing. I thought this was a fun book, and I highly recommend it."—Jackie Layton, author of Lowcountry Dog Walker Mysteries, Texas Flower Farms Cozy Mysteries, and Organized Crime Cozy Mysteries

"Stolen antiquities, counterfeit art, and murder. Mia Reid is back and finds herself in the middle of an investigation that's a little too close to home in *Murder of an Antiquarian*."—Heather Weidner, Author of the Pearly Girls Mysteries and the Jules Keene Glamping Mysteries

"A spectacular entry in the Mia Reid, Archaeologist Mystery series! *Murder of an Antiquarian* is a masterclass in plotting, offering a sophisticated and thrilling journey through the murky world of artifact smuggling, complete with satisfying twists and turns. A must read!"—Christina Romeril, author of The Killer Chocolate Shop Mysteries

"Equally intriguing and engaging as the first, book 2 in the Mia Reed

Archaeology Mystery series will pull you in right from the start. With a smart, savvy sleuth with a unique profession, interesting characters, and a compelling mystery, *Death of an Antiquarian* offers a fun, fresh spin on cozy mysteries."—Kylie Forsythe, author of *Murder at the Agency*, A Cassidy Blayne Mystery

Chapter One

Wednesday Morning

Mia pushed away from her desk and walked to the far wall of her office. She looked at the plans on the wall. In less than a week, this exhibit had to be ready. Marketing and promotion were well underway. Interest from all over Lakeview City was growing. Ticket sales were doing well. The artifacts were on loan from the Mexico City Museum. It was the first time the museum had loaned them out.

Mia tapped a pencil to her chin and examined the floor plans for the exhibit. They just needed a little tweaking. She made an adjustment to two of the display cases and stepped back to look at the plans again. That looked better. Patrons would have a bit more space to move around the exhibit.

Her cell phone rang with Gran's ringtone. A clear, light piano riff. She picked it up and smiled as she heard Gran's voice. "Mia, could you come with me to Timeless Treasures tonight? There's an event at the store, and I think you might find a few pieces for your apartment."

Gran never wasted time on the phone; she cut through all the pleasantries and got straight to the point.

"Sure, what time do you want to go?"

"Why don't we meet for dinner around five-thirty? The event starts at seven, but the doors open at six-thirty. I don't want to be late."

"That works. Do you want to meet at Syd's? It's close enough to the shop that we could walk."

"Perfect. I'll take a cab and meet you there."

"Great. It'll be nice to see you again."

"I'll talk to you then. Don't work too hard, dear." Gran hung up.

By the end of her workday, Mia was pleased with the work she'd done. The project she'd been working on, featuring artifacts discovered in the mid-twentieth century from Central America, was going to be displayed in a manner that allowed people to view them and to learn about them interactively. She still had to wrap up listening to the script for the displays. Photos would accompany the artifacts, showing how the archaeologists had discovered the objects, removed them from the ground, cleaned them, and catalogued them. The script would be read in several different languages, and the museum was fortunate to have translators who could do the work.

Mia hurried downstairs and got her bike out of the employee's lot. She put her helmet on, made sure her backpack was secured, and headed out. The bike paths in the city meant she had a fifteen-minute commute instead of thirty minutes sitting in traffic.

Stopping in the lobby of her building, she picked up her mail. Tossing the flyers in the recycle bin, she noticed an official-looking letter from a law firm in Chicago. Tucking the envelope in her bag, she took the elevator to the fourteenth floor and made her way to her apartment. It was a nice corner unit overlooking Lake Ontario.

She hefted her bike on the rack in the utility room, dropped her keys in the dish on the sideboard in the hallway, and toed off her shoes. In the kitchen, she poured herself a large glass of ice water and added a couple of lemon slices. She grabbed the envelope out of her bag, walked to the balcony doors, and sat in one of the comfortable patio chairs. After taking a long drink of water, she set the glass on the rattan table in front of the chairs. She opened the envelope and read the enclosed letter.

She read it twice, and the second time, tears welled up. Ethan Carter, one of her closest friends, had died a few months ago. It happened on their dig, on the Isle of Skye, and Mia had been instrumental in discovering who his killer had been. Ethan had left her his personal journals of the digs they'd both been on. It was such a wonderful gift.

Mia sent a text to Shelly, Ethan's widow, and her good friend.

Mia: Just received the lawyer's letter regarding Ethan's gift to me. I'm so touched.

Mia's phone rang a few minutes later. It was Shelly.

"I want to make sure you're okay with his bequest."

"I am. I wasn't expecting this."

"He wanted you to have the journals. I've packaged them up and will send them to you. I've made copies for Henry to have when he's older." Shelly sighed. "It's been a busy few months. How are you doing? How's the new job?"

"If Henry wants the originals, I'll gladly give them to him."

"Well, he's not old enough for them now, maybe when he gets older. Now, how are you? What's happening with work and Luke?"

Mia smiled. "Work is good. I'm settling into it. There's more to do than I originally thought, but nothing I can't handle. And Luke is coming back this weekend. He'll be here for at least two weeks. He's going to be training police on what to look for when dealing with thefts of artifacts. I'm looking forward to him being here again. I've missed him this past month."

"Do you think he'd move to North America?"

"That would be great. I know he's asked his supervisor to let him know if there's an opportunity for him to work in Canada. That's how this latest job came up. We'll see how things work this trip." Mia took a drink of water. "How are you and Henry coping?"

"We're okay. Henry's health is stable. The cancer hasn't returned. He's getting ready for school and looking forward to seeing his friends. The nightmares have stopped." Shelly paused and then said, "I'm going back to work. The university called and offered me a part-time position in the English department. I'm looking forward to returning to work. My parents are close by and are still helping me out with everything to deal with Ethan's death. Mom thought it would be good for me to get back into teaching again."

They chatted for a few more minutes. It was good to talk to Shelly. They'd been friends for a long time. Ethan's gift was something Mia would treasure.

Mia glanced at her watch. Time to get ready for dinner.

***

Wednesday Evening

Thirty minutes later, Mia and Gran were seated at their favorite table at Syd's. The restaurant offered a variety of pasta dishes. The server returned with their drinks and took their food order.

"Cheers." Gran raised her wine glass to Mia.

Mia smiled and raised her glass. "Cheers! What can you tell me about this event tonight?"

Gran swallowed her wine and set her glass down. "It's by invitation only, and everyone is permitted one guest. Tim organized this event a few weeks ago. I decided at the last minute to attend. He's got several nice pieces for sale that I'm looking at, and I thought there would be something for you as well. He's brought in some art déco pieces out of New York, and I know you like that era."

"I wonder what the price range is?"

"He's crafty. No prices were listed in the email or on the information sheet he sent. But the photos were exquisite."

The server arrived with their food.

While they were eating, Mia told Gran about Ethan's bequest.

"Well, that was kind of him. They'll mean a lot to you." Gran put her napkin down on the table.

They settled up the bill and walked to the antique store. It was a block down the street, and they took their time looking in the shop windows in the area. Most of the shops on this street were specialty shops. There were a few gift shops displaying works by local artists. One shop specialized in fibre arts. It had several colorful quilts in the window. The next store had artwork and ceramic wares made by local artists. Mia slowed down in front of this one. She admired the ceramic pieces. They were bright, and she had a few of them at home.

"Mia, they're having a sale." Gran pointed to the sign in the window.

"It looks like they're closing. Darn it. I liked this shop." Mia peered in the window. "I can't see anyone working."

"The sign says the sale starts this weekend, and everything has to go."

Mia pulled out her phone and made herself a note. "It was a cooperative. I wonder what the artists and craftspeople are going to do now. I'm going to check this out. I hope I have time this weekend."

They continued along the street. The other stores specialized in antiques of all kinds. All were closed for the day. Mia and Gran checked the window displays as they strolled by.

"That's Martha Jones's shop. It's All I've Got," Gran said. "I'm glad to see she's still in business. She was starting when I was selling my shop."

They strolled down to Timeless Treasures. A middle-aged woman wearing all black and a name tag that said Cheryl greeted them. Her chestnut hair was pulled back in a ponytail, and her fingernails painted a deep red. Her face was carefully made up, and her lipstick matched her nail polish.

She took their names and checked them off a list. "You can go right in. Mr. Fraser is in the store and will answer any questions you have."

They stepped in, and Mia noticed there were about twenty other people in the store. She wondered how many more were expected. The store appeared crowded. Mia spotted Alex Bennett across the room. Alex was Mia's best friend. Had been for as long as they could remember. Alex made sure Mia took time off to enjoy life and wasn't working all the time. She was also Tim Fraser's niece. Alex smiled and nodded at Mia as she chatted with a couple who were browsing a jewelry display. Alex wore a blue dress and heels. Mia winced at the thought of walking in the heels. Alex made it look effortless.

Mr. Fraser came up to them. "Marie, Mia. Thank you for coming. Are you in the market for anything in particular?" He was a slender man with a touch of gray at the temples of his dark brown hair. His brown eyes shone behind black-rimmed glasses. He wore a dark blue business suit with a soft blue shirt and a red tie. His hands were soft and carefully manicured.

Gran glanced up at him. "I'm looking for a mirror for my hallway. I'm not sure exactly what I want, but I'll know it when I see it."

"I have a few mirrors, a couple are here on this level, but I also have some in the loft. Mia, are you looking for something?"

"I'd love to find some classic art déco pieces. Depending on the size and price of course."

"Understandable. I have a variety in the shop. Both on the main floor and upstairs."

"I didn't realize there was a loft. Is that a recent addition?" Mia looked at the ceiling.

"Yes. I opened it up this spring. The space was being wasted. It didn't take a lot of work. Just added a floor, staircase, and a bit of electrical work."

"Do you own the building?" Mia asked.

"Yes. I've been here a long time. I'm happy I do. I've heard the rents in the area are going up, and shop owners are having to leave. They can't afford the increases." He glanced around the room.

"We won't keep you, Tim. We'll wander around, and if we see anything, we'll let you know." Gran put her hand on his arm.

"Excellent. Either I or Cheryl, my salesclerk, can help you. Oh, Steve can give you a hand as well. Danielle's husband, you know. He's taking an interest in the business." Tim walked to the front of the store, where Cheryl was greeting people.

Mia and Gran wandered through the store. Tim had organized the store into sections by antique type, age, and era. There were expensive items mixed in with less expensive stock.

"Mia, hi! Can I offer you some wine?"

Mia turned toward the woman's voice. "Danielle! How are you? It's been a while." Danielle was Tim's daughter and Alex's cousin. The three women had all gone to the same high school and university. They'd been friends for a long time.

"Yes, at least a couple of years. I'm in estate management at a bank downtown. Are you still in archaeology?" Danielle moved the cart holding the wine and glasses to the side.

"Yes, I'm working at the city museum. On a contract for a while. You remember my Gran, Marie Tremblay?"

"Of course. We spent lots of time at your house when we were in school."

Gran gave Danielle a hug. "You look wonderful. Marriage agrees with you."

"It does. We're expecting our first baby in the new year. Dad's looking forward to being a grandfather." Danielle smiled. "Here's Steve. He's helping Dad with some work in the shop."

Mia noticed Danielle's husband. He was almost six feet tall and still had an athletic build. He and Danielle had met on one of the golf courses in the city. Danielle had been an excellent golfer. Mia noticed they both looked tanned and relaxed. Danielle's black dress showed off her toned arms.

Steve nodded. "Nice to see you. I'm learning about the business and seeing where I can help Tim with his investments."

"That's right. Are you still in investment banking?" Mia asked.

"I am. I'm just helping Tim out on weekends and evenings when I have time."

"How are you enjoying the antique trade?" Gran asked.

There was a shout from the front of the store.

"What do you mean I can't come in? I helped build this damn store. Of course I can." The woman speaking looked to be in her late fifties.

"Oh no. Not again." Danielle said.

"Excuse me. I'll go see if Tim needs my help." Steve hurried to the front of the store.

Mia looked at the woman causing the commotion. She was as tall as Tim, about five feet eight inches, blond hair, and had a voluptuous figure. Her clothing was elegant, and she projected an air of authority. "Who is that?"

"That's my dad's first wife. They were married for a year, and then they split up. Not amicably, as you can see." Danielle shook her head. "She's been nothing but trouble. Even going to a lawyer and claiming she owns part of the store. There's no way she does. Dad's the one who did all the work."

The woman pushed her way past Cheryl, the store clerk, and strode up to Tim. "I told you I'd be back. And I am. I want what's mine, and I want it now."

Chapter Two

Wednesday Evening

Tim put his hands on his hips. "Barbara, lower your voice. I've told you not to come here again. You need to leave."

Steve stood next to Tim, arms crossed.

Barbara scanned the store. "Seems like there's a lot of people here. What are you doing?"

"Conducting business. Occasionally, I host an event where clients can come in to buy specially priced merchandise. It gives them the opportunity to browse and shop outside of normal shop hours."

Barbara moved her large black purse to her right shoulder and tucked her blonde hair behind her ear. "Seems as if this is something I should know about. After all, I am a silent partner."

Tim shook his head. "No, you aren't. I paid you what you had put into the business as part of our divorce settlement. Now I need you to leave immediately, or I'll call the police."

"You haven't heard the last of me. I want what's mine. You cheated me."

Steve grabbed her by the arm. Cheryl came up behind her and grabbed her other arm. "You need to leave. Now!" Steve pulled Barbara toward the door and shoved her out. Cheryl closed the door while Barbara scowled at them.

Mia saw Barbara raising her fist in the air and shaking it. Yelling at Cheryl. Cheryl opened the door and said something to her. Then she closed the door and locked it. Cheryl spoke to Steve, and he nodded in apparent agreement.

"Cheryl, if she returns or tries to get in, please call the police." Tim turned back to the people in the store. "Sorry about that, folks. A bit of a misunderstanding. Danielle, some wine for our guests."

Danielle walked toward the people gathered in the store, offering wine.

Gran leaned close to Mia. "I wouldn't want to deal with that woman. She looks like she has a temper."

Mia chuckled. "Yeah. Rather embarrassing, isn't it?"

Gran nodded. "Oh well. Live and let live. Let's go upstairs. I haven't seen a mirror here that would work for me."

Mia followed Gran to the loft. As she climbed the stairs, she noticed Steve speaking quietly to Tim. Tim rubbed the back of his neck and then nodded at whatever Steve had said. She shook her head. None of her business what they were discussing. She just hoped Tim wasn't in financial difficulties.

Reaching the top of the stairs, she looked around the loft. It was almost as big as the main floor. Along a side wall were bookcases filled with books, small statues, and what Gran called knick-knacks. Dining tables and chairs were arranged in the center of the room. Beautiful bone china and silverware decorated the tables. On the walls were portraits, paintings, and mirrors. Mia thought the portraits were creepy. She shivered in spite of the heat. It felt as if their eyes followed her. The paintings were typical hunting scenes from England or garden scenes. Mia noticed a small painting tucked away in a bookcase. This one was different. The seaside scene included a cliff, a calm sea beneath, and a schooner at anchor offshore. The lighting was beautiful and peaceful. She picked it up and looked at the price. Very reasonable. The artist wasn't one that Mia recognized. She did a quick online search and learned the artist had started painting later in life. She painted mostly seascapes. This one was off the coast of England, and Mia thought it was soothing and pretty.

"Mia, could you give me a hand, please?" Gran called out.

Mia hurried over. "What do you need?"

Gran was rooting around in her purse. "I have a tape measure in here somewhere. Ah, here it is." Gran pulled out the tape measure. "Can you measure this mirror for me? I can't reach the top."

Mia took the tape measure and read out the measurements for Gran.

"That'll fit nicely. I like the mirror's frame too. Let's find Tim and see if he can deliver it."

"My place isn't far. I can get my Jeep and take both you and the mirror home tonight."

"Are you sure?"

"Of course. Let's tell him we've found something we want and see about getting them home." Mia picked up the painting she had her eye on and led Gran downstairs to find Tim.

Tim was standing behind the counter, "Marie, can I help you?" he asked.

"I've found the mirror I was looking for. It was upstairs." Gran pointed to the loft.

"Excellent! I'm so glad you found something." Tim glanced at his phone. "I have my inventory here. Let me pull up the pictures. Is this it?"

He showed Gran a photo of the mirror.

"Yes, that's it. How much is it?"

Tim quoted her a price.

"That seems a little low. Are you sure that's the right piece?" Gran asked.

"I do. And yes, it's a little low. You've been a wonderful customer and have sent many people to my shop. My way of saying thank you."

"In that case, consider it sold," Gran said.

Mia pointed to the painting she was holding. "And I'd like to buy this."

Tim scribbled the prices on two pieces of paper and gave them to Gran and Mia. "Cheryl will take care of the sale. Marie, did you want me to arrange delivery for the mirror?"

"I'm going to get my Jeep and will be able to take it and Gran home shortly. Gran, will you be okay here while I do that?" Mia asked.

"Of course. I'll enjoy a glass of wine and chat with a few people here."

Tim nodded. "Marie can stay as long as necessary. Don't worry."

"Perfect. I won't be long. My building isn't far from here."

Mia gave Cheryl her piece of paper and the painting. After the transaction was completed, Cheryl wrapped the painting carefully.

Steve carried the mirror down for Cheryl to wrap.

"Mia, you can park around the back of the store when you return. There's a side street around the block that will lead you to the back. Just look for the number twelve hundred. That's the street number for the store." Tim said.

"Thanks. Gran, I'll be back soon. I'll come in when I return." Mia hurried out the door and scooted home.

Ten minutes later, she was in front of the antique store. There wasn't any parking available at the front of the store, so she followed Tim's directions and found parking in the back.

Gran was chatting with a couple when Mia walked into the store. When Gran saw her, she said her goodbyes and stood in front of the register. Mia picked up her purchase. Steve led them to a back door carrying Gran's mirror. They stowed the mirror safely in the back seat and then Mia and Gran left.

Traffic was light, making the drive to Gran's condo quick.

"Who were you talking to when I arrived?"

Gran twisted in her seat. "Tom and Fran Esly. They live in my building. I think you've met them."

Mia nodded. "I remember them. He was involved with Charles Gordon's board of directors, wasn't he?"

"That's right. What a mess that turned out to be. He still hasn't received compensation for the money he invested in Charles's company. He may never get it back."

"That's awful. Are they going to be all right financially?"

Gran nodded. "I think so. His investment wasn't large. But it's frustrating he's lost it. He told me if he sees Charles again, he'll call the police immediately."

"I'm not sure where Charles Gordon is. There are a lot of people looking for him. Being involved in artifact smuggling puts a target on a person. He'll turn up somewhere and get caught." Mia navigated the turn to Gran's building and parked her Jeep in a visitor's parking spot. "I'll help you with the mirror."

Mia picked up the mirror and then locked her Jeep. She and Gran made their way to the entrance, where a doorman was holding the door open.

"Good evening, Mrs. Tremblay, Miss Reid. How are you tonight?"

"Good evening, Mitch. We're doing well. I found a mirror that will fit perfectly in my hallway." Gran smiled.

"Do you need help carrying it to your apartment?"

Mia shook her head. "I've got it. It's not heavy, just awkward. I won't let it drop."

Mitch laughed. "I hope not! That would be seven years of bad luck!"

Gran chuckled. "Mitch, that's such an old superstition. You don't believe that, do you?"

Mitch accompanied them to the elevator and held the doors open while Mia maneuvered the mirror in. "No, I don't. But I couldn't resist!"

"Thanks for the help. See you later." Gran smiled as she pushed the floor number to her apartment.

At her floor, Gran held the elevator door open while Mia got out, and they hurried down the hall. The hallway was wide, and the tile floor shone. Gran unlocked her apartment, and they entered.

Mia gently put the mirror down. "Where do you want the mirror? We can put it up tonight."

Gran's cat, Cleo, a Maine Coon cat, greeted them at the door. Cleo was big and affectionate. She had the pointed, upright ears of the breed, and her black and white fur was long. She meowed, talking to Gran and Mia as they came in. Mia reached out and scratched Cleo under her chin. "Hey there. What have you been doing?" Cleo shut her green eyes in pleasure and answered with a loud purr, rubbing herself against Mia and then Gran.

Gran laughed. "She expects a treat. Let me put my jacket away, and I'll give her something. Then I'll show you where I want the mirror." Gran hung her jacket in the closet. She walked to the kitchen, reached into a glass jar on the counter, and gave Cleo a treat. Satisfied, Cleo sauntered to her bed in the living room.

Mia left the mirror against the wall and followed Gran. There was a table at the end of the hall, and the space above the table was perfect for the mirror.

"Let me get the tools, and I'll hang it for you." Mia walked to the small storeroom off the kitchen and found what she needed. Everything in Gran's apartment had its place.

Mia put the tools on the table and then went to get the mirror. She unwrapped the mirror and placed it on the kitchen countertop. She carefully measured the wall and the mirror and then held the mirror up for Gran to decide exactly where she wanted it. After a few tries, they settled on the position.

Mia put the mirror down and got to work.

"Have you heard from Luke?" Gran asked.

"We spoke at lunchtime today. He arrives Friday afternoon." Mia told Gran what he'd be doing for work while she finished up her measurements and then picked up the hanging kit. "It's going to be different having him here while we're both working."

"Do you have plans while he's here?"

"Nothing firm, but there's so much to do at this time of year." Mia smiled. "I won't monopolize him completely. I promise you'll get to see him, too."

"Well, I'd better! I like him, and I hope the two of you can make this relationship work."

Mia picked up the mirror and hung it. She looked at it critically and made a few slight adjustments. "Looks good. What do you think?"

"Perfect. Thank you for doing this. Don't we look great together?"

Mia looked at their reflection. In her eighties, Gran was still fit and vibrant. She was slightly built, and her blond hair was now snow white. Her blue eyes sparkled behind her glasses, and her makeup carefully applied. At five feet three inches, Gran appeared tiny next to Mia's five feet eight inches. Gran had worn a well-cut pantsuit in a bold blue that suited her perfectly. Mia's looks were a mix of her Gran and her grandfather. Her eyes mirrored Gran's, while her dark brown, wavy hair came from her grandfather's side of the family. Gran's style was elegant, whereas Mia's was more casual elegance. At least that's how Alex had described Mia's style. Mia and Alex had recently gone shopping and had upgraded Mia's wardrobe. The dressy tank top and ankle-length pants were slimming, and she felt attractive in them.

"We do." Mia grinned. "I'll get some cleaning solution and wipe down the mirror." Comfortable in Gran's apartment, she strode to the kitchen and pulled out a cleaning spray and a microfiber towel. It took her just a few minutes to get the mirror sparkling. "It looks great."

"You spoil me. I could have done that." Gran said as they put the cleaning supplies away.

Mia shrugged. "I know. But I'd rather do it than have you climb a stepladder. And you know you'd do that."

Gran chuckled. "Yes, you know me too well. Do you want a cup of tea?"

Mia checked her watch. "Sure."

Gran busied herself in the kitchen, and they were soon sitting in the living room with some tea and cookies that Gran had pulled out of the freezer.

"These are good. Did you make them?"

Gran raised an eyebrow. "Ah, no. I haven't baked since you left for university. I picked these up at the new bakery down the street. And yes, they're very good. Now, tell me about work."

"I think the exhibit is ready. It launches a week from today. I had a meeting with the public relations manager today, and the media blast for next week is ready to go. One of the morning shows will be in on Tuesday, and I'll be taking them through the exhibit."

"That sounds like fun. Are you going to be working Wednesday evening as well?"

"No, the museum closes at five-thirty." Mia took a sip of tea. "You remember the special event scheduled for Friday evening?"

Gran nodded.

"Christine Marks, the museum CEO, is expecting it to be well attended. There's been tremendous interest in this exhibit. Some of the artifacts were discovered when developers started building a new resort. The artifacts include everything from daily utensils to weapons and jewelry. We even have ceremonial clothing and have been busy dressing mannequins. The museum labels are ready, and we're producing a limited-edition exhibition catalogue that will be for sale in the gift shop."

"You have been busy. Are you enjoying it?"

Mia put her teacup down. "Yes, it's been great. The staff person who started the project left a detailed plan before taking their sick leave. And the other staff members have been helpful. It's made this project go smoothly."

"It sounds like it's going to take up a lot of room."

"We've got three separate areas on the main floor. Two larger rooms and the hallway connecting the rooms. I'm concerned about space, but we're going to start to put everything together tomorrow morning. We'll make it work." Mia picked up a cookie. "Did you know that Barbara woman who crashed the event? She said Tim owed her money and that the store was half hers."

"Yes. His first wife. They were married very young, and I remember his parents weren't happy they had gotten married. They divorced, and a short time later, Tim married Rita. Rita was Alex's mother's sister. I remember wondering if Barbara was going to make life difficult for them. I'd heard he'd paid Barbara for her share of the store. I don't know what it was worth at the time, but apparently that was part of the divorce agreement. She left for British Columbia shortly after he remarried."

"Has she ever been back to Lakeview?"

"I don't know. I had heard she had opened a shop in the town she moved to, but I don't know how it worked out. She had family in Lakeview. It's possible she came back. Why do you ask?"

"I'm just curious. It's strange that she thinks Mr. Fraser owes her money."

"Well, Steve and Cheryl took care of removing her from the store. I doubt she'll show up again."

"I hope she doesn't cause problems for him." Mia finished her tea and then went home.

Chapter Three

Thursday Morning

Mia's phone rang just as she was getting ready to leave for work. "Morning, Mia. Do you have a few minutes to talk?" Luke asked.

"For you, always."

"My flight arrives at Pearson Airport tomorrow afternoon at four. I've planned for a car service to pick me up. I just need to know where they should bring me?"

"My place. I could have picked you up. I'll be home, and I may even attempt cooking a meal."

Luke laughed. "I don't want you to go to any trouble. We can always get take-away."

"We'll see. Message me when you arrive. I'll leave work then. When do you have to start work?"

"Not until Monday morning. I'll be meeting with the city's police chief and members of his team."

"Perfect. We'll have the weekend together. I know Gran and Alex will want to see you."

They chatted a few minutes longer, and then Mia left for work.

As she swiped her security card, she saw Heather McCloud, the public relations manager, walking down the hall.

"Heather, do you have a minute?" Mia called out.

Heather stopped and looked back at Mia. "Sure, are you ready for today?"

Mia hustled to her side. "Yes. When did you want to start?"

"I have the videographer coming in about thirty minutes. I'd like to start in one of the rooms where the exhibit will be set up."

"And you still want to film in my office as well?"

"I'd like the option. Maybe give viewers a behind-the-scenes look."

"That's fine. I'll remove any personal items I don't want seen in the video."

"Good idea. We'll see you in room 231 C shortly." Heather hurried down the hall as Mia took the stairs to her office.

She stowed her lunch in the lunchroom fridge and then checked her office for anything she didn't want on display.

Her bookcases had a variety of journals and books. Nothing needed to be removed. The prints on the walls had come with the space.

The desk was presentable. Papers had been put away in their folders, and her filing was up to date. Her desk had a lamp, computer monitor, and a notepad close by. She had a funky mug she'd found in Brazil several years ago. It was full of pens. And the coffee machine was tucked next to the bookcase.

Mia took a few minutes to check her email messages. Nothing that couldn't wait until later. She glanced at her watch and changed her voicemail for the day, advising she was in the office but unavailable to take the call. This video session would be fun. Heather planned to use it across the museum's social media platforms to promote the exhibit.

She picked up her water bottle, made sure it was full, and hurried out.

Mia stood in the doorway of room 231 C. Heather and the videographer were setting up the camera. There were several pieces from the exhibit, and Mia noticed they had one of the mannequins wearing a ceremonial costume.

Heather turned to the door. "Mia, there you are. We're just about ready. Is it all right if we show this mannequin?"

"Yes, definitely. We have several costumes, but this one is the most striking. The workmanship on it is excellent. Are we showing the exhibits we have in place?"

"I thought it would be a good idea. We can start with you and then pan over to a few of the exhibits while you talk about them. Then we can move down the hall. When will the rest of the exhibit be up?"

"Everything will be ready by Monday at noon."

"I'll have someone come in and take photos for our social media accounts Monday afternoon. Does that work?"

"That would be perfect."

"Heather, I'm all set to go." The videographer cleared her throat.

"Thanks, Susan. Mia Reid, meet Susan Barnstoff. She's our in-house videographer and photographer."

Susan extended her hand to Mia. "Good to meet you."

"Likewise." Mia shook Susan's hand.

"Let's get started. Don't worry about making a mistake. Just keep talking. We can edit it out when we're finished," Heather said.

Mia took a drink of water. "Where do you want me?"

Susan led Mia to one of the tables that had been set up. "We'll start here. Just talk about the exhibits and then walk down to the next table. I'll follow you along. And like Heather said, just keep going if you make a mistake."

They began, and for the next hour, Mia went through the exhibit they had set up. They took a break, and Mia took a drink of water.

"That's a lot harder than I thought. Is it always this tough?" Mia asked.

Susan chuckled. "No, sometimes it's harder. You're doing well. We have a lot of information to convey."

Heather had been reviewing the video. "She's right. You're engaging and knowledgeable on the video. Here, take a look."

Mia walked to the camera and watched herself on the screen. "Oh, that's much better than I thought! Phew. Thanks for showing me that."

Susan glanced at her watch. "Ready for the next one?"

"Let's do it." Mia took her place and handled the next session like a pro.

By the end of the morning, they had done several videos and had finished up in Mia's office. Susan connected the camera to a monitor, and they watched the videos.

"Now remember, this is raw footage, and I'll take care of editing it," Susan said.

Mia and Heather watched the videos, and Heather nodded her approval. "Really good work. Both of you. Mia, you're excellent on camera. I'm glad we have you speaking with the morning news show on Tuesday. You'll do very well."

"Thanks. I'm glad it went smoothly."

Susan packed up her equipment. "I'll send the edited version no later than tomorrow morning."

"It'll go up on our platforms in the afternoon. Mia, I'll let you know when it goes up so you can share it too."

"Thanks for making this morning so easy and fun."

Heather and Susan left Mia's office, and Mia dropped in her office chair with a deep sigh. "Thank goodness that's over!"

Her cell phone pinged with a text.

Alex: Lunch at the Sandwich Bar?

Mia: Sure, when?

Alex: 30 min

Mia: Yes

Mia had enough time to check her email and voice messages. Nothing urgent. She enjoyed the pace of working at the museum. It was busy, but nothing she couldn't handle. Upper management wasn't looking over her shoulder. At least not yet. She'd met with her supervisor when she started a week ago and had been told if she needed anything to ask for it.

With a grimace, she remembered she'd brought her lunch. Oh well. It would keep in the fridge, and she'd eat it for dinner.

She wrapped up a couple of items and then hurried off to meet Alex. Office workers on their lunch break and sightseeing tourists congested the sidewalks. Mia almost bumped into a couple when they stopped in front of a street performer playing the saxophone. She sidestepped the couple and then crossed the street, where it was slightly less busy.

A few minutes later, she arrived. The Sandwich Bar was a converted tavern that offered patrons a variety of sandwiches and sides. The restaurant gained recognition due to its quick table service and good food.

Alex was waiting for Mia outside the door. "Let's see if we can get a table.

Hey, you look great! Is that one of the new outfits we put together?" Alex asked as they walked into the restaurant.

"Yes. I had a video session this morning. We did several segments on the exhibit. Heather, the public relations manager, gave me suggestions about what to wear, so it was easy to pull this together."

"That color of shirt looks gorgeous on you."

"A table for two?" the hostess asked.

"Please. A booth would be great." Alex replied.

The hostess led them to a small corner booth tucked by the bar. "Will this do?"

"Yes, thank you," Mia said.

"Your server will be here shortly."

"I already know what I want." Alex closed the menu.

Mia checked the menu to make sure nothing new was added.

Their server arrived, and Alex ordered smoked meat on a bun, curly fries, and seasoning salt.

Mia's order of a poutine and a roast beef sandwich was her go-to at this restaurant. The poutine was always piping hot. The gravy and cheese curds melted together over the fries. It was delicious.

The server returned quickly with their drinks, and Mia waited until she'd left.

"I didn't expect to see you at Timeless Treasures last night. How did that happen?"

Alex rolled her eyes. "I wasn't planning on it, but at the last minute, Uncle Tim called to see if I'd lend a hand. He wasn't sure Steve could attend. Thank goodness they didn't expect me to know anything about the antiques. He wanted me there to give Danielle a hand if needed."

"How is she feeling?"

"I guess she's been tired. No morning sickness, just exhausted."

"Why was she there at all? I know Tim's excited about the baby, but maybe Danielle should have been at home resting."

The server returned with their meals.

"He's been hoping Danielle would take some interest in the shop. But I think he's given up on that. She loves her work at the bank. But he did tell me that Steve has been helping a bit around the store and learning more about the world of antiques."

"I was surprised Steve was there. I thought he was happy in his field." Mia shrugged. "I guess he could always switch careers if he was really interested." Mia took a forkful of her poutine, the cheese curds making long strings as she pulled it up.

"I'm not sure about Steve and his career. Danielle has mentioned he's been away from his office lately. She says he keeps telling her everything is fine."

"How old is your uncle? Is he thinking of retiring?"

"He's in his mid-sixties, so maybe that's it. I don't know if he'd sell the shop or if he'd cut back to part-time. I'd hate to think he's sick or something." Alex took a drink of water. "When does Luke arrive?"

"His flight comes in tomorrow at four, and he's arranged for a car service to drop him off at my place."

"Do you have plans tomorrow night?"

"I'm going to try to cook dinner."

Alex shook her head. "I'm sorry, what did you say? You're going to cook dinner?"

"I can cook. Some things. Spaghetti is easy. And I'll get some sourdough bread and toss a salad."

"What about the sauce?"

Mia rolled her eyes. "I'll make that. I have Gran's recipe, and it never fails. I'll make sure to get all the ingredients from the store."

"Do you want to get together for brunch on Sunday? Zack's off in the morning, and I know he'd like to see Luke again."

"Sure. Pick a restaurant and let me know. We'll meet you there."

Alex's phone rang. "Excuse me, it's Danielle."

Mia finished her meal while Alex took the call.

Alex looked up at Mia when she hung up. Her eyes were filled with tears.

"What happened?" Mia asked.

Alex took a drink of water. "It's Uncle Tim. He's dead." Her voice broke.

"How did that happen?"

Alex shook her head. "Danielle said Cheryl showed up at work this morning and found him in the office. He was dead. They think it's a heart attack."

Mia put her hand over Alex's. "I'm so sorry. That was sudden."

Alex nodded. "He was fine last night, and I don't think he had any signs of heart disease. Danielle's really upset. I have to go to her." Alex looked around for the server.

"Don't worry about lunch. I've got it. Are you okay to drive to Danielle's?"

"Yes, I'm going to meet her at home. She's really upset and can't get hold of Steve."

Alex picked up her purse, and Mia stood and gave her a hug. "Call me if you or Danielle need anything."

"Thanks, I will."

Mia watched as Alex hurried away.

The server arrived. "Is everything all right?"

"It's fine, could you please bring me both bills? I'll take care of it."

"Not a problem."

Mia called Gran on her way back to work and told her what Alex had said.

"That's so sad," Gran said. "Danielle is going to have a tough time with this."

"I know Alex and her mom will help her, but it's got to be a shock. He looked fine last night."

"Heart disease can creep up if you don't keep an eye on it." Gran sighed. "I'll see if they need help with anything. Tim was a good man."

"I'll talk to you soon. I'm almost back at work."

Chapter Four

Thursday Afternoon

At the museum, Mia couldn't shake the sadness that enveloped her when Alex told her Mr. Fraser was dead. He'd seemed so well last night. She focused her attention on the details she was working on. Listening to the script that had been recorded for each exhibit. She had to backtrack several times because she'd gotten lost in thoughts about Danielle and Mr. Fraser. What would she do with the store? How was she going to deal with her only parent gone?

She rolled her shoulders and glanced at the wall clock. She'd been struggling for the last forty minutes. Time to put things away. She hadn't found any errors in the recordings.

She wondered if Gran had heard any more about Tim's death. Alex hadn't called her back either. Maybe a call to Alex on the way home.

She put her things away, remembered to pick up her lunch from the fridge, and made her way to her Jeep. On her way out, she called Alex.

"Hi Alex. Just on my way home from work, and I'm wondering how things are with Danielle?"

Alex's sigh came across the line. "She's pretty upset. The paramedics were at the shop, and they felt Uncle Tim's death wasn't normal. The coroner's involved now, and we're waiting to hear the results. Danielle says he didn't have heart disease. And she finally reached Steve. His phone was off until about fifteen minutes ago. I'm so ticked off at him."

"Why are you ticked off at Steve?"

"He wasn't available because he was out of the office. And he hasn't told Danielle where he's been." Alex blew out a breath.

"Hey, are you okay? You seem really ticked about Steve. He couldn't have known Tim was going to die."

"I know, I know. I'm just frustrated and upset. Danielle was told there's going to be an autopsy." Alex cleared her throat.

"That's upsetting. I'm sorry to hear that. But then Danielle will know what happened."

"Yes, she will. I'm going to go home shortly. I have to drive by the store and make sure everything's locked up."

"Do you want me to meet you there?" Mia asked.

"Do you mind? I don't really want to go there by myself, but Danielle asked me to check on it."

"No problem. I'll meet you there shortly. If I'm later than you are, just wait for me in your car."

"Okay. Thanks."

Mia hung up and changed directions. It would take her a little longer to get to Timeless Treasures from her current location, but Alex would wait.

Mia arrived at the store and didn't see Alex's car nearby. She pulled into a parking spot a few yards away from the store and got out of her Jeep. There were two women in front of Timeless Treasures, and Mia didn't recognize them. They appeared to be in their fifties or sixties. One woman had light brown hair that curled around her head, and she wore a pair of black pants with a red shirt. Over the shirt, she had a black apron with the words "It's All I've Got" across the top. The other woman had black hair that was so dark, Mia was sure it came from a bottle. She had a green wrap dress and matching ballet flats.

As she approached the store, she overheard one of the women talking.

"And I knew something was wrong when I didn't see Tim drive up this morning. You know my apartment overlooks the street. I always see him arrive before I open my shop."

Mia cleared her throat. Both women turned in her direction. "Excuse me, did you need any help?" she asked them.

The woman who'd been speaking shook her head. "No. I was just telling Bev about Tim Fraser. Do I know you?"

"I'm Mia Reid. I'm afraid I don't know you."

"Martha Jones. I have a shop down the street. I knew Tim Fraser. You're Marie Tremblay's granddaughter, aren't you?"

"Yes. And I remember Gran mentioning you. I was surprised by Mr. Fraser's death. We were here last night for his soirée. Gran and I both bought something."

"I'm Bev Matheson. I own the tea shop across from Martha's shop. We've both been on this street for fifteen years. Opened our shops within a month of each other."

"You must have known Mr. Fraser well," Mia said.

"He was a kind man. He helped me out quite a bit when I started. My shop specializes in jewelry and smaller pieces. We weren't in competition with each other. Most of the shopkeepers along the street support each other. If a client wants something we don't have, we always suggest the shop that does." Martha paused to take a breath.

"Martha was just telling me she hadn't seen Tim come to work this morning," Bev said.

"Was that something you'd always see?"

"I live above my shop. I purchased the building when I started selling antiques. My apartment has a small balcony that overlooks the street. In the summer, I have coffee there in the morning. Tim was usually at the shop by eight or eight-thirty, but this morning I didn't see him drive by. I should have known something was wrong." Martha glanced in the store window. "Do you know how he died?"

"Apparently, a heart attack," Mia said.

"Well, why would the coroner and police show up? I saw the van marked coroner arrive after the paramedics were here." Martha crossed her arms over her chest.

"I don't know. Maybe regular procedure? I wasn't here." Mia looked at her watch. Where was Alex?

"Did something happen last night at the soirée?" Martha asked.

"His first wife showed up. She wasn't happy about something. Did you know her?" Mia asked.

Martha's face cleared up. "I've met her. She was gone long before I arrived, but she kept returning to Lakeview."

"What do you mean?"

"Like I said, I've been here about fifteen years. I remember I'd just opened my shop, and she came to see me. She had a shop in Kelowna, British Columbia, and was having problems getting stock. She was looking for someone to partner with her. She asked if I'd be interested in that. I'd work from a list of antiques she was looking for and ship them to her."

Mia frowned. "That doesn't sound like a good business model. It would be more cost-effective for her to have the items go directly to her shop."

"That's what I told her. And I didn't have the extra capital needed to purchase the antiques and then send them on to her. I told her she'd be better off working for someone else if she was having trouble keeping her store afloat."

"Did you see her again?"

"Frequently. She was in and out of the area several times a year. I don't know if she saw Tim every time she was in the city or not. I remember going to a meeting of the local antique dealers, and someone mentioned her name. There weren't a lot of good things said about her at that meeting. Someone, and I can't remember who, said she'd been gambling in Kelowna and had lost her store. She'd declared bankruptcy."

"When was this?" Mia asked.

"Maybe eight or ten years ago. I can't remember exactly."

"Did she approach anyone else to work with her?"

"I'm not sure. I can tell you the shop owners on our street work well together. We're there for each other if anything happens. We each have our own specialty and often refer customers to someone else if we don't have what the customer is looking for. Tim specialized in furniture. It wasn't until later he started bringing in antiquities from Europe and Asia. I don't know how he managed to make money with those. They were very expensive to bring in. But he carried on and did well."

"Mia, sorry I'm late," Alex called out.

Mia turned and saw Alex hurrying across the street.

Martha and Bev looked at Alex. "That's Tim's niece, Alex Bennett," Martha said to Bev.

Mia hid a smile. Martha seemed to know everyone and everything.

Alex stopped in front of the store. "Hi, Mrs. Jones."

"Alex, my sincere condolences. How are you and Danielle doing?"

Alex shrugged. "As well as we can be. Danielle's pretty upset. Uncle Tim's death is unexpected."

"If there's anything I can do to help, please let me know. Bev and I were checking on the storefront. There's been a lot of flowers dropped off since the police left this afternoon."

"Thanks, I'll let Danielle know. The store's going to be closed until after Tuesday and maybe later. I'll gather the flowers for Danielle. I need to get in the store and make sure everything's been properly locked."

"Of course. We'll let you be on your way. Mia, it was nice to meet you. Please give my regards to Marie." Martha and Bev turned from the store and walked down the street toward Martha's shop.

Alex leaned against the front door. "Okay, let me get us inside, and we'll do a quick check."

"What do you want to do with the flowers and cards?"

"We'll pick them up, and I'll take them to Danielle in the morning." Alex unlocked the door and hurried to turn off the alarm.

Mia followed, then locked the door behind them.

Alex snapped on the lights and said, "I have to check the back door."

"Wait, I'll go with you."

They hustled to the back of the store. Alex tried the large door at the back and found it securely locked. "Good. That's a relief. Danielle knew we'd locked it last night, but didn't know if it had been unlocked overnight."

Mia looked around. "Is there anything else we need to do?"

"We need to check the windows, and there's a side door too."

"I'll look at the windows. Do you know where the side door is?"

"Yes. I won't be long." Alex hurried off toward the office, and Mia strode across the store to check the windows.

All the windows were secured on the main floor. Mia remembered there was a window in the loft, so she climbed the stairs to check it. The lights were on upstairs, and Mia was grateful for that. It would have been difficult to walk through the dining room displays without knocking into a table or chairs. She checked the window. This one could be opened and wasn't locked. She tugged on the old-fashioned locking mechanism and then tried the window. It held.

"Mia, where are you?" Alex called.

Mia hurried to the stairs. "I was checking on the window up here. I made sure to lock it."

"I didn't even think of the loft. Thanks. I'm ready to go."

Mia hurried down the stairs. "I'll help with the flowers at the front door. Should we put up a sign that the store's closed?"

"That's a good idea." Alex walked to the cash register. "There should be paper here." She opened a cupboard and pulled out a piece of paper and a marker. She quickly printed out that the store was closed until further notice. "I don't want to put a date yet. Danielle needs to decide what she's going to do next." Alex added tape to the sign and attached it to the door. They turned out the lights, set the alarm, and then locked the door. Mia and Alex collected the flowers and placed them in Alex's car.

"Thanks for coming. I didn't feel like being here alone."

Mia gave Alex a hug. "It's okay. I don't mind. If you need anything, let me know."

"Thanks. I called mom to tell her. She'll be here for the service. She can't get away until then." Alex got in her car and drove away.

Mia headed home. She kept thinking back to the conversation she'd had with Martha. Something Martha had said kept bothering her, but she couldn't remember what it was. She shrugged. It would come to her.

Chapter Five

Thursday Evening

At home, Mia pulled out her lunch that she'd taken to work. Gross. It had sat too long in her car and wasn't safe to eat anymore. After disposing of it in the compost, she opened the fridge and shook her head. Not a lot of choice. Opening the freezer, she found a container of chili. It would have to do. And groceries needed to be done before Luke got in. Picking up her phone, she dictated a grocery list and sent it off to her favorite grocery store. She loved the service they provided. Place the order, and they promised delivery in two hours. She'd be all set for when Luke arrived tomorrow. There would be plenty of time for her to make her pasta sauce for their dinner. She heated up the chili and then ate her meal at the table. From her dining room, she could see flights landing at the Island Airport, boats leaving the marina, and people walking along the boardwalk. The neighborhood was settling into its nighttime routine. People returning home from work, going out for dinner, or hurrying to get a run in before ending their day.

Mia's building was one of several condo towers. Her condo afforded her a view of Lake Ontario and the hustle and bustle that came from living in the downtown area. The Rogers Centre, where the Blue Jays baseball team played, was close enough to walk to. And if she sat on her balcony when there was a game, she could hear the music from the street performers outside the Rogers Centre.

She finished her meal and tidied up the kitchen. Glancing at her Timex, she knew she had time to touch base with Gran. Mia smiled when she remembered Alex insisting she get rid of her Timex. She said it didn't match the image they were going for. Mia refused to let go of the watch but had agreed to a new watch band. The watch had belonged to her grandfather and had sentimental value. She poured herself a glass of wine and took it and her phone to the balcony. Gran picked up the phone almost immediately.

Mia told her about the conversation she'd had with Martha Jones while she was waiting for Alex.

"I remember that. I was one of the people Barbara approached." Gran sighed. "I must be getting old."

Mia chuckled. "You're far from old. Do you remember anything else about Barbara?"

"It was just as I was selling my shop. There was so much happening at that time. Your grandfather was sick, and I needed to be with him. So, maybe around fifteen years ago."

"I've never heard this before, Gran. What happened?"

"Honestly, there was so much happening when I sold the shop, I'd forgotten about it completely. Tim's death has me thinking about the past. Anyway, Barbara was trying to get someone to work with her as a partner. The partner would buy the antiques and then ship them to Barbara for her to sell on the West Coast. The markup she planned was criminal. After I turned her down, she went up and down the street asking the shopkeepers if any of them were interested. Martha had just opened her shop, and Barbara pressed her hard." Gran coughed. "I need a drink of water. Just a moment."

Mia waited until Gran returned.

"Where was I?" Gran asked.

"Barbara was pressing Martha about partnering with her."

"Yes, Martha called me for some help with her store. She had a few questions. Then she mentioned the scheme Barbara had proposed. I told Martha to stay away from it, that it was a half-baked idea. Then Martha told me she'd learned that Barbara had lost a lot of money. She'd started gambling and had lost her store. A few weeks later, I asked Martha what

Barbara had said when she turned her down. Apparently, she told Martha she'd have to take the deal with the devil. Martha didn't know what that meant, but it was the last she heard from Barbara. Although she has seen her in Lakeview several times a year over the last ten years."

"Wow, Gran. That's a lot of information. Martha didn't tell me all that. I wonder if Barbara was meeting with Tim when she was coming into town?"

"I remember seeing her when Rita passed away. She'd been in Lakeview for a few months. Tim told me Barbara tried to get him to work with her. He didn't want to. He might have kept records of his meetings with her. I know he kept track of people he worked with or who wanted to work with him."

"Do you know how he tracked that information?"

"He had a notebook by his side whenever he was working. I had one too. It's something I had told him about. It's a good way to remember things. Although I suppose now a computer program would make it easier." Gran cleared her throat. "Now, I'd like to see you and Luke for dinner this weekend. Does Sunday work?"

"Yes, that should work. I know he's looking forward to seeing you again."

"Excellent. I'll plan dinner for five o'clock. Come early, maybe around three, and we'll catch up. I'll invite Alex and Zack as well."

"Okay, I'll be in touch."

Mia sat back and thought about the conversation with Gran. Barbara had been in Lakeview over the last ten years. Could she have been meeting with Tim and neither of them talking about it? And what was the deal with the devil Barbara had mentioned? Would it have been Tim or someone from British Columbia?

She grabbed a notepad and started writing down some items to check. First, any correspondence between Tim and Barbara. What kind of work did Barbara do? Could she get access to Tim's notebooks? Or had he moved everything to a computer? Mia put her pen down and shook her head. What was she thinking? She shouldn't get involved in this. With a sigh, she put the notepad away and finished her wine.

Her phone rang. "Grocery delivery for you, Dr. Reid."

"Thanks. Send them up, please." She pulled her wallet out of her purse and took out some cash for a tip. The delivery person arrived with the groceries. Mia tipped them and then brought the bags in the kitchen.

"You'd think I was having a family of four show up." Luke had a good appetite, and she'd stocked up on some of his favorite foods. Pasta, vegetables, baked goods. She sighed. "I'd better not gain weight while he's here. I can't afford to buy a new wardrobe."

By the time she'd put away the groceries and arranged a loose meal plan, it was almost ten.

Time to call it a day. Tomorrow would be busy enough, and she was looking forward to seeing Luke.

* * *

Friday Morning

Mia arrived at worked and Heather met up with her while she was walking to her office. "I just wanted to let you know the video you did was great! The edits look excellent. I'll send you a copy of the final videos this afternoon."

"I'm glad to hear that. Video isn't my favorite medium, but I'm getting better. Do you have the press releases for the event?"

"I just sent them for you to review. If there's any changes, let me know before ten this morning. They go out this afternoon."

"I'll look at them when I get to my desk. Is there anything else you need from me today?"

"No. Don't forget you have the interview Tuesday morning for The Morning Show."

"I remember. I'll be here bright and early."

They parted ways, and Mia hurried to her office.

She closed her office door and opened the blinds. The plant sitting by the window needed a good drink of water. Mia poured a generous serving of water over the dirt. She looked around her space and felt the rushed feeling leave her. Her office was quiet, away from the daily hum of the museum. She took a deep breath and turned on the sound system, letting soft rock music come through the speakers. The silence was wonderful, but this morning she needed the boost from the music.

She turned her attention to her email program and found the press releases. She read them through and made a few minor corrections for clarity and returned them to Heather.

There were a few other emails she needed to address. One was for the school program she was working on with schools in Northern Ontario. Mia was leveraging technology to bring programming to the students who couldn't travel to Lakeview. Some communities were in remote locations with no road access throughout the winter months. She was looking forward to using the technology to work with the students. The school boards were excited to work with her.

Mia'd been working steadily when her phone rang. It was Alex.

"Hi, what's up? Is everything all right?"

"I wanted to say thanks again for coming with me last night. I probably could have done it by myself, but it felt good to have you with me."

"Not a problem. Have you heard any more from Danielle?"

"She and Steve are meeting with the lawyer this morning. She's hoping to get the service done on Tuesday but hasn't heard from the coroner's office yet."

"How long is that going to take?"

"I don't know. Depends on how busy they are, I guess."

"Are we still on for brunch on Sunday?"

"Definitely. Zack is off, and he wants to see Luke again. I'll let you know where and when."

"Sounds good. You take care. I've got to finish up some work since I need to leave early."

Mia spent the rest of the morning doing administrative work on the projects she was managing. Lunch was picked up at the museum cafeteria. The food was good, not too expensive, and she could be back at her desk in ten minutes. She'd planned to take the afternoon to go over the exhibits once more. She had to leave work no later than three-thirty today to get home and start dinner.

By three, she was sure the exhibits would be ready. She went back to her office and checked her email. Heather had sent the videos for her to review. They would be released after five that afternoon.

Mia clicked on the videos and watched them. It was hard to see herself on camera, but she focused on what she was saying and watched them a couple of times.

She emailed Heather, letting her know she was happy with the videos.

The videos were professional, and she sounded knowledgeable and excited about the topics at hand.

Mia checked her office, making certain she had the office laptop and any information she might need. Luke would be jet-lagged, and she might have the opportunity to get some work done.

A quick walk down to the parking lot, and she was on her way home.

Chapter Six

Friday Afternoon/Evening

Mia hurried upstairs to her apartment. She ran through her to-do list in her head as the elevator stopped on different floors to let passengers out. Living in the city, she felt anonymous and loved it. The building's tenants were people in their late thirties, early forties. Working to get ahead in life and eventually find a house in the burbs. Mia didn't think that was in her future. She owned her condo outright and enjoyed living in the city. There was so much to see and do. When she needed to get away, there was her grandparents' cottage in Muskoka, about a two-hour drive north of the city. She was fortunate to be able to use it whenever she needed it.

Arriving at her floor, she nodded to the rest of the passengers and walked down the hall. She glanced at her watch and saw that Luke's plane should have arrived at Pearson. He'd still have to go through Customs.

Her phone pinged with a text from him.

Luke: Just landed. Will let you know when I'm leaving the airport.

Mia: Glad you're here! I just got home.

She walked to her bedroom and changed her clothes, putting everything away. There was room in the second dresser for Luke to put his clothes, and there was space in the closet as well.

In the living room, Mia said, "Siri, play soft rock." Siri complied, shuffling a playlist Mia had put together. Mia watered several plants in the living room and dining room. They were drought-tolerant and could handle weeks of no water if necessary. Handy when she was away on a dig, although Alex checked on her place when she was away.

Mia pulled the ingredients out for the spaghetti sauce. The recipe had been handed down from Gran and was a favorite of Mia's. It was one of her can't-miss meals. She browned the meat, added chopped vegetables, spices, tomatoes, and tomato paste. Stirred everything together and lowered the heat to have it all simmer together. The sourdough boule the grocery store had delivered would need to be reheated, but it could wait until just before they ate.

Mia put together a tossed salad. The ingredients were fresh and crisp. She put that in the fridge to keep cold and then whipped up a simple vinaigrette for the salad.

Her phone rang.

"I'm in the car, and we should be at your place in about forty minutes," Luke said.

"That's great! I'm looking forward to seeing you again!"

"I am too. Do we have anything planned for tonight or tomorrow?"

"Not tonight. And I thought we'd see how you're doing in the morning before we make plans. Alex has suggested brunch on Sunday, and we're expected at Gran's for dinner Sunday afternoon."

"That's fine. I'd like to take it easy tomorrow if we can."

"We can do that. When do you have to be at work?"

"Monday morning at nine. I think they're being kind for the first day because the remainder of the week, I start at eight."

"You'll acclimatize quickly."

"Right then, I'll let you go and see you shortly."

Mia disconnected the call and smiled. "I hope we can make things work." She busied herself getting the table ready for dinner and pulled out a good bottle of red wine.

Half an hour later, her intercom rang.

"Dr. Reid, it's the concierge at the front desk. Mr. Forbes is here."

"Thanks. Please send him up."

Mia stopped at the hall mirror and checked her hair and makeup. She shook her head. "I need to relax. I look great."

She heard footsteps approaching her door and opened it just as Luke stopped in front of it.

"Mia." He dropped his suitcase and pulled her in his arms. A few moments later, Mia stepped away.

"Come on in."

Luke walked in with his suitcase. Mia picked up his backpack. "Ugh. What do you have in here? It weighs a ton."

"Couldn't be helped. I needed to bring artifacts from my office, and they're heavy." Familiar with Mia's home, Luke walked down the hall and dropped his suitcase in the bedroom closet.

"Did you want to unpack?" Mia asked.

"Later. Do we have time to relax before dinner?"

"Of course. Let's go out on the balcony. Do you want some wine?" Mia lowered the flame on the sauce.

"Sure. Can I do anything for dinner?"

"Everything's done." Mia gave Luke the bottle of red wine. "Can you take this out to the balcony, and I'll bring the glasses and some appetizers." Mia opened the fridge and took out a tray of appetizers she'd ordered from the store, and then grabbed the wine glasses. She joined Luke on the balcony where he was watching the activity in the neighborhood.

"How was your week?" Luke asked, reaching for her hand.

Mia smiled. Luke was a touchy-feely guy. It was a surprise because he'd never been like that when they been together at university. "Work's going well. I have an exhibit opening next week, and that's kept me busy. I told you about the soirée Gran and I went to on Wednesday night." Mia paused and took a drink of wine.

"I remember that. We haven't talked too much since then. Has anything happened?"

"I'm afraid so," Mia told him about Tim Fraser's death.

"And the coroner's doing an autopsy?"

"Yes. I'm not sure how long it takes. Danielle wants to hold his service on

Tuesday."

"I guess it depends on what they're looking for." Luke poured them each another glass of wine. "Something else is bothering you. What is it?"

"I don't know. I keep thinking his death was sudden. He seemed fine on Wednesday night."

"It's possible he had health issues that no one knew about. He may not have shared that with Danielle. Was anything missing from the shop?"

"Nothing that the police could see. Danielle didn't think anything was missing either." Mia took a drink of wine. "I don't want us focusing on this. If there's a problem, the police will deal with it. I'm so glad you're back."

"I am too. I'm looking forward to spending time with you."

"What are your hours going to be like?"

"I'll be working regular hours during the week. There's one weekend I'll have to do a seminar. That's scheduled for one day."

Mia glanced at her watch. "Are you ready for dinner?"

"Famished. Can I help?"

"Everything's almost ready. I need to cook the pasta and heat up the bread. It won't take long."

They went into the kitchen, and Mia got the rest of the meal prepared. The sauce was the perfect consistency, thick and chunky with lots of vegetables.

"It smells like an Italian restaurant in here," Luke said.

"I hope it tastes as good! The sauce is a recipe from Gran, and it's not difficult to make." Mia stirred the pasta, checking to see if it was ready. "It's ready."

Mia dished out the pasta and sauce and took the sourdough out to the table.

Shortly after dinner, they went to bed.

* * *

Saturday Morning

The next morning, Mia was awake before Luke was. He'd fallen asleep quickly last night and had slept through the night. She got dressed and left him sleeping.

Coffee in hand, she went out on the balcony with her cell phone. She wanted to check some attractions nearby. There wasn't a shortage of things to do; it would depend on Luke's energy levels. They'd done a few touristy things when he'd been here in early July, but there was a lot more they could take in. She looked through the growing list and narrowed it down.

The patio door opened. "Good morning. What are you doing out here?" Luke asked.

"Hey. I didn't want to wake you. You looked so peaceful." Mia glanced at her watch. "You had a long sleep. How are you feeling?"

Luke smiled. "Famished. And in desperate need of coffee."

"I can help with both." Mia rose from her chair, and Luke pulled her in a hug.

"Let's get some food in you, and then we'll go out for a walk. The weather's gorgeous."

Luke followed her in the kitchen. "I can help."

"You get a pass today. Did you want coffee or tea?"

"Coffee will help more than tea this morning."

"You can get your coffee. Do you remember where everything is?"

Luke grabbed a mug from the cupboard. He opened the drawer under the coffee machine, selected a dark roast coffee pod, slipped his mug under the spout, and pressed the button. "What were you working on so intently?" he asked as he waited for his coffee to finish.

Mia looked up from the bowl of eggs she was scrambling. "Checking out some tourist attractions. I'm not sure what you feel up to, though." She poured the eggs into a pan, swirling them around.

Luke drank deeply from his coffee. "Mmm, that's good coffee. What did you have in mind?"

Mia dropped slices of the sourdough bread in the toaster. "I'd like to go to the Farmers Market. I can pick up a few items. And we didn't go to the CN Tower the last time you were here. And there's the Beaches area that we could go to. The weather is perfect for the beach." She shook the pan of eggs and added peppers and shredded cheese.

"That sounds like a full day."

The toast popped, and Mia added butter to the toast and then set it on a plate, covered with a paper towel. Two more pieces of bread went in the toaster. "We can do as much or as little as you'd like. We don't have to do it all in a day."

"Let's go to the Farmers Market after breakfast and see how the day rolls out," Luke said.

Mia buttered the last two pieces of toast and plated the toast. "Could you put these on the table?"

Luke took the toast and set it on the table. Mia pulled a fruit salad out of the fridge and handed it to him.

They sat down and ate their food.

"The Farmers Market isn't too far from here, but we'll need to take the Jeep. Especially if we decide to go somewhere else after. The Beaches is a distance from here. There are some cute shops and restaurants. We could do lunch there. If we decide to do the CN Tower, I can book us a time slot."

"Sounds like a good plan. Are we meeting up with Gran today?"

"We're having dinner with her tomorrow. She wants us to go see her around three so we can spend time with her. And, on Sunday, Alex wants us to have brunch with her and Zack."

"Great. So today is just the two of us?"

"Yes."

"Excellent." Luke took her hand and kissed it. "I've missed you."

Mia smiled, "I've missed you too."

They finished breakfast. "I need to check my email to see if anything's come across I have to be aware of," Luke said.

They cleared off the table, and Mia loaded the dishwasher. "I'm going to have a shower and get dressed while you look through your email. Will you be ready to leave in forty-five minutes?"

"Yes, I'll shower after you get dressed." Luke made himself another coffee and settled out on the deck with his laptop.

Mia was out of the shower, with her hair dried in fifteen minutes. She glanced at the bed. Luke had made it with military precision. She smiled. He'd been like that when they'd been together in grad school. He said it was boarding school that had drilled that in him. She added the toss pillows and fluffed them up. She pulled out a sundress from her closet and some comfortable sandals. The dress was a light blue flowered print that was made of a soft material. It had deep pockets as well. A delicate gold chain and gold hoop earrings completed the look. Her face had just a touch of makeup.

"You look nice," Luke said as she walked out to the balcony.

"Thanks. Anything you need to deal with before we go out?"

"No. All's good in my world. I won't be long." Luke leaned in and kissed Mia. "You really look lovely."

Mia made herself a coffee and sat out on the balcony waiting for Luke.

When he came out of the bedroom, he looked fresh and alert. He'd dressed in lightweight shorts and a short-sleeved golf shirt.

"Are you ready to go?" Mia asked.

"Yes, let's get to the Farmers Market."

Mia grabbed her crossbody bag. They left her apartment and drove to the Farmers Market.

She found a parking spot close to the market. Mia pulled some reuseable shopping bags out of the car and took them with her.

They walked down the street toward the market. There were people going in and out of the entrance, and Mia could hear music playing. There were over one hundred vendors at the market. They stopped at the entrance, and Mia took a map of the market. The market had recently undergone extensive renovations. An addition had been added made largely of glass and brick. It provided additional space for meetings and events. There was an art gallery in the new space.

"It's much bigger than I imagined," Luke said.

Mia grinned. "It is. There are vendors upstairs as well. Let's wander around and see what there is."

"Is there something you need in particular?" Luke asked.

"I'd like some honey, but apart from that, we can just look around. If I see something else, I'll pick it up. You never know what you'll find."

They wandered among the fresh fruit and vegetable vendors. At this time of year, there were many options to choose from. Each stall had their speciality and Mia knew a few of the vendors, having been a regular customer of the market for a few years.

She stopped at Abbott's Apiary and chatted with Sara, one of the owners.

"Mia, how are you?" Sara asked.

"I'm well. Sara, meet Luke Forbes. He's here from England for a few weeks."

"Pleased to meet you." Sara held out her hand.

Luke shook her hand and said, "Nice to meet you, too. How long have you kept bees?"

"My husband and I have had our hives for about ten years."

"Abbott's Apiary makes the most wonderful honey. And I need two more bottles of honey. One for me and one for Gran."

Sara pulled two jars of honey and set them in Mia's bag. She added a couple of index cards. "New recipes we've developed. I think you'll like them. Oh, and here's a sample of a salad dressing we've been testing. It's nice and light."

"Thanks, Sara." Mia paid for her purchases, and she and Luke continued on their way.

They walked past other food vendors, and they included vendors with preserves, baking, and chocolate. They sampled different foods, and Luke couldn't resist picking up chocolates and preserves for Gran.

Beyond the food stalls were crafts. And the artisans had a wide variety. From felted animals to stained glass windows and everything in between. Mia stopped at a booth displaying ceramic mugs and plates. "I love this stuff. I wish I could do it myself." She picked up a mug and wrapped her hand around the mug. "Fits my hand perfectly." She glanced at the price. "Not unreasonable." There were four mugs in beautiful shades of blue. The pattern on the mugs resembled waves along the lakeshore. She pulled out her credit card to purchase them. The potter wrapped the mugs carefully, and Mia placed them in one of her bags.

Mia and Luke stopped for an iced coffee on their way out. They sat at a bistro table and watched people go in and out of the market. Mia's phone rang. It was Alex.

"Mia, I'm sorry to disturb you and Luke, but Danielle just called me, really upset." Alex drew a breath. "The coroner's report says that Uncle Tim was murdered!"

Chapter Seven

Saturday Morning

“Oh no! How?”

“He had cyanide in his system. I don't know how that happened or who killed him. Danielle's so upset. The police are going to his house with a search warrant. Danielle asked if you could come by and help.”

“I can come by, but I'm not sure how I can help. What does she need?”

“She remembers that you figured out who killed Ethan and thinks that you could help with this.”

Mia frowned. “But that was different. And I'm not a police officer.”

Luke leaned forward. “What's wrong?”

“Alex, hang on a minute. I need to fill Luke in.” Mia quickly told Luke what she knew.

“It won't hurt to be there for Danielle. I don't mind going with you.”

“Are you sure?”

“Yes. Tell Alex we'll meet her there.”

“Alex, we'll meet you at Danielle's.”

“You'll need to meet us at Uncle Tim's house.” Alex rattled off the address, and Mia scribbled it on a napkin.

“Okay, we'll meet you there as soon as I can get us there.”

Mia hung up and looked at Luke. “This isn't good news. We'd better head out.” Mia gathered her things, and they hustled to the car.

Mia entered the address into the Jeep's navigation system. "Okay, not too far from here."

As Mia navigated the drive, she asked Luke, "Do you know anything about cyanide poisoning?"

"No, just that it's not something you normally come back from. Did Alex say how it was administered?"

"No. She was really upset. And I don't blame her. A sudden death is stressful, but to think he's been murdered is even worse."

They arrived at Tim's home and found Danielle and Alex's cars in the driveway. It was on a beautiful tree-lined street. Most of the homes in the area were Victorian in style and had well-landscaped, but small yards. The street was quiet. There were two police cars and a forensics van parked on the street.

They hurried out of the Jeep and walked to the front door.

Alex opened the door. "Thanks for coming. The police just got here. Come on in."

Mia and Luke followed Alex to the living room.

Danielle was reading a document, and there were several police officers in the room. There was one man dressed in a suit, and he had a police badge attached to his jacket pocket.

The man in the suit looked at them as they walked in. "Who are you and why are you here?"

"Mia Reid, I'm a friend of Danielle's. This is Luke Forbes, he's with me."

"You wouldn't be Dr. Forbes from Interpol?"

"I am. And you would be?"

"I'm Detective Joe Martin. Good to meet you. I'm scheduled to take your sessions next week." The two men shook hands.

"We're here because Danielle asked Mia to come. Can you tell me what's going on?" Luke asked.

"Ms. Fraser, is it all right if I tell them what we've learned?"

Danielle glanced at him and noticed Mia and Luke. "Sorry, Mia. I didn't see you there. Yes, of course. You can tell them anything. I'm still trying to understand what you're looking for."

"The autopsy report on Mr. Fraser came back with signs of cyanide in his system. We're here to look for possible sources of cyanide in his home and outbuildings. Once we're through here, we'll need to go to the store and do the same search."

Luke nodded. "Danielle, may I look at the document?"

Danielle turned the document over to him.

Luke read it through. "It says you need to look through the home for any substance that could be cyanide in a powder or liquid form. The document is a legal document. There's nothing to stop them from their search."

"Let me get this search started. Ms. Fraser, we'll try to keep the disruption to a minimum." Detective Martin gave orders to the officers, they put on protective gear, and they scattered in the house.

Danielle was in tears.

Alex took her by the shoulders. "Come, sit down. I'll get you some water."

Mia helped Danielle on the couch. "Danielle, I'm so sorry."

"I can't believe someone poisoned him." She sobbed.

"Did your dad say if anyone was coming to see him after the event on Wednesday night?" Mia asked.

Danielle shook her head.

"Did you notice anyone hanging around outside when you left?"

"No." Danielle gulped a breath. "There wasn't anyone around. Alex, Steve, and I walked to our cars. Cheryl stayed behind to lock up. Dad didn't say anything about meeting with anyone. His plan was to update his files and have a drink before going home."

Alex arrived with a bottle of water. "They think the poison was in his drink."

Danielle opened the bottle. "He always had a whiskey after one of the evening events. It helped relax him after his day. And I guess the whiskey would have concealed the taste of the cyanide." She drank from the bottle. "The police are going to search the store, too. Detective Martin said that when he arrived."

"Where's Steve?" Mia asked.

"He was going to the store to check on something. He left early this morning."

"Have you contacted him about this?"

"I've called and left a message and texted him too. But I haven't heard from him." Danielle frowned. "He should be here by now."

They sat in the living room while the police went about the search.

"What happens now?" Alex asked.

"The police will investigate. This means it's murder or suicide," Luke said.

Danielle drew a breath. "There's no way he would have killed himself. He was so excited about this baby. You could see it in the way he talked. No. I won't believe that." Danielle turned to Mia. "Mia, I need your help. I want you to look into this. You know how to look for things that people miss. You did that in Scotland this summer. You figured out who killed Ethan. Please, can you help me?"

Mia paused a moment. Danielle grabbed her by the arm. "Mia, please."

"I'm not sure what I can do that the police won't be able to do. I'd like to help, but..."

"I'm convinced it has to do with the store. I think someone wanted something that was in there. Dad had been getting antiques from Europe and Asia. That was something new for him. And there's been different people working with him. Not Cheryl. She's been there for more than five years now, but people I'd never seen before."

"Do you think someone stole an item from the store, and they killed him for it?" Mia asked.

"I don't know. I just know things were different at the shop. Dad had been asking me to help, and when he found out I was pregnant, he stopped asking. He said Steve was going to help him out. Steve was there on the weekends and evenings, helping Dad move stuff in the store. At least that's what he said. He'd come home, and his clothes were dirty and messed up."

"What about his job with the investment company?"

"He's still working there. He said something the other day about making sure our money was bulletproof. I'm not sure what he meant." Danielle sighed. "I think he's stressed about the baby coming and wants to make sure we're okay financially."

"Have you let your lawyer know the police are here?" Alex asked.

"Ah! No, I need to do that right now." Danielle grabbed her phone and made the call. Alex, Mia, and Luke moved to the dining room to give her some privacy.

"Can you help her out?" Alex asked.

"I'm really not sure I can. If he was murdered, it's a matter for the police."

"What if there's something happening at the store that ties to the murder?" Alex asked.

"Like what?"

"I don't know. I know you're great at finding things out. You've always been able to look at a puzzle and come up with a different solution." Alex crossed her arms. "Would you be willing to look at his files at the store and whatever he had on his laptop?"

Mia glanced at Luke. "What do you think?"

"So long as you aren't interfering in the investigation, there shouldn't be any problem. And if you find anything, you connect with the police immediately."

Danielle came back to the living room. "The lawyer said to cooperate with the police. They can search the house and the store too."

"Danielle, I'll help where I can. Do you think I could look through the files in the office and on your father's laptop?"

"That would be wonderful. Yes, of course, you can have access to his files and laptop. Will you go to the store when the police go there?"

"I will. You need to know that if I find anything that will help the police in their investigation, I'll have to turn it over to them."

Danielle nodded. "That makes sense. I'll let the detective know I've given you permission to take the laptop. I think most of the files that are in the store are also stored on his laptop."

"Did your father have an office at home?" Mia asked.

"Yes. It's just off the kitchen. I took some of the files out of the cabinets. They're on the table here if you need them."

"Are they personal files or are they work files?"

"The ones on the table are all work files. I was going to bring them to the office so Cheryl could help me with them, but if you can look at them, I'd appreciate it."

Mia looked through the files scattered on the table.

One folder was filled with information on antiquities from Central America. Mia looked through it carefully. Tim had contact names and addresses in the folder for people in Belize, Honduras, and Mexico. Mia took her phone and snapped a photo of the information. None of the names were familiar to her, but that didn't mean anything. Central America had a large group of people who were involved in the antiquities market. And that's what it was. A market. There were many individuals who worked hard to protect the antiquities and made certain that any of them were dispersed around the world correctly, with proper documentation and distribution. Others weren't so scrupulous. And valuable artifacts were copied and sold illegally around the world.

Mia did a search with one of the names. His store address and a website showed up. When she clicked on the website, it gave a 404 error code. A further search came up with a newspaper obituary for the man. He'd died in a car accident a few months ago.

A search of the two other men listed gave her the same results. This was alarming. Were all of Tim's contacts dead? Were they accidents, or was someone systematically getting rid of the people Tim had worked with?

Mia put the folder aside and opened the next one. Again, a list of names of people Tim had worked with. These were from the U.S. and in Canada. Mia scanned the list; the names weren't familiar. They could be clients, or they could be dealers as well. She checked a few names on her phone with the same results. The individuals she looked at had all died in the last six months. Most had died in accidents or suddenly at home, according to their obituaries. None had had a long-term illness.

Mia sat back in her chair, conscious that Danielle and Alex were watching her.

"Did you find anything?" Alex asked.

"I don't know. These two files have lists of people, phone numbers, addresses, websites. They seem to have been involved in the antique world as buyers or clients. But the ones I've checked out are all dead."

Danielle raised her head. "How?"

"Some were accidents, like a car accident or a hunting accident. But some don't give a cause of death." Mia frowned. "When I look at when your dad printed these out, it looks as if he started printing them several months ago."

"Can you show me?" Danielle asked.

"Sure, look at this file. You can see the date on the bottom of the page when he printed it. The people who are dead died during the last year."

Alex frowned. "Well, that's not unexpected. None of them were living in the same place, right? And did they know each other or belong to the same organization?"

"Not everyone belongs to the Antique Dealers Association. Dad was a member for a long time, and he let his membership go." Danielle took a drink of water. "It isn't necessary to belong, but you do get some benefits. There's a Canadian Association and an International Association. Dad took some courses before he started his shop, and he worked with a dealer who was a member of the Canadian Association at the beginning of his career. He had a business degree as well. When he picked a new piece or was looking to purchase something, he studied it and learned as much as he could about that period. He said that's how you learned."

Mia nodded. "Gran was a member of the Canadian Association when she was in business."

Luke came down the stairs. "Mia, could you come here, please?"

"Of course." She put the folders on the table and joined him and the detective in the office.

"Detective Martin has a question regarding something he found in the desk."

"Sure. What did you find?"

He held up a man's ring. It had a red gemstone in the center. The gemstone was surrounded by small diamonds and emeralds. There was no inscription on the inside of the ring. "What can you tell me about this ring?" he asked.

Mia took the ring and held it up to the light. "This seems to be the same ring that we found on the Isle of Skye this summer. But it can't be. That ring's on display in the museum on the island."

Luke nodded. "It's possible this is a fake. A good one, but nonetheless, a fake."

"I can't tell. I don't have any tools here to examine it." Mia looked at Luke. "This is more your specialty. Can you identify it as a fake?"

"Not without more careful examination. I'll need to ask Danielle if we can take this ring and examine it. If it's a fake, then I'd like to know where Tim got it."

"Did you find other items?" Mia asked.

Detective Martin shook his head. "No, we've confined our search to the parameters of the search warrant."

"Have you found anything that shows Tim had cyanide in the house?"

"Nothing."

"Let me ask Danielle about the ring and see if we can bring it with us to examine it more carefully." Luke took the ring and left Mia and the detective.

"Does this mean that the cyanide didn't come from Tim? And if that's the case, someone else would have had to introduce it?"

"That's right. Or it could be at his office."

"I was going through some of his files, and I found a couple of files with lists of contacts. I checked several of them online, and they're all dead. They died within the last year, and not many by natural causes."

Detective Martin raised an eyebrow. "And this is of interest to us how?"

"What if someone were killing these dealers one by one? Luke's working on exposing a smuggling ring. It could be possible that they're all part of the ring and had auctions like Tim did. When they outlived their usefulness, someone had them killed."

"That's pretty far-fetched."

"I know. But if this is part of a bigger picture, a large smuggling ring, and people aren't needed anymore, it could happen. Just get rid of the people that were working for you to eliminate any loose ends."

The police officers came downstairs, carrying several bags with them. "We took everything out of the medicine chests in both bathrooms."

"Good. I've got a few items here as well. Let's give a receipt to Ms. Fraser, and we'll let her be."

The officers left the house, and Detective Martin met Danielle and Alex in the living room.

"Here's a receipt of the items we've taken. Everything will be returned once they've been tested, provided they don't return as positive for cyanide." He handed Danielle the paperwork, and Danielle signed where he indicated.

"Have you been able to help Luke with the ring?" he asked.

Danielle shook her head. "I've never seen that ring before. Dad didn't wear rings anymore. The only one I've ever seen him wear was his wedding ring, and he just stopped wearing that one last year."

"It looks like the one we found at the dig this summer. But I know it can't be that ring." Mia said.

"I sent a message to D. I. Anderson about the ring. He's going to verify it's still in the museum." Luke looked up from his phone. "Danielle has given me permission to examine the ring. I'll look at it today and see if I can learn anything from it. I have equipment at your place that I can use."

"Sounds good. Danielle, I'm sorry about all this. Hopefully, we can learn more about this ring."

Alex had her hand on Danielle's back. "If the police are finished, I'd like to get Danielle home for a rest."

Detective Martin nodded. "Not a problem. We're done here, and we'll check the store now. Did you want someone present to monitor the search?"

"I've asked Mia and Luke to go with you," Danielle said.

"I'll give you a receipt for the ring," Luke said.

Danielle shook her head. "Don't bother. And you don't have to rush to get this done on my account. If that's all, I'd like to get home."

Mia picked up the folders and grabbed her purse. "Alex, can you give me the alarm code to the store? And I'll call you when we're done at the shop."

"Give me your phone."

Mia complied, and Alex added the alarm code and the password for Tim's laptop under her contact information. She handed a set of keys to Mia. "These are to the store."

"Thanks. I'll talk to you soon."

Chapter Eight

Saturday Afternoon

Mia and Luke drove to the store. "I'm sorry, this isn't what I had planned for your first day back," Mia said.

"No problem. I think it will help Danielle if we're there just to verify everything is being done according to protocol." Luke shifted in his seat. "What are you thinking about the people who died in the past year?"

"I wonder if they were colleagues that he worked with to find new antiques. Their locations lead me to believe they would have been able to deal with antiquities and possibly artifacts. Tim didn't deal with those items. He was strictly antiques."

"Perhaps. In the world of smuggling, it's not unusual to eliminate someone when they stop being useful. I'm not saying Mr. Fraser was involved in smuggling, but the other people might have been."

They pulled in front of the store. The detective and police officers were waiting for them.

"We'll get started. The search is going to focus on the office, break room, and powder room," Detective Martin said.

The officers went in and began their search.

"Is it okay if we just sit and watch?" Mia asked.

"Of course. You won't be in the way." Detective Martin directed his officers to get started.

Mia watched as the officers went through the office and break room.

"Do you think they'll find anything?" she asked Luke.

Luke shrugged. "Hard to tell. I don't know that whoever killed Tim would have been careless enough to leave cyanide in the shop. But they could have slipped up."

Mia leaned against him. He felt solid under her. "You must be getting hungry."

"I could eat."

Mia snorted. "You can always eat. That hasn't changed since our grad school years."

"Well, I am more careful. I can't eat a full pizza like I used to." Luke grinned.

Detective Martin came around a short time later. "We're done. I didn't think we'd find anything. Nothing that looked like cyanide. We are taking the bottle of whiskey and the two glasses. We'll test them in the lab to see if they contain traces of cyanide." He looked around the store. "I'd say we're done here. Mr. Forbes, I'll see you next week. Enjoy the rest of the weekend." The police left the store.

"I'm going to check on the files in the office and get his laptop."

"I'll lend a hand."

The office was a small windowless room. A large antique desk dominated the room. There was a computer monitor in the centre of the desk. Family photographs occupied the left-hand side of the desk. A magnifying lamp was on the right-hand side. Two ceiling-height oak bookcases were located on the wall behind the desk. The books appeared to be reference materials. Wooden filing cabinets were on the right wall of the office and stood about five feet tall and three feet wide.

Mia opened the filing cabinets in the desk and glanced through them quickly. "Most of these are for payroll, personnel, and basic running of the store." She looked at the row of filing cabinets. "I really don't want to go through all of those today."

"Why don't we start with the laptop and the files you brought from his home office? That should give us enough to work on later today and tomorrow."

"That's a good plan. I don't think we'll have time to check every file in this office." Mia picked up the laptop and power cord.

They left the office, and Mia set the alarm and locked the door.

"I'll call Alex and let her know everything's done. I'm sure the detective will let Danielle know when she can access the store again." Mia made the call while they were walking to her car. Alex's phone went to voicemail, and Mia left a detailed message.

"Done. Let's find somewhere to eat," Mia said as she unlocked her car. "What do you feel like eating?"

"Well, now that you mention it, I'd love some pizza," Luke said.

Mia chuckled. "No kidding. Let's go to the Beaches area. It's not far. There's a few nice restaurants, and I know there's an excellent pizza place. We can walk along the boardwalk afterwards."

Mia drove efficiently through the traffic. There were several streets closed due to special events. They arrived at their destination and found that parking was at a premium. Mia circled a couple of blocks before she found a space.

They held hands as they walked down the sidewalk. There were restaurants and quirky little shops lining each side of the street. The shops had awnings providing some protection from the weather. Most of the shops were painted in bright, colorful shades of blue, red, and yellow. Several of the restaurants had sidewalk tables.

Mia led Luke down a path. "This goes to the beach. And there's a great pizza place right around the corner." They passed an ice cream shop called "Moos" which had a line up going out the door and down the street. There was a statue of a black and white cow next to the shop.

"Must be good ice cream," Luke said.

"It's excellent. Rich and creamy, and they have over sixty flavors. It's popular for good reason. We can stop in on our way back." Mia pointed down the street. "The pizza place I'm thinking about is down here. There's a terrace behind it that overlooks the water."

"Sounds great."

They stopped in front of the pizza restaurant where the hostess greeted them.

"We have room on the terrace if you'd like to sit there."

"That's perfect. Thanks."

The hostess smiled. "You arrived at the right time. Follow me."

Mia and Luke followed her to the back of the restaurant and out on the terrace. The hostess led them to a table for two with excellent views of the lake. A large umbrella provided protection from the sun's rays and heat. The hostess gave them menus and said, "Your server will be here shortly."

Mia smiled her thanks.

"What's good?"

"Every type of pizza is excellent. You can order a full pie, or you can get slices of different ones to taste. I always like doing that. Alex and I come here often, and it's a great way to sample different pizzas."

"Do you want to try the sampler pizza?"

"Sure. Do you want beer or sangria?"

"A cold beer would be good."

The server arrived, and Mia gave her their orders. She promised to return with a pitcher of beer for them.

Mia sat back in her chair and watched people stroll down the beach. There were several volleyball games going on, and there was boisterous cheering for two of the teams.

"Are you all right?" Luke asked.

Mia glanced in his direction. "Sort of. I'm thinking about who killed Tim and why. If he was poisoned, it could have been in his whiskey, but who did it? And how could he not notice?"

The server arrived with their beer, and Luke poured them each a glass.

"There's a lot to look at. I'll help you look through his files to see if there's any information there." Luke took a drink of beer. "I'm interested in learning more about the contacts he had in other countries that have died. I'll be following up on that with my people to see if there was foul play."

Mia frowned. "Do you think they were part of the smuggling ring?"

"We'll check their activities in the months before they died. Who they worked with, who visited their shops. We'll need to access their email accounts. That might provide more information."

"It doesn't sound like it's going to be done quickly."

"It depends. We have a lot of resources available, and we have people on the ground in those countries as well. Has Alex messaged you?"

Mia checked her phone. "Not yet. I know she was going to organize the memorial service. She'll get back to me if she needs to."

"So, tell me how Gran's been doing?"

Mia grinned. "She's amazing. She's still active on several boards, including the Lakeview Museum. And she's involved with her condo board, too. I'm continually in awe of her energy."

"She obviously enjoys what she's doing."

"Yes. Although Tim's death has shaken her up more than she's let on. She helped him when he was starting in the business. She was his go-to when he needed something and wasn't sure how to do it. At least for the first few years. And she was there for Danielle and him when her mom passed away."

The server arrived with their sampler pizza. There were eight pieces in total, all different varieties of the pizzas available. "Let me know if you need anything else," she said after dropping off their meal.

They made short work of their pizza. Luke insisted on paying for lunch, and they left for a walk along the beach. Mia took off her sandals.

There was a breeze coming off the lake, and Mia could see families flying kites along the beach. There were several large kites in different shapes that filled the sky.

"Oh, oh, I think there's going to be a crash." Luke pointed to two large rectangular kites that appeared to be on a collision course.

They watched as the parents hurried to help their kids and averted tangled lines and downed kites.

Further down the beach, they discovered a sandcastle building contest. There were prizes to be won. They sat on bleachers to watch the teams build their castles. The sand was hard-packed and made building tall sandcastles easy.

Mia glanced at Luke and noticed he seemed to be tiring.

"Ready to head back?"

"I think so. Between the beer and the pizza, the carbs are making me sleepy."

"No problem. Let's go back, and we can take a break."

"Let's not forget the ice cream, though." Luke took her hand as they turned and walked back.

A short time later, they were in front of the ice cream shop. They stood in line and debated on the merits of the different flavors available and argued over cones or cups.

"Ice cream is meant to be eaten in a cone." Luke insisted.

Mia shook her head. "The portion sizes are enormous, and the ice cream melts before you can eat it all." She pointed to a family walking away with their cones. "See, there's no way they'll be able to eat all that before it runs down the cone."

At the order window, Luke asked for a strawberry and chocolate cone. He looked at Mia, "I dare you to have a cone."

"Not happening. I've made too many messes in the last few years. I'll take a serving of maple pecan in a cup."

The server chuckled. "We always have people who debate about the right way to eat our ice cream. We don't care, so long as you enjoy it."

They paid and walked a short distance to a bench to enjoy their treat. They watched families go by with kids who had had a bit too much sun and were tired out, who didn't want to leave. Luke struggled to keep ahead of his melting ice cream.

"Told you." Mia laughed.

Luke checked the area for a place to wash his hands and found a fountain where he could wet the napkins from Moos to clean up. "You were right. But it was delicious ice cream."

"Ready to head back?" Mia put on her sandals.

"Definitely."

Arriving at Mia's, Luke said, "I'm going to grab some shut-eye."

Mia made herself an iced tea and took Tim's laptop out on the balcony. She entered the passcode Alex had given her, and the laptop came to life. A few minutes of searching, and she found folders on his desktop. She clicked on the email icon.

The screen populated with the emails in his inbox. On the left-hand side of the screen, there were a few folders. Mia glanced at the emails in his inbox. Most of them were unread. They had come in since Wednesday evening.

She looked at the folders. They appeared to be store business, electricity bills, city taxes, requests for specific items from clients. Not a lot there to explain his death.

"I wonder," she thought to herself. It wasn't unusual for people to have more than one email account. Mia hovered her mouse over Tim's email account icon, and another account popped up. She clicked on it. When asked for a password, she shook her head. Ugh. Would he have used the same password as his laptop? She tried it, and it worked. *"Thank goodness for sloppy password management."*

She glanced at the emails in the account and was surprised to find a large number of folders with dates on them. Mia clicked on the first folder, and emails popped up. The correspondence was between Tim and someone named Josh Humphries. She read through several of the emails. They were all about tracking shipments of antiques that were enroute to Tim's shop. The information showed the shipments were originating in the Philippines. Mia sat back and thought about the stock Tim had in his shop. Nothing there was from the Philippines. Could it have been a location where the antiques were shipped and then distributed to the buyers?

She skimmed through the emails. They went back eight years. There were twenty different folders in this email account. If she went through them all, she'd be reading emails for days. Mia thought about what she needed to know. Barbara had been in the store on Wednesday evening. Did she and Tim correspond at all? She typed the name 'Barbara' in the search bar and hit enter.

A list of emails appeared. The most recent was dated two weeks ago. Mia clicked it open.

'Charles is concerned with your store not keeping up with the specifications that were outlined in your agreement with him. I'll be back in Lakeview next week and expect to meet with you to discuss the next steps.

I trust we'll be able to come to a mutually beneficial solution.'

Mia blew out a breath. Okay, that was vague enough. What agreement did Tim have with a Charles, and why was Barbara in the middle of it? She looked through the folder this email had been in and discovered emails going back ten years. She knew she didn't have time to read through all the emails this afternoon. She went to her desk in the second bedroom, opened one of the drawers, and found a new thumb drive. Back on the balcony, she inserted the thumb drive and began copying all the emails in the second account. Mia was going to copy everything on the laptop as backup and would make a copy for Danielle if she wanted.

While the files were copying, Mia opened a folder labeled CG Auctions. There were over a hundred emails in the folder. Opening one at random, Mia saw it was a list of potential buyers for the auctions. Email addresses, last names, and mailing addresses were listed. Opening an email from one person revealed the man was from Hungary, another one was from Colombia. Mia's eyebrows raised. This list was worldwide, and the men and women on the list were wealthy individuals. Some were high-ranking government officials. There were emails with photos of the items that would be available at the auctions, and Mia's heart sank. She recognized several items. They had been reported stolen a few years ago and had never been recovered.

Could Tim have been dealing with smuggled antiquities? How could he have gotten involved with them? He didn't have connections to that world. Mia would know. Or she thought she would know.

This presented a problem. If Tim was involved in selling smuggled artifacts or antiquities, it would hurt Danielle. Was there any way he didn't know what he was doing?

Mia shook her head. The wording in the emails sent out as invitations to the auctions was clear. The artifacts were rare and unavailable for sale anywhere else. The recipients of the emails were each assigned a code to take part in the auctions. They could attend the auction in Lakeview, or they could send a delegate. In about half the cases, a delegate attended. That provided the email recipient with a cover that they wouldn't be exposed. It wasn't a complicated affair.

Mia started digging further into the emails. She found more folders with information on the auctions. They went back just over eight years. Every year had its own folder. Mia thought back. That was about the time Danielle's mother was very ill with MS. Mia wondered if Tim had started the auctions to make more money. And had he made money on them? He would have needed someone else to work with. An operation the size she had seen in the emails was big. She glanced at the clock. Luke should be up soon. She'd bring it up with him.

She found it hard to believe Tim could have worked the auctions on his own. He'd need access to the antiquities and a way to bring them in. More and more, it appeared he might have been involved in a smuggling ring. It made sense that he would have been part of Charles Gordon's organization.

She did a search for 'Charles Gordon'. The search box flooded with emails from him. Mia opened one of the emails. Reading it, her heart sank. Here was the proof Tim was involved with Charles and the smuggling ring in Canada.

The email outlined the antiquities Tim would need to auction off. A list of instructions for inviting the clients to the auction and the reserve price for each antiquity. Mia knew that meant the lowest figure the dealer would accept. There were photos of the antiquities Tim would be responsible for selling.

She opened one of the most recent emails. Charles was reprimanding Tim, reminding him of their shared history with antiquity auctions. And he reminded Tim of the agreement they had. He didn't get into specifics in the email.

Mia knew Charles Gordon. He'd been the sponsor for the dig Mia and Ethan were supposed to work on the Isle of Skye in June. He had a large international construction and design firm. Mia had discovered a cache of stolen antiquities and had tied Charles to them. That's when they discovered he'd been behind a smuggling ring that operated out of Canada.

They didn't know who'd been involved in selling the antiquities. And Mia thought she had found him, or at least one of the individuals.

She continued her dive into the files on the auctions. She noted the number of auctions had dwindled in the last year. Could Tim have been trying to get out of doing the auctions?

Mia sat back. She'd have to go through the rest of the emails in the file, but it appeared this was the proof that Charles Gordon was smuggling antiquities and selling them in Lakeview. She made a note to let Luke know about this when he woke up.

Mia's phone rang. It was Danielle.

Chapter Nine

Saturday Evening

"Hey, Mia. Alex told me the police went through the office. Did they say anything about when I'd have access there?"

"Detective Martin didn't say anything about that. He said he'd be in touch with you if anything showed up and would send you a list of the items they'd taken."

"Okay. I'll check my email. I need to figure out what I'm going to do with the shop."

"Are you going to keep it open?"

"I'm not sure. I had a phone call from Martha Jones. She has a store down the street, and she's interested in buying some of the stock Dad had."

"What did you tell her?"

"That I needed some time to figure things out. I know I don't want to run the store, and I don't think I have time to deal with it. Steve had just started to work with Dad, getting to know some of the stock. But I'm not sure if he wants to take it on. I also had a call from a real estate agent. He wanted to know if I was interested in selling. He told me the location is very good, and the store would sell quickly."

"Wow. I guess I didn't think people would be interested in buying it right away."

"I didn't even think of selling until I got those two calls. It's something I need to talk to Steve and our lawyer about." Danielle sighed. "Anyway, I just wanted to say thanks for going to the store with the police."

"No problem. Have you decided on when the service is going to be?"

"Tuesday evening at seven. Alex is organizing it. Once she's got everything finalized, she'll be sending out the information."

"Thanks. Gran, Luke, and I will be there."

"I'll let you go. I've got a few more things to deal with. Again, thank you for going to the store." Danielle disconnected the call.

Mia called Gran.

"Mia, how are you?"

"I'm well. Luke and I had a busy morning." Mia filled Gran in on their day. When she told her about Tim being poisoned, Gran gasped.

"Who would do that? What are the police going to do?"

"We don't know who did it. The police went to the store to check for cyanide. Luke and I went with them. They were thorough. Detective Martin is going to get back to Danielle about anything they find. This changes how the police are investigating. It's ruled a homicide."

Gran sighed. "It's deliberate. No one can make a mistake like that. Danielle doesn't believe Tim did this himself, does she?"

"No. She was clear about that. Her father was excited about her pregnancy. His service is going to be on Tuesday evening. Alex is organizing it and will send me the information."

"I want to go."

"Of course. I'll let you know the details, and I'll make sure to pick you up."

They chatted a few minutes longer and then hung up.

Luke joined her on the balcony.

"Did you get some rest?"

"Yes. I fell asleep, and I feel much better." Luke glanced toward the water. "What did you get up to?"

Mia pointed to Tim's laptop. "I did some digging in Tim's files. I found some information that you may find useful." She opened the files and handed the laptop to Luke.

He spent a few minutes reading through the emails. Looking up at Mia, he said, "This is excellent. It ties Charles Gordon to the smuggling ring and

Tim as well. I don't think Danielle will be happy with the news. But I am, and so will my superiors."

"What are you going to do now?"

"I'll copy these and then send them on to my supervisor. I expect to have some feedback from them in the morning."

"Are they going to send you away when they read this?"

"No. They may send another agent here to help me, but there are agents around the world working on this. I'll go get a thumb drive to copy this information." Luke set the laptop on the patio table and kissed Mia. "Thanks, love. This is going to be very helpful."

Mia watched as he hurried back with a thumb drive and copied the files he needed. He grabbed his laptop. "I'll send these off now, and then maybe we can figure out dinner?" he asked.

"Yes, there's a nice pub a short walk from here. It's got steak, seafood, and vegetarian dishes. I think you'll enjoy it."

A few minutes later, Luke looked up from his laptop. "Done. Did you want to go out now?"

"Yes. I'm hungry, and it's a nice evening. We can go for a walk after dinner."

The pub was casual and had good food. After a short wait, they were seated at an outside table that overlooked the water. Mia enjoyed the atmosphere at the pub. The servers were friendly and knowledgeable about the meals. She ordered a seafood dish, and Luke ordered a steak.

Dinner was a leisurely affair with wine and appetizers to begin with.

"Is there something you'd like to do or see while you're here?" Mia asked.

Luke put his glass of wine down. "Not especially. Work is going to keep me tied up during the week. I know you're busy as well. And with this latest information on Mr. Gordon's affairs, well, who knows what will turn up."

"When will you hear back from your supervisor?"

"Possibly tomorrow morning. Right now, I want to enjoy this evening."

* * *

Sunday Morning

Mia's phone pinged with a text.

Alex: Are we still on for brunch?

Mia: Yes. Where do you want to meet?

Alex: Marco's at 11:00?

Mia: Perfect. We'll meet you there.

Alex: Zack will be with me. He's looking forward to talking to Luke.

Mia: See you soon.

Alex and Zack were waiting for them outside the restaurant. Zack extended his hand to Luke, "Hi, good to see you again."

Luke shook his hand. "Thanks. How've you been?"

They walked into the restaurant. Alex headed to the hostess station while Zack and Luke caught up.

The hostess led them to their table, handed them menus, and left after telling them the server would be by shortly.

"You're going to be in Lakeview for a few weeks?" Zack asked Luke.

"That's the plan at the moment. I'll be working next weekend. We're having officers from Montreal and Vancouver come here for an intensive workshop."

The server arrived, and after filling their coffee cups, she took their orders and hurried off.

Alex leaned forward. "I told him what happened with Uncle Tim."

"I knew something was wrong the minute I saw her last night. Unfortunately, this type of death is a difficult one."

"Do you know anything about cyanide poisoning?" Mia asked. Zack was a doctor and might know more about cyanide poisoning.

"I know the basics. Most people don't recover from cyanide poisoning. It depends how it's administered. I take it in this case it was mixed with his whiskey?"

"That's what we think happened." Luke put his coffee cup down.

"As I told Alex, it would have been a quick death. He'd start gasping, struggle to breathe, and then lapse into unconsciousness. Ultimately, he suffocated."

"So, there was no way to save him?" Mia asked.

"Unfortunately, not at that stage. I'd like to know who did it and where they got the cyanide. Cyanide's a controlled substance. It's used in different industries."

"That's the question. No one knows if there was someone with him. And Danielle says her father wouldn't have killed himself. He was too excited about the new baby coming," Mia said.

"Danielle's focused on getting through the next few days. She can't believe someone would do this to her father. And honestly, I can't either. Uncle Tim wasn't perfect, but he was a nice guy." Alex's voice shook.

Mia looked at Luke. He nodded.

"I was able to access his email account. He had two. One was for the day-to-day operation of the store. The other one, he used for a separate purpose."

Alex put her coffee cup down. "What other purpose?"

"There's no easy way to say this. I think he was involved in auctions that involved stolen antiquities." Mia watched Alex. Her friend's face paled.

"What do you mean, stolen antiquities?" she whispered.

Mia explained to Alex and Zack what she'd found in the emails. She took them through the process she'd used to access the email account and the emails that were in there.

"It looks as if he's been involved for the last eight years. I'm so sorry, Alex. This isn't the type of news I wanted to share with you."

"Have you spoken to Danielle about this?"

"No, I haven't. I don't want to bring this up with her until we know more. I knew I couldn't hide this from you. If he was mixed up with Charles Gordon, then he was with a ruthless group." Mia put her hand on Alex's arm. "You need to be prepared for that, and so does Danielle."

"Mia's right. I've had experience with Mr. Gordon's smuggling ring, and ruthless is a good way to describe it," Luke said.

Zack looked at Alex. "Did you know any of this?"

"No. And I'm sure Danielle doesn't know either. Aunt Rita was very sick with her MS eight years ago. There was an experimental treatment available in the U.S., and Uncle Tim wanted her to do it. I know it was very expensive. I never knew where he got the money for the treatments." Alex took a drink of her coffee. "Is Danielle going to be responsible for anything he did?"

"No. We'll figure this out. My supervisor connected with me this morning and has given me the go-ahead to work with the police here. He believes the artifacts at the auctions were part of the smuggling ring. We may not be done with Charles Gordon yet," Luke said.

"I agree. I think Charles Gordon is behind all of this. I'd love to know where he's hiding," Mia said.

Luke squeezed her hand. "Like I said, we'll figure this out."

"What do I say to Danielle?" Alex asked.

Mia bit her lip. "I think it needs to come from me and Luke. I have the facts that I found on his laptop, and Luke's connected through AART with Interpol."

Alex nodded. "I want to be with you when you tell her."

Mia nodded. "We'll find a time to tell her together."

The server arrived with their food.

"What are you going to be doing here, Luke?" Zack asked.

Mia was grateful Zack was changing the subject.

"I'll be working with a team of officers and detectives doing training on antiquity smuggling. The RCMP will be involved as well. My department at Interpol finds and returns antiquities that were illegally taken. We're aware of a smuggling ring operating out of Canada. Three of the largest cities are involved: Montreal, Lakeview, and Vancouver."

"Are you going to Montreal and Vancouver?" Alex asked.

"Not that I know of. They're coming here. I may have to go there for some follow-up. That hasn't been determined yet."

"How did you get involved with this?" Zack asked.

Luke told them how he'd been approached by a patron at the British Museum to sell an illegally obtained artifact. The patron was shocked that Luke wouldn't sell the artifact for him. Luke and his supervisor at the museum contacted Interpol, and they worked together to return the artifact.

Luke's expertise led Interpol to ask him to join their team.

"Are you happy with what you're doing?" Zack asked.

"Yes. I'm making a difference. Artifact smuggling isn't just about someone stealing an artifact. It finances many underground operations, including drugs, guns, human trafficking, and terrorism. You name it, the money from artifact smuggling reaches into all sorts of other criminal organizations. When we close one, we effectively hurt others."

"Are you in danger?" Alex asked.

"I guess it depends on your definition of danger. I've received some basic training. How to use a gun, self-defense tactics, surveillance. But most of what I do is done with computers and following the money trails. When I'm in the field, I usually have the local police with me."

"That sounds dangerous enough to me," Zack said.

"Zack, what have you been up to?" Mia asked.

"I'm settling in well at Lakeview General. I'm working with the cardiology team for the next two weeks, and then I'll be working with another department. As an anesthesiologist, the hospital is going to have me rotate departments. They're short-staffed right now. It's been busy, but I'm enjoying it. The facilities are state-of-the art."

"Have you been home to Huntsville lately?" Mia prodded.

"I was there earlier this week. My sister and her family were at the cottage. Her kids are a lot of fun. We took them fishing, and I taught the oldest some basic canoeing skills."

"How old are her kids?" Mia asked.

"From four to eight. She has two boys and a girl. The oldest is the girl, and she couldn't wait to get in a canoe." Zack grinned. "She had a great time. I heard all about her friends in skating."

"We're hoping to get away to the cottage next weekend. It depends on Zack's schedule," Alex said.

"My hours are all over the place right now. Once I'm on a rotation, I'll be able to plan ahead. The hospital administrator said it would be a month or so before my schedule is settled."

Zack asked about Mia's job at the museum. "What will you do after the contract?"

"I'm not sure. There are always options, and by then, there might be a new dig that I'd be interested in working on."

"Or something else might come up. You never know what's around the corner," Alex said, pushing aside her plate.

"True enough. Who knows where I'll be in a year, or where any of us could be."

They spent the next twenty minutes chatting about plans for the week.

"We have Uncle Tim's memorial on Tuesday evening. And we're going to your Gran's for dinner tonight."

Mia sat back in her seat. "I have the Museum After Hours event for the exhibit on Friday night. The museum thought they'd get more people coming in on a Friday night than a Wednesday. It's ticketed, and I think it's close to being sold out. I need to be there to talk to patrons about the exhibit."

"I'll be there. Gran asked me to go with her," Alex said.

"I have to work on the weekend as well." Luke said.

"We could still get together for dinner, though. Let's chat later this week, and we'll figure something out." Alex suggested.

Mia made a note in her phone. "I'll touch base with you on Thursday morning, okay?"

"That works for me."

They left and went their separate directions. Mia and Luke walked along the waterfront. People were getting out on their boats. Sailboats dotted the lake. Families were biking along the bike paths. The outdoor patios were open and filling up quickly. In the nearby park, there was a softball game getting underway. Mia and Luke stopped by the benches to take in the game.

Mia's phone pinged with a text from Danielle.

Danielle: Police have said I can get in the store again. Would you mind coming by after 1:30 to check something with me?

Mia read the text out loud to Luke, "Do you mind going?"

"Of course not. When do we have to be at Gran's?"

"At three. I'll let Danielle know."

Mia: Sure. We have to be at my Gran's at 3, though.

Danielle: Thanks, and it shouldn't take long.

"Does she say what she wants to show us?"

Mia shook her head. "No, just that it shouldn't take long. Let's go back to my place and get ready to meet her. We'll only have about thirty minutes to get there."

At Mia's condo, she and Luke went directly to the parking garage to get her Jeep. Timeless Treasures was too far to walk to. While Mia drove, Luke checked his email.

"I've heard back from my supervisor about those names that were in the auction folder."

"What does he say?"

"Several of them are connected to illegally obtained artifacts. There's a strong possibility that they're still involved and actively looking to purchase more artifacts. He wants me to look at Tim's activities more closely. In particular, the last three years."

"Well, I guess he's confirming that Tim was involved with smuggling artifacts. Right?"

"It appears that way. I don't want to say anything in front of Danielle. Her father's dead and can't be prosecuted, but we'll have to look closely at the stock in the shop."

"You think he'd keep them at the store? I know he had a storage unit, too."

"Either one. I'm not sure about accessing the storage unit. We'll need information from Danielle."

"I'll ask her if she knows anything about it." Mia pulled into a parking spot just shy of the shop. "Are you getting involved in this investigation?"

"Yes. I'm here, and my supervisor is going to follow up with the city police to make certain we work together."

"What's going to happen with the training you're supposed to do?"

"It's still going to take place. The police who are taking the training will be getting hands-on exposure since we're going to include them in this development."

They knocked on the front door of the store, and Steve appeared to open it for them.

"Hey, Danielle's in the office."

They followed him in, and Mia noticed all the lights were on in the store and the loft.

"Mia, Luke, thanks for coming on such short notice. I found something in one of Dad's ledgers, and it doesn't make sense to me. Let me show you." Danielle opened the ledger and pointed to a column. "This says to check the second ledger. Did you see another ledger in his office? Or maybe on his computer?"

Mia leaned forward for a better look. The ledger had several columns and showed sales for antiques from the store. It also had a column that showed online sales.

"What's the online sales column?" she asked.

"I know the store's website had items for sale. They were usually small and easy to mail. Dad rarely sold larger pieces of furniture online. He preferred for people to come in and see them, and then he'd arrange for their transportation."

"Okay. I didn't see anything in his computer files that would indicate another ledger. Could it be a different ledger that he used for the storage unit?"

Danielle frowned. "I haven't had time to get to the storage unit. I don't know what's in there. And honestly, I wouldn't know the value of any of the things there either."

"Is there someone you'd trust to help you assess the items?" Luke asked.

"You and Mia. Could you do that?"

Mia shook her head. "I'm great at antiquities but not antiques. There's a skill set you need for that. I could ask Gran if she knows anyone who could do it."

"I never thought to ask your Gran. Do you mind?"

"Of course not. I'll ask her this afternoon."

"Thanks. I didn't ask you to come here just for this. Mia, I know you were here for Dad's sale the other night, and you were in the loft. Did you notice anything strange up there?"

Mia frowned. "Strange, like how?"

Danielle sighed. "I noticed one bookcase appeared to be pulled away from the wall. I asked Steve to push it back, and he couldn't move it. Steve, could you show them?"

"Of course. Why don't you come with me?" Steve motioned to them to follow him.

They went up to the loft, and Steve turned on additional lights. Immediately, Mia could see the bookcase in question. It was against the wall that adjoined to the shop next door, and it was at a thirty-three-degree angle away from the wall.

"I know that wasn't like that when we were here on Wednesday evening," Mia said. She walked to the bookcase and examined it. There were still books in it and a few small antiques. Items that would be used on a desk or as ornaments. She peered around the back. "This is weird. The bookcase is attached to the wall, and this opening appears to go into the wall. Luke, can you help me?"

Luke hurried to her side, and they tried to move it further. The bookcase wouldn't budge.

"I wonder if there's a latch that opens it further?" Mia looked around the edges of the bookcase and felt around with her fingers. She felt a depression along the top edge and pressed it down. She heard a click, and the bookcase moved toward the center of the room, and the wall moved with it.

"Oh my! What's that?" Danielle cried out.

Chapter Ten

Sunday Afternoon

Mia and Luke used the flashlight apps from their phones to look in the opening. "It looks like a narrow staircase," Mia said. "Shall we?" she asked Luke.

"Right behind you."

"Wait, let me get some stronger flashlights," Steve called out. "I'll be back in a minute, and I'm going with you guys."

"I am too," Danielle said.

A few moments later, Steve returned with two large flashlights. "These should help. Danielle, you stay right behind me. Hang onto my waistband."

Luke took the other light. "Mia, do you want to go first?"

"Yes. Just be careful. I don't know how far it goes, and watch your heads."

They started down the steps, and Luke shone the light along the staircase. Mia used her phone's flashlight to see the stairs.

The staircase was built out of concrete. There were a few spots where the stairs were crumbling and loose. A metal railing ran along the staircase, but Mia didn't trust it for support. She had no way of knowing how old it was. After going down about twenty steps, they arrived at a landing. The landing opened against the wall of the store next door. There was an entrance with a large door that had a padlock on it. Luke shone the light on the padlock, and Mia noticed it appeared rusted. She gave the handle a yank, but it didn't budge. Along the wall of the staircase, there were caged lights at various intervals.

"Have you seen a switch to turn on the lights?" Mia asked.

"No," Steve answered.

"We might have missed it at the top of the staircase. Danielle, are you okay?" Mia asked.

"I'm fine. Let's keep going."

They continued down the staircase, and twenty steps later, they arrived in a large open room. They shone the flashlights around, and Mia noticed industrial lighting on the ceiling of the room.

"Right, there's got to be a switch somewhere. Let's split up and find it," Luke said.

A few minutes later, Steve called out, "Found it." And then the lights went on.

Mia blinked as her eyes adjusted to the light. She looked around. There were large tubs on one side of the room, a massive table with work stools in the center and strong lights hanging from the ceiling above the table, three large kilns on the other side of the room, supplies stacked against the backwall, and a table with what Mia recognized as a state-of-the-art 3D printer on it. There was a large garage door at the end of the room.

"What is this?" Danielle asked.

Mia walked to the table and examined the items on it. They appeared to be molds, and under the table were supplies to use for the molds. She looked at Luke, and he nodded.

"I hate to say this, but I think this place was used to make copies," Mia said.

"Copies of what?" Danielle asked.

"Probably antiques or artifacts. Molds were made, materials poured into the mold, then they'd go into the kilns to be fired. If you look at the supplies, there's clay and metal. They can all be used to make reproductions that can be made to look old." Luke picked up one of the paints. "This paint can be used to duplicate Aztec pottery."

Danielle sat on one of the stools. "Was Dad involved in fakes?" Her voice broke.

Mia glared at Luke. He shrugged.

"I don't know if he was or not. But this is in the basement of his store. It's unlikely he didn't know something about it," Mia said.

Danielle shook her head. "Mia, don't sugarcoat it. If Dad was involved, I need to get to the bottom of this."

"Let's take a closer look around the room. We may be able to find something that gives us more information," Luke said.

"I'll look around the table." Danielle stood.

"I think you need to be careful. There could be all kinds of chemicals here that wouldn't be good for a pregnant woman to be around." Mia bent down under the table. "Yeah, Danielle, I think you need to move away from the table. There are some caustic chemicals under here."

"Are any of the containers opened?" Steve asked.

"No, they're all closed. There are some rags in a box, though, and that's not covered."

"Danielle, I wish you'd go back upstairs and in the office. Just to be safe." Steve put his arm around Danielle and tried to guide her to the staircase.

"I don't want to be by myself in the office. I'll go sit on the stairs and just watch." Danielle moved to the stairs and sat down. She watched as the other three started looking around.

Mia searched under the table and found a variety of items that could be used to age items quickly. Bottles of bleach, vinegar, sandpaper, steel wool, paint, and glazes. A box held work gloves, a dust mask, a respirator, and safety goggles. At least he was careful with safety when he was antiquing items. She'd taken a seminar a few years ago on how people could age items and pass them off as antiquities. It wasn't a stretch to imagine Tim being involved in this aspect. He could copy artifacts and sell them anywhere. The 3D printer could produce smaller items and would be much faster than working with molds. He didn't need the actual item. The printer could work from a photo.

She stood and looked around the room. Steve was checking items that were stored on shelves, and Luke was examining the kilns.

She strode to Steve's side. "What have you found?"

Steve pulled a small box off the shelf. "It looks like these are all copies of the same item." He pulled out a small statue. It was gold in color, but Steve was able to toss it from one hand to another. "It's not real gold. It's way too light. I don't know a lot about antiques, but it looks old."

"Can I see it?" Mia held it in her hands. It was about six inches tall, gold in color, and the male figure was garbed in ceremonial clothing decorated with paint. The paint appeared old.

"It's a good replica. Are all these boxes filled with the same item?"

"The ones on this shelf are. I think there's twenty. The top shelf has boxes filled with a different figure." He stretched his arm and took another box off the top shelf. "See, this isn't the same."

Mia glanced in the box. It was a Buddha. Mia shook her head. "Not good. I think Luke's going to have to get involved with this."

Luke appeared next to her. "Did you say something about me?"

Mia snorted. "You have incredible hearing. Always did. Yes. You need to look at these." Mia pointed to the shelves.

Luke took a few minutes to examine the contents of several boxes. "The originals were reported stolen last year. I wonder how many others Tim worked with."

"What would these sell for?" Steve asked.

"It depends on the need. They're well made, and although they wouldn't fool an expert, they would look nice in a display cabinet under lights."

Danielle walked toward them. "What have you found?"

Mia explained the finds.

Danielle sighed. "Why would Dad do this? I didn't think he needed money. He always said the shop was doing well. He planned to retire in a couple of years."

Mia put her hand on Danielle's shoulder. "He may have been forced to do this."

"By whom?"

"Maybe whoever was getting him to sell the artifacts at auction." Luke cleared his throat. "It's not difficult to imagine they would have pressured him into this. The setup here is ideal." He pointed to the far wall with the garage door. "Does this open to a back alley where trucks could come in and out easily?"

"Yes. That's how the shipments for the large pieces come in. But I didn't know anything about this room or that staircase." Danielle looked around the room.

"Then how did the larger furniture pieces get in the shop?" Mia asked.

"There's an elevator off to the side." Danielle walked to the garage door. She pressed a button, and a large door closed behind them, effectively closing off the workroom. When that happened, another door opened, and Mia could see a large industrial elevator. "This is what I knew about. I've been here when shipments have come in. Dad would ride down the elevator, and I'd wait upstairs."

Mia walked to the elevator and pressed the button. The doors opened, and the interior of the elevator was padded to protect pieces of furniture. It was larger than the elevator in her condo and looked as if it could accommodate several pieces at a time. "Where does it go?" she asked.

"The main floor. Dad kept the larger pieces of furniture there. He didn't have the loft built until this spring, and he wanted to use the loft for smaller items."

"That makes sense." Mia closed the door, and then the wall opened to the workroom.

"What do we do now?" Danielle asked.

"I'll bring this up with the police and my supervisor. From what I've seen of the molds, this was quite the operation. I don't think your father was working alone." Luke nodded toward the boxes on the shelves. "He would have needed some help, especially to decorate the pieces. One person working at this would have taken too long. And this looks like it was an enterprise that worked on speed."

Mia glanced at her watch. "We're going to have to get going. Gran's expecting us shortly."

They headed upstairs, and Mia and Luke closed the bookcase properly. It fit seamlessly against the wall, and it would be difficult to believe there was a secret staircase.

"Could I get a sticky note to show where the latch is?" Mia asked.

"I'll be right back," Steve hurried down to the office. He returned with a package of bright yellow sticky notes.

"Perfect." Mia placed the sticky on the depression on top of the bookcase. It would be easy to find again.

"Danielle, I'll be in touch with you later today. The police will need to come in, most likely tomorrow morning," Luke said.

"That's not a problem. I'm not planning on opening the store for a few weeks. I'm still trying to decide what to do."

"Do you have the keys to the storage unit?" Luke asked.

"I'm not sure where they are. And I'm not clear where the unit is." Danielle blew out a breath.

Mia put her hand on Luke's arm. "Why don't we give Danielle some time to rest, and then we can check into the storage unit. Whatever's in there isn't going anywhere."

Luke nodded. "Good idea. Steve, Danielle, I'll be in touch."

"Thank you both for coming in. I didn't expect this."

"Don't forget to check your dad's home office for a second ledger. There must be one somewhere."

Danielle picked up her purse. "I wonder if Dad's accountant has it?"

Luke shook his head. "Then he'd be complicit as well."

"Okay. I'll look around Dad's place."

"Whatever you do, please don't come to the store alone. I think your dad was involved with some shady people, and if the store isn't open, they might try to get in." Mia's brow furrowed. "At least have Cheryl come in with you."

"You're right. I'll talk to you later. Thanks, Mia, Luke."

They left the premises, and Mia and Luke walked back to her car. "Not a good situation at all." Mia unlocked her Jeep.

"Unfortunately, not. I'm going to send a message to my supervisor and to Detective Martin, letting them know what we've found. I have a feeling we'll be going to the store to check things out tomorrow. It'll be a good field experience for the officers to see an operation like this."

Chapter Eleven

Sunday Afternoon/Evening

Gran had cold drinks and hors d'oeuvres waiting for them on the balcony. Mia hurried off to clean herself up a bit, and Luke joined Gran.

"Well, that was the adventure this afternoon. What do you make of it?" Gran asked.

"It appears the store was used to make copies of artifacts or antiques. If it wasn't Tim, someone was using his basement."

"Will Danielle be held liable for this?" Gran asked.

"No. She wasn't involved in the day-to-day operation of the store. From what I can tell, she only helped as needed."

Gran nodded. "She worked there a couple of summers, but she didn't like the trade."

Mia joined them on the balcony. "I remember she said it felt like she was spending all her time with dead people's stuff."

"I wonder what she would have said if your parents had taken her on a dig like they did with you?" Gran asked.

Luke shook his head. "I doubt she would have enjoyed it. She's a nice person, though, and I don't like to see her upset like this."

"Did you hear from anyone you messaged?" Mia asked.

"Yes, Detective Martin said it will be the first order of business in the morning."

Mia reached for an appetizer. "Gran, these look wonderful. Thanks for having us."

Gran smiled. "You're welcome. I'm glad we could get together. Now tell me what you've been up to apart from dealing with Timeless Treasures."

Mia and Luke entertained Gran with what they'd been doing since Luke arrived. They spent a pleasant couple of hours on her balcony, enjoying the quiet Sunday afternoon. The birds were chirping, and the squirrels were chattering. Gran's building was set behind trees, and the traffic was muffled. The complex was designed for seniors who could still live on their own. And was complete with a gym, pool, recreation room, barbeque area, a dining room where residents could have their meals, and a party room if needed. Gran's apartment had a kitchen with a full-sized fridge and stove that let her cook meals for herself and invite friends over.

Alex arrived shortly before five, and Gran led her to the balcony.

"Zack sends his apologies. He was called in for an emergency." Alex picked up the drink Gran had brought her. "Thanks, Gran. What happened at the shop this afternoon? I called Danielle, and she was upset."

"We found some things that don't add up. Luke is going to go tomorrow with the police, and they'll do a thorough search. Unfortunately, it seems Tim was involved with smuggling and dealing with fakes."

Alex's eyes widened. "Dealing with fakes? How?"

Mia explained what they'd discovered. "The 3D printer and the molds show he, or someone he worked with, were involved with making reproductions. We found a few boxes with artifacts that were fakes."

"Is it easy to tell they are?"

"In this case, yes. You'd never find twelve artifacts that were identical unless they were mass-produced. And at that time in history, it couldn't have been done. The statues we found were clearly faked." Mia put her glass down. "I'm sorry, Alex. There's no doubt in our minds about this."

Alex shook her head. "Why would he have done this?"

"He may not have had a choice in the matter," Luke said. "The information Mia's found in his files and email correspondence points to him being involved in a smuggling ring. We just need to figure out if it's the same one Charles Gordon is in charge of."

Gran rubbed Alex's back. "Are you all right?"

"I will be. I'm worried about Danielle, though. She didn't know anything about this, and she sounded exhausted this afternoon when I spoke with her. And Steve left her alone at home to get some rest. I don't know where he went."

"Maybe he only went out for a little while," Gran said. "Mia, would you help me in the kitchen? Dinner should almost be ready."

Gran and Mia left Alex and Luke on the balcony and went into the kitchen.

"Do you think Danielle will be all right?" Mia asked Gran.

"She'll have to be, won't she? You don't know what you're capable of until you're tested." Gran handed Mia some potholders. "Can you pull the pan out and set it on the trivet on the counter? I need to make some gravy. And then, can you get the serving dishes out of the cupboard and get the food in them?"

"Do you want me to carve the roast?"

"Yes, please."

Mia opened the cupboard and removed the serving dishes Gran needed. Then she pulled the carving knife out of the block and sliced the roast beef into thin slices. The juice from the meat dribbled out onto the cutting board. "This is perfectly cooked, Gran."

"I'm glad to hear that. Once you're done, can you make the glaze for the carrots?"

"Sure." Mia tented the roast beef with foil to keep it warm. Opening the cupboard, she found honey and took some butter out of the fridge. The carrots were already in the serving dish, and once she had the glaze made up, she poured it over the carrots.

Mia carried the food out to the dining room and called Alex and Luke in.

Gran added the gravy and asked Luke to open the wine.

They sat at the table, and dishes passed around as they helped themselves.

"What's the glaze on the carrots?" Luke asked.

"A honey glaze. It's the only way Mia would eat them as a child. I've kept making that recipe all these years."

Mia rolled her eyes. "It's good, and it isn't overly sweet."

Luke smiled. "I'm sure it is. My mom used to do Brussels sprouts with bacon and onions. It was the only way we'd eat them."

"The beef is so tender. How did you cook it?" Alex asked.

"A low oven for the afternoon. I added some beef broth and spices, too," Gran said.

"It's delicious. Thanks for going to all this trouble!" Alex said.

"No trouble. I enjoy having you to cook for." Gran smiled.

Gran steered the conversation away from Tim's death and the problems Mia had uncovered. She asked Mia about the exhibit she was working on.

"I've been doing videos the museum is going to use to promote the exhibit, and everything's falling into place. We finish getting all the exhibits up on Monday, and on Tuesday, the exhibition cases will be ready. I have an interview with The Morning Show on Tuesday morning, and I'll be showing them some of the exhibits." Mia paused to take a drink of wine. "The marketing department has been working hard to get this exhibit in the news. And then Friday evening, we have the Museum After Hours. Tickets for the event are almost sold out."

"I'm looking forward to Friday evening. Alex, are you still able to come with me?"

"Yes. I've got my outfit ready for it. I can't wait to celebrate something fun."

Mia grinned. "I don't doubt you have your outfit ready."

"What are you wearing?" Alex asked Mia.

"The blue and gold dress you helped me pick out. It's pretty and comfortable. I don't have to wear high heels with it either."

"Good choice. That will look stunning on you. Especially with your tan."

"How dressy is this occasion? Do I need a tux?" Luke asked.

"You'll be fine in a business suit. Did you bring one?" Mia asked.

"Yes."

"With your good looks and accent, if you wore a tux, people might call you James Bond," Gran said.

Mia and Alex chuckled while Luke's jaw dropped.

"Don't pull any punches there, Gran." Mia laughed.

"Well, it's true!"

While they ate their meal, Gran kept them entertained with stories from her days as an antique dealer.

Mia looked toward the kitchen. "Is there dessert?"

Luke groaned. "Mia. I don't think I could eat anything else."

Alex laughed. "You don't know Gran's desserts. They're worth the indulgence."

Gran stood, "Help me clear the table. We have chocolate lava cakes and vanilla bean ice cream."

They made quick work of clearing the table. Alex and Mia shooed Luke and Gran out of the kitchen. "Let us clean up Gran. You and Luke go out and enjoy some fresh air. We'll bring coffee and dessert out shortly." Mia was loading dishes in the dishwasher, and Alex was wrapping up leftovers. Both of them very comfortable in Gran's kitchen.

"Fine. Come on, Luke. Let's sit out, and you can tell me some of your adventures."

A short while later, Mia and Alex joined them with dessert.

Dessert was individual chocolate lava cakes. Mia had scooped vanilla bean ice cream over them. After checking what people wanted to drink, Alex had made tea.

"This looks decadent," Luke said as Mia handed him his plate.

"The bake shop down the street specializes in chocolate. When I went in this afternoon, I knew this would be the perfect dessert."

They made short work of their desserts and were enjoying their tea.

Gran set her teacup down and asked, "Mia, have you considered Tim's first wife? She was at the soirée on Wednesday evening."

"What about her?" Mia asked.

"Could she be involved with the illegal auctions? She was living in British Columbia, but I've heard that she's been in Lakeview for the last several years. So I'm not sure if she's still in British Columbia or not."

"Danielle asked me to look through her father's laptop. I found a lot of emails from Barbara, his first wife. They were still in touch with each other.

And she seemed to be aware of the auctions."

"We'll be looking at all of Mr. Fraser's contacts. Mia learned a few things yesterday about some of his contacts." Luke looked at Mia.

"Like what?" Alex asked.

Mia put her napkin down and took a drink of tea. "Several of his contacts have died or been killed in the last eighteen months. None of them were living in Canada. They were in the U.S., Mexico, Belize, Honduras, Colombia. Some of them died under suspicious circumstances, and others it isn't mentioned. It seemed strange to me that they all seemed to be dying in the last eighteen months. Luke's going to investigate their deaths."

"We've started looking at several of them. And their deaths are suspicious. In most cases, though, there wasn't an investigation by the local police."

"Do you think this ties to Tim's death?" Gran asked.

"I do. I'm not sure how, but it warrants further investigation."

They were silent for a few minutes.

"Did Danielle talk anymore about the store? She's been getting calls from realtors about selling it." Alex asked.

"It's in an excellent location. If she doesn't want to keep it going, she would get a good price. Especially with today's real estate market. I'll let her know I don't mind helping her if she decides to sell. I don't want her to be taken advantage of," Gran said.

They all left shortly afterwards. Before leaving, Alex filled them in on the particulars of Tim's service.

"It's going to be at the Monroe's Funeral Home, Tuesday evening at seven. They'll do the service, and there's a room where they can hold the reception afterward. Danielle wanted it there. The internment on Wednesday morning will be private with just Steve, Danielle, Mom, and me."

"Thanks, Alex. Gran, I can pick you up if you'd like."

"Yes, please. And I'll get in touch with Danielle to let her know if she needs any help with the store, I can give her a hand. I still know people in the business."

"I'll let her know. I think she'd like your expertise."

Luke's phone rang. "Excuse me, I need to take this. It's my supervisor."

He returned a few minutes later. "Sorry about that. Apparently, the list of names you found in the files are known associates of Charles Gordon. That ties Tim Fraser to the smuggling ring."

Chapter Twelve

Sunday Evening

Gran shook her head. "I'm sorry to hear that. I was hoping he wasn't involved."

Alex sighed. "So, what happens next?"

"We're going to move forward with the investigation. I'll keep Danielle informed about what we're doing. I'll touch base with her in the morning. The information Mia found on the laptop will be helpful to the investigation."

"All right. I'm going to head home. I won't discuss this with Danielle, at least not until you've had an opportunity to speak with her." Alex said her goodbyes.

"We'd better get going, too. We both have a busy week ahead of us. I'll talk to you tomorrow, Gran." Mia leaned into Gran for a hug.

"Yes. Let me know if Danielle needs anything from me."

* * *

Monday

The following morning, Mia and Luke left for work. Luke was taking a cab to the police station. Mia waited with him outside the building with her bike ready to leave.

"I'll text you when I'm done for the day. I'm not entirely sure how today is going to go."

"That's fine. I have a lot of last-minute details I need to address today. And I also have to prep for that interview scheduled for tomorrow morning."

Luke's cab arrived, they exchanged a quick kiss, and he left. Mia got on her bike and hurried to work.

Mia's morning was busy and productive. She did more prep work on the school projects and was satisfied with the results. She sent final documents to the school boards and principals for their review.

In the afternoon, Mia checked over the display for the new exhibition, making certain everything was in order. There would be plenty of time to chat about the display during tomorrow morning's interview.

Luke texted her shortly after two.

Luke: Will be through by four.

Mia: Sounds good. I'll meet you at my place.

"Hmm, what to do about dinner?" Mia mused as she glanced outside. The sun was shining, and it looked as if it would be a nice evening. *"We could go out or get takeout. Either one. I'll see how he feels."*

Mia was shutting down her computer when Heather popped in.

"Are you set for tomorrow?" she asked.

Mia grinned. "I'd better be. I've gone over the information on the exhibition this afternoon. I should be all right."

"Did you have a good weekend?"

"I did. Luke's here, and I showed him around a bit. We went to the Farmers Market and to the lake too."

"How long is he here for?"

"At least two weeks. How was your weekend?"

"Good. I heard about the death of Mr. Fraser. And that they're looking at it as murder. That's awful."

"It is. Did you know him?"

"Yes. He volunteered here a few times for some events. He was knowledgeable about Aztec artifacts."

"How so?" Mia asked.

"He knew a lot about the history behind the artifacts. I don't know how he learned about them, but he was very good."

Mia paused for a moment. She didn't want to tell Heather any information she shouldn't. "Did he handle any of the artifacts or take them out of the museum?"

Heather shook her head. "That I don't know. He came in on Mondays. He took that day off from his shop. Why are you asking?"

"I just wondered. I know the protocol is that no artifacts leave the building, and I wasn't sure when that was put in place."

"Oh, that's been around forever. Apparently, a patron who volunteered some ten years ago stole the original pieces he'd worked on. He replaced them with fakes. Very good fakes, but fakes nonetheless."

"Wow. That's bold to do something like that. Do you know who it was?"

"I can't remember the name. But I do know it was someone who was wealthy and thought he could get away with it."

Mia chuckled. "I hope they caught him." She closed her backpack and slung it over her shoulder.

"They did. That's when they started adding security cameras everywhere in the building. And more security guards. Now, no one works with important artifacts except our staff. If someone wants to volunteer, they're vetted carefully and put through a rigorous training program."

"Glad to hear that. I'm going to head home. Was there anything else?" Mia asked.

"No, I'm on my way out too. Tomorrow's an early start."

They parted ways in the lobby, and Mia hopped on her bike and began her commute home. On her ride home, she wondered why Tim would have volunteered his time at the museum. Before learning about the smuggling, Mia would have thought he'd been doing it out of the goodness of his heart. Now, she thought he might have done it to steal artifacts, make copies, and sell the copies. Or worse, replace the original with a copy.

She checked her side mirror and noticed a white car following her closely. She stopped at the stoplight before crossing the street to her building, and the car drove by slowly. *"Hmm, maybe they're lost."* The light turned green, and she crossed to her building. Getting off her bike, she stopped in the lobby to check her mailbox and then went up the elevator.

She walked her bike into the condo and hung it up on the bike rack in her utility room. Glancing at the mail, she saw it was mostly flyers. She found a letter addressed to her with no postmark.

It was a regular white envelope, her name and address handwritten in block letters. Opening it up, there was a single piece of paper in it.

LEAVE FRASER'S DEATH ALONE OR YOU AND GRANNY WILL REGRET IT.

Who was threatening her and Gran? And who knew she was even involved?

Mia grabbed her phone and called Gran's number. It rang a couple of times before Mia heard Gran's voice.

"Gran, are you all right?" Mia spit out the words.

"Mia, of course I am. What's wrong?"

Mia gulped. "I just got home from work and found a threatening message in my mail. Telling me to leave Fraser's death alone, or you and I would regret it. Gran, if anything happens to you, I couldn't take it."

"Mia. I'm fine. No one can get in my building without going through Mitch or the other doormen. And at night we have security guards out there."

"I know. I'm just worried." Mia's voice grew bolder. "Something's not right. I'm going to talk to Luke about this. And Gran, please don't go out tonight."

"I don't have plans. And before you say anything, I won't open my door to anyone unless I know they're coming. Now you be careful as well, you've got me concerned for your safety.

"I'll call you after I've spoken with Luke."

They hung up, and Mia paced the floor waiting for Luke to get in. How dare they threaten her and Gran? Whoever 'they' were, she'd figure it out. She stopped pacing and looked at the envelope again. Could it have been hand-delivered? There wasn't a postmark or a stamp.

She called the front desk.

"It's Mia Reid. I'm calling about an envelope I received in my mail today. There's no postmark or stamp on it. Could someone have hand-delivered it to the front?"

"Let me check the records." The concierge could be heard asking the other two people at the desk. "Apparently, someone did. It was a woman in her fifties. I can look it up on the cameras and check to see if it's someone you know."

"Please do. Once you've located it, could you send it to my email?"

"Is everything all right?" the concierge asked.

"I'm not sure. I'd like to see who dropped this off, and then I'll know more."

"No problem. We'll send you the clip as soon as we find it."

"Thanks."

Mia disconnected the call. She took two clear plastic bags and slipped the envelope and the letter into the bags. She wanted to avoid getting her fingerprints on it or smudging any prints already there. Who could have done this? Who knew Danielle had asked her to look into things?

Mia heard a key in her door. Luke was home.

Mia hurried to greet him. He put his backpack on the chair in the hall and locked the door behind him.

"Hey, how was your day?"

"Productive. Yours?"

Mia shrugged. "Good until I got home. Let me get us a drink, and I'll tell you."

She opened a couple of craft beers and poured them in pilsner glasses. "Let's go out on the balcony."

Luke put his suit jacket aside and took his glass. "What happened?"

They sat in the comfortable deck chairs, and Mia showed him the envelope and the letter in the plastic bags.

Luke read the message. "Are you all right? And is Gran all right?"

"Yes, I checked with her immediately."

"This isn't good. Someone suspects you're looking into Fraser's death. Who did you speak with?"

Mia shook her head. "Alex, Zack, Gran, Danielle, Steve. That's it. No one at work knows I'm looking into this for Danielle."

"I'm going to call Detective Martin and let him know about this." Luke pulled out his phone and made a call.

Mia waited as he left a message for the detective to call him back.

"Hopefully, he returns my call soon. I'll have the police check this for fingerprints." Luke looked at the envelope and paper.

"I touched both the envelope and the letter. And someone from my building would have touched the envelope."

"That's fine. We'll take your prints and run them against the ones on the letter. Maybe the writer didn't take precautions and left their prints."

Mia shrugged. "It still doesn't tell me who knows about this."

"Are you worried about Gran?"

"I know she's safe in her building. Nobody's getting in unless she knows them. But it still concerns me."

Luke watched Mia for a minute. "All right. Let's see if we can think of someone who would write this."

Mia shook her head. "I don't think Danielle or Steve would do this. The clerk at the store, Cheryl, only knows me from the soirée on Wednesday night. I doubt Danielle mentioned anything to her about asking me to investigate. And I don't know the ex-wife."

"It's a puzzle."

"Do you think it's safe to go to Tim's service?"

"I'll be there with you and Gran. And the police will have a presence there as well."

"You don't think anyone would try anything while we're there?" Mia's eyes widened.

"I doubt it. However, we might be able to see someone who stands out."

"That makes sense. Okay, so what do we do now?"

"We need to wait and hear from Detective Martin. But we can work through some of the information we have. And let's figure out something for dinner, and we'll talk this through. Is there someplace that does a good takeaway?"

Mia grinned. "It's takeout in Canada. And yes, there are a lot of options. Let me get some menus."

Mia returned with a fistful of menus from takeout restaurants close by. They settled on a Chinese food restaurant, and Mia placed the order. "Dinner in thirty minutes. They promised."

While they waited, Luke told Mia about his day. There had been officers from the city, provincial, and federal departments. The experience the officers had was varied, and there had been discussion on the challenges with antiquity smuggling.

"It's not something they learned in their training. We've discussed how artifacts are stolen, why they are, and how they're sold. Then we went to Timeless Treasures, and that was an experience for them. They got a first-hand look at Tim's basement. The molds, kilns, and tools he had for replicating artifacts were an education in themselves. We went through everything in the basement. We spent most of the morning and part of the afternoon there."

"How many officers were there?"

"There were six. Detective Martin was in the group as well."

"I thought he was a homicide detective. Why is he there?"

"He's one of the most senior detectives the city has, and he's involved with Tim's death."

Dinner arrived. "I'll get it," Luke said.

Mia got plates out, and they sat at the dining room table for dinner.

"This looks great."

Mia handed Luke one of the containers. "It's very good, I order from them frequently."

Mia waited until Luke had started eating and then asked, "How will we figure out where the note came from? There's no postmark, and the envelope is a regular letter-sized envelope."

"True, but it tells us it's someone local. Could it be someone who was at the event on Wednesday evening at Timeless Treasures?"

Mia put her chopsticks down and thought for a minute. "There were twenty to thirty people there while we were in the shop. I didn't know most of them, Gran did. She's well-connected with that world. I told you about Barbara, Tim's first wife, right?"

"You mentioned she'd shown up and made a scene. Do you think she's involved with Tim's death?"

"Who knows? She's supposed to have been in British Columbia for the last thirty-plus years, but we know she's been in Lakeview frequently."

"And there are the emails you found in Tim's email account."

"There was a lot from her. And she did mention a Charles. I suppose that could be Charles Gordon. Which means that she's worked with him as well."

"That would be a given. I believe she's an integral part of his operation.

"Danielle doesn't think Tim was ready to get out of the business either. So you may be right about the auctions. But isn't it the opinion that Lakeview was chosen by the smuggling ring because of the airport and ease of bringing artifacts in either by air, water, or rail?"

"That's the consensus. The same reasons apply to Montreal and Vancouver. If this Barbara was in Vancouver, she may be looking to step in and take it over."

Mia snorted. "She didn't look like someone who could be part of a smuggling operation. But then neither did Mr. Fraser." She sighed. "I hate this."

Luke's phone rang. "It's Detective Martin. Let me talk to him about this." Luke answered the phone, and Mia sat and listened to his side of the conversation. The call was brief. He gave the detective Mia's address.

Luke disconnected the call. "He's coming here and will take the envelope and letter in to be fingerprinted and processed. He should be here in ten minutes."

"That's fast."

"He's on his way home and lives close by."

Mia stood, "I'm going to clean up."

Luke gave her a hand, and the kitchen and balcony were tidied up quickly. Mia's buzzer rang. "Yes."

"Dr. Reid, there's a gentleman here from the city police. A Detective Martin."

"Send him up, please."

"And Dr. Reid, we just sent a video clip to your personal email as you requested."

"Thank you."

Detective Martin arrived at Mia's door a few minutes later. Luke showed him in. Mia was busy on her laptop watching the video clip sent by the front desk.

"Hi, Detective Martin. Can I get you anything?" Mia asked.

"No thanks. When did you receive this letter?"

"It came in today's mail. It was in my mailbox, and the mail is sorted at the front by two in the afternoon. There wasn't a postmark or a stamp on it."

Detective Martin held out his hand, and Mia gave him the plastic bags.

He looked at both the envelope and the letter. "Hmm, it looks like they were both printed by hand. You've spoken to your grandmother?"

"I have, and she's fine. She lives in a secure building with a doorman and security guards. I don't think anyone could get into her building, and she won't open the door to someone she doesn't know."

"Yes, that's fine. But what if this person is someone she knows or that you know? She'd let them in, wouldn't she?"

Mia sighed. "Yes. But I don't think it's someone who knows her well."

"All right. I'll take this in and have the lab go over it. You handled both items?"

"I did. And my fingerprints are on file because of some of the work I've done."

"Okay, if we need them for elimination purposes, we'll get them."

"There's something else. The front desk sent me a clip of the person who dropped off the envelope. It's not great, but it shows a woman in her fifties leaving it with the front desk staff."

"Can you show me?"

Mia turned her laptop and enlarged the video. After watching it, Mia said, "I don't recognize that woman."

"Can you send it to me? We'll examine it at the station. The lab might be able to clean it up."

"Sure. Can I have your email?"

Detective Martin gave her his business card, and Mia forwarded the email to him.

"Thanks. Luke, I'll see you in the morning. Have a good evening." He left the apartment.

Mia looked at Luke. "Do you think Gran needs more security?"

"I think this isn't a threat that's to be taken lightly. But I also think Gran is safe for now. I'm concerned about your safety. You're out and about and could be targeted."

"I'll be careful. When I'm at work, I should be safe. There's security everywhere in the museum. Tomorrow, I have to be at the office early, by six-thirty. I have that morning show interview."

"That's right. Are you ready for it?"

"I should be fine. I know the items that we have on exhibit well. And I'm an expert in that era."

"I was going to suggest we go out for a walk, but given this development, I think we should stay in."

Mia smiled. "I think we can come up with a few things to do."

Chapter Thirteen

Tuesday

Five-thirty came early the next morning.

"Ugh." Mia pushed the covers off and looked at Luke. How could he sleep through that alarm? She turned the alarm off and hurried to the bathroom, where she showered and dried her hair. She got dressed in the clothes she'd laid out the night before. A nice pair of navy pants, a green silk blouse, ballet flats, and minimal jewelry. A bit more makeup than she normally wore took longer than she expected. She was in the kitchen having a coffee when Luke came in.

"Morning, you look great."

"Morning and thanks. I've got to leave soon."

"No problem. I wanted to see you before you left."

Mia smiled. "I'll see you back here before the service?"

"Yes. I'll be back by four-thirty."

"How are you getting back and forth?"

"I'm taking the subway. That should be an adventure." Luke leaned in for a kiss. "I'll see you later. Be safe."

Mia was cautious in the parking garage of her building. There weren't many people around at this time of day. She got into her Jeep, locked the doors, and drove off to work. Traffic was light, and she arrived at work in fifteen minutes. She parked the Jeep and headed to the museum.

* * *

Mia arrived at her office and tucked her bag in a drawer of her desk. She took a moment to check her appearance in the mirror in the ladies' room and nodded to herself. It was the best she could do. She walked to the conference room they'd be using to film part of the interview.

The room was busy. The interviewer was there with the cameraman, and they were talking about where they should set up. Heather was making coffee and had water bottles in ice. A blonde woman looked up when Mia walked in. "Dr. Reid, hi, I'm Sally Clark. I'm looking forward to our interview this morning."

"Thank you for coming. Please call me Mia. I'm a fan of your work."

"Thanks so much. How are you feeling this morning?"

"I'm good."

Sally grinned. "We're going to get started soon. I was chatting with the studio, and they'll be ready for us in about ten minutes. I just need to fix my makeup, and we'll be ready."

Mia watched as Sally pulled out a small makeup bag and a pocket mirror. She expertly applied makeup, combed her hair, and then shoved everything back in her purse.

The cameraman had a microphone for Sally and one for Mia. He showed Mia how to attach it to her shirt and then stepped off to the side.

"Have you done interviews before?" Sally asked Mia.

"Yes. Most of them at digs. I enjoy talking about the work that I do. And my contract with the museum has me working in several areas."

"How long have you been here?"

"About three weeks. I started at the beginning of August. It's been a lot of fun."

Sally put her hand against her ear. "We're ready when you are." She looked at Mia, "That was the producer. We're going to be live in a minute. Are you ready?"

Mia nodded.

The cameraman counted them down, and Sally faced the camera. "Good morning, everyone! We're at Lakeview Museum this morning with Dr. Mia Reid, an archaeologist who's working with the museum on several of the exhibits. There's an exciting new exhibition opening tomorrow, and I can't wait to let you all know about it. But first, a bit about Dr. Reid. I understand you've spent a lot of time in the field. How different is working in a museum than what you normally do?"

"Good morning, Sally, thanks for coming in. There are a lot of differences in my work in the field and the work I do in the museum. In the field, we're digging and searching for artifacts. We're responsible for the site and for making certain that all the work is done according to our standards. If we have students, we're responsible for their safety as well. When I'm at the museum, it's a completely different workplace. I'm working with artifacts that have been collected, and we're making sure they're catalogued correctly. We develop the exhibits to inform and educate, but to make it fun as well. I'm working with different people every day."

"Which do you prefer?"

Mia shrugged. "I enjoy being out in the field, but you can't be there all the time. The museum is a nice change. I'm developing new skills and testing my knowledge in different ways. It's always a bonus to work with new people. Everyone here is great to work with."

"I understand you were on a dig this summer and you found treasure. Can you tell me what that was like?"

"We did. It's not something that happens all the time. Our dig was on the Isle of Skye. And we found loose gemstones, gold coins, jewelry, and a sgian-dubh. It was exciting for me and for the students who were there."

"What happens to the treasure?"

"In this case, it stayed in the country. They have a display at the local historical society, and I understand that Scotland is going to permit the items to be displayed in different locations throughout the year."

"So, no finder's fee?"

Mia laughed. "I'm afraid not! The student who found the gemstones was surprised they were gems. At first, he thought they were small rocks."

"Lucky they didn't get thrown away." Sally looked at her notes. "Let's talk about the exhibition we have here today."

Mia skillfully explained the artifacts that were in front of them, showing them to the camera and explaining how they had been found and where. She provided their history and what they were used for.

Sally pointed to one of the artifacts, a necklace. "And this piece? How old is it?"

"That necklace is just over fifteen hundred years old. It was worn by a high priest in the Aztec community for specific ceremonies. There were times in the calendar year where sacrifices were made, and that necklace is part of the costume the priest wore while celebrating the sacrifice."

"Are all the items here part of the ritual for the sacrifice?"

"Not all of them. A few are." Mia pointed to several pieces. "These are the ones used. You have to remember sacrifices were made to ensure a prosperous year for the tribe. They were offerings to the gods. And the offerings could be an animal, grains, gold, or semi-precious stones, or statues."

They chatted for a few more minutes, and then the interview was over.

"You did great!" Sally said to Mia.

"Thanks. It's been a while since I've been in front of a camera."

"You're a natural. Heather, I think you have a winner here. You should get Mia to do all the interviews for the museum!"

"I'll be working on that. Mia, you were very good. Don't be surprised if I call on you to do some more interviews."

"Thanks, both of you. That's good feedback to hear."

"It was an excellent segment. I think the numbers are going to be very good for this one," Sally said.

Heather grinned. "Awesome! I hope that translates to more people coming in to see the exhibition."

They chatted a few more minutes, and then they all left to get back to work.

When Mia returned to her office, she had messages from Gran and Alex about the segment. Both expressed how well she'd done and that they were proud of her.

The rest of the morning was spent making sure the exhibit was ready for its opening the next afternoon.

At lunchtime, Mia called Gran to verify when she wanted Mia to pick her up.

"Can you be here by six-fifteen tonight?" Gran asked.

"Yes. That works. Luke's coming as well. Alex and her mom will be there with Danielle and Steve. How's everything going today?"

"All's well here. No one has tried to kidnap me!" Gran chuckled. "They'd have a hard time getting past Mitch at the door."

"Gran, it's not funny. I would hate it if anything happened to you. And mom would never forgive me either."

"I'm kidding, Mia. I've taken some precautions. I did have to go out this morning for a hair appointment, and instead of walking, I took a cab. Mitch was very careful with me. I told him about the note. He's added it to the book they keep at the front, and he'll make sure everyone who works the front desk is aware of the threat."

"I'm glad you're taking this seriously. Hopefully, the police will be able to identify the woman who dropped off the envelope. I didn't recognize her."

"Do you have a photo you can share?"

"No. I'll ask Detective Martin if they've been able to discover anything or have a photo I can look at. Gran, I need to finish a couple of emails. I'll see you shortly."

Mia finished up her work and hurried to the parking lot. She checked her surroundings carefully, taking note of the people nearby. Once she got to her Jeep, she got in quickly and drew a breath. She shook her head; the threatening message had got to her. She'd feel better once she was home.

* * *

Luke arrived shortly after she did. They met on the balcony and recapped their day. Luke was curious about the morning news show. Mia had recorded the program, so they went in and watched. Her segment was on for ten minutes.

Mia was critical of herself when she watched it and then relaxed. "I did all right. Heather told me I had, but I didn't believe it."

"You came across very professional. You answered all the questions in terminology that anyone could understand. I hope the museum appreciates your skills. Not everyone can do that." Luke leaned across and hugged Mia close. "You were great."

"Thanks. I was a bit nervous. I've never done an interview like this before." Mia leaned back. "Are you hungry? Gran wants us to pick her up at six-fifteen. And she doesn't want us to be late."

"I could eat, but I'm not overly hungry."

"There'll be food served after the service. How about if I heat up some leftover Chinese food?"

"Perfect. And the dress code for the service?"

"Business casual will work. What you have on is fine." Mia walked into the kitchen to heat up the leftovers.

Luke came in and took a beer out of the fridge. "Did you want one?"

"I'd better not. I'm going to be driving. I'll stick to mineral water."

Luke poured her a glass with a slice of lime and ice cubes. "Do you want to hear about what I've learned about the woman who dropped off the envelope?"

"Yes! My goodness, why didn't you start with that? Did Detective Martin get a clearer photo of her?"

"I wanted to check on your day first." He selected a photo on his phone. "It's clearer than the video the front desk sent. Take a look."

Mia checked the photo. The woman had her back to the camera. She had short, blond hair that was covered with a Blue Jays baseball hat. She was wearing a pair of black shorts and a Blue Jays T-shirt. A brown purse was slung cross-body. On her feet were sneakers. "Well, that's disappointing. I can't make any features out."

"Whoever she is, she tried to look non-descript. The police don't have any leads on who she might be. The next photo isn't much better. She keeps her head down the entire time, as if she knows where the camera is located."

"It isn't difficult to see the cameras. The building management wants people to be aware they're on film. There are signs in the lobby about them."

Mia sighed. "Too bad. It would have been nice to place her."

"There's still the fingerprints. They might turn something up."

The convection oven beeped.

"Supper's ready. I'll grab some plates, and we can eat outside."

Luke took their drinks and napkins out on the balcony.

"What did you do today? Did you go back to Timeless Treasures?"

"We did. There were a few things we had to look at. I felt it was important for the officers to see the tools used to replicate artifacts. I spent a few hours explaining the process someone would use. In this case, Tim Fraser. Bringing the artifacts in, then making the copies, aging them, and then selling them to different clients. It was an opportunity that I didn't want to miss. The officers had a lot of good questions." Luke took a drink of beer. "I think we're done at Timeless Treasures. We're going to focus our attention on some of the files I've worked on over the last few years."

"Can you talk about your cases?"

"The ones that are closed, I can. I can go back several years. They're particularly interested in how their department can work with us when they suspect smuggling is happening."

"Are you happy you're doing this type of work? Any regrets leaving archaeology?"

"I enjoy what I'm doing. I think I'm making a difference and bringing criminals to account for their crimes. We don't get them all, but we are getting better. As for regrets, I do miss working in the field. Being with you and the students on the Isle of Skye this summer reminded me how much I enjoyed it. The excitement of being on a dig and working with students. Seeing archaeology through their eyes. Most of them are so happy to be in the field. But I wouldn't want to be working as a professor at university. That wouldn't be for me."

"I learned that as well." Mia finished her meal. "I'm going to touch base with Gran and let her know we'll be there shortly."

"Hi Gran, just wanted to let you know we'll be leaving here in about ten minutes. I'll have Mitch buzz you when we get there."

"Perfect. I'm just finishing getting ready. See you soon."

They arrived at Gran's building, Mia parked her Jeep, and they walked in. Gran was in the lobby chatting with Mitch.

"Hope we didn't keep you waiting," Mia said as she leaned in to hug Gran.

"No. I just got here. I thought I'd save a little bit of time."

"We'd better get going. I'll need to find parking when we get there."

Luke helped Gran get in the front seat and settled himself in the back.

"Do you have enough leg room?" Gran asked.

"Yes, don't worry about me. I'm fine."

Mia looked at him in the rear-view mirror and smiled. He was adaptable; that was a good thing about him.

The drive to the funeral home didn't take long. Mia dropped Gran and Luke off at the front. "I'll be right back. There's parking behind the building. You go on in and wait for me inside."

Luke took Gran's arm, and Mia watched as he escorted her in.

She joined them inside and looked around for information on the service. Mia saw a sign with the name Tim Fraser pointing to a room on the left. "There's the room. Shall we go in?"

They walked in and took a seat toward the middle of the room. The room was filling up. Mia leaned toward Gran, "Do you know anyone here?"

Gran nodded. "The four rows ahead of us are all members of the local antique dealers association. I haven't seen many of them since I closed my business. But they're here, and that's good." Gran looked around. "The front row is Danielle and her husband. Alex and her mother are with them."

Across the aisle, the seats were filling up as well. Mia gasped.

"What? Who did you see?" Gran asked.

"Sorry, I thought I saw his first wife. Why would she be here?" Mia asked.

"I'm surprised Danielle let her come after the scene at the store."

Luke leaned forward. "What are you two whispering about?"

Gran turned to him. "Tim's first wife is here. I didn't think Danielle wanted her to come."

"Where is she?" Luke asked.

"Across the aisle. She's about five rows up from us. And she's got blond hair and is wearing a black jacket and pants."

Luke looked for the woman. "I see her. How long have they been divorced?"

Mia sniffed. "At least forty years."

"Strange that she would show up like this."

"We'd better shush. The service is ready to start." Gran nudged Mia.

The service was simple. There were a few readings from the minister and then a eulogy from Steve. It was poignant and had a few humorous moments when he recounted how he'd met Tim for the first time.

At the end of the service, the minister invited them to stay for the reception. Mia, Gran, and Luke made their way to pay their respects to the family.

"Mia, thank you for coming. I'm glad you're here. Can I talk to you in a little while?" Danielle asked.

"Of course. I'm in no hurry. We're going to get a bite to eat and chat with some people Gran knows. How are you doing?"

Danielle shrugged. "All right, I guess. The police have been keeping me in the loop. That's part of what I want to talk to you about."

"That's okay. Look, if we don't talk tonight, we can get together for lunch tomorrow if that works.

"We'll see. I'd like to talk more tonight."

Mia nodded. "We'll work it out."

She followed Luke and Gran into the reception area and saw Alex and her mother speaking with a couple of women. She hurried to Alex's side. "How are you doing?"

Alex smiled. "I'm okay."

Mrs. Bennett shrugged. "It's been challenging. I'm glad the police are on the investigation. I hope they resolve it soon."

"Are you going back home tonight?" Mia asked her.

"I'm going to stay with Alex overnight and go to the internment tomorrow morning. I'll head back home tomorrow afternoon. I have to get back to the hospital tomorrow." Mrs. Bennett was a hospital administrator in Huntsville. "Alex and Danielle tell me you're looking into Tim's death. Have you learned anything?"

"Nothing conclusive. I've shared the information with the police and with

Luke as well."

Mrs. Bennett raised an eyebrow. "Why Luke?"

"It seems Uncle Tim was involved with some antiquities that may have been stolen." Alex looked at her mom.

Mrs. Bennett bit her lip. "I warned him to be careful who he worked with. He was so intent on making money for Rita's treatments."

"Did you know about what he was doing?" Mia asked.

"No. He wouldn't tell me where he was getting the money from. I could always tell when he was hiding something." Mrs. Bennett sighed. "Make sure Danielle's okay, will you?" She looked at Alex when she said that.

"I will, Mom. Maybe we should look at getting back home?"

"Yes. I'm exhausted. Mia, it was good to see you again. Give my best to your Gran and to Luke." Mrs. Bennett leaned into Mia and gave her a warm embrace. "Thank you for helping with this." She whispered in Mia's ear.

Mia nodded. "We'll see you soon." Mia watched as Alex and her mom left the room.

Chapter Fourteen

Tuesday Evening

She looked around for Gran and Luke. There were tables set up for people to sit, eat, and chat. There were side tables laden with food. Mia noticed that Gran had been pulled aside by one of her antique dealer friends, and they were speaking in hushed tones.

Luke sidled up to her. "Gran's friend just pulled her away from me. I take it that's a friend?"

Mia smiled. "Yes, I recognize her. It's Martha Jones. Her shop is smaller than Tim's. She sells different stock. She and Gran worked together for a couple of events a few years ago."

Mia walked up to Gran. "Did you want me to make up a plate and find us all a table?"

"Oh, Mia. You remember, Martha Jones from It's All I've Got!"

"I do. Hello, Mrs. Jones. Good to see you again, despite the circumstances."

"Hello, Mia. Nice to see you. Your Gran was telling me that you've been looking into Tim's death. You could have knocked me down with a feather when I heard Tim had been poisoned! What's going on?"

Mia raised her eyebrows and looked at Gran. Gran just rolled her eyes. "Well, we're not sure. The police are looking into his death."

"I asked Martha if she'd heard from Barbara, Tim's first wife, lately. Martha, why don't you tell Mia what you told me?"

Mia looked around. They were gathering interest from different people.

"Why don't we grab a table. Luke and I will get some food for us, and we can chat?"

Gran nodded. "That's a good idea. Come on, Martha."

Mia took Luke's hand.

"I take it we're eating with Martha?" He asked with a grin.

"I have a feeling she has lots to tell us."

They each took a plate and filled it with sandwiches and desserts. Mia spotted some fruit and added a small plate as well. She looked around for something to drink and noticed that each table had a coffee carafe and a teapot. The tables had cups and spoons as well as milk and sugar.

Back at the table, Mia and Luke deposited the food and took a seat. Mia was sitting next to Martha and Luke between Gran and Mia.

They helped themselves to the food, and Mia poured out tea for all of them.

"Now, Martha. Tell Mia what you told me."

Martha swallowed her bite of Nanaimo bar. "It's like I told Marie, Tim and I had talked last week about Barbara. That's his first wife, you know." She looked at Mia, and Mia nodded in agreement. "Apparently, she's been living in Lakeview for the last year, and she's been working with him in some kind of new venture. And she claims that she owns part of Timeless Treasures."

Mia frowned. "But I remember him saying that he'd given her what she'd asked for in the divorce. Why would she say she owns part of it if she doesn't?"

"She claims that with their latest work together, he told her he would leave her the store and the stock in his will."

Mia shook her head. "There's no way he did that. I've been speaking with Danielle, and he didn't make a new will. Everything goes to her."

"I'm only repeating what she told me yesterday when she stopped by my shop."

"Is that all she said?" Mia asked.

Martha put down her teacup. "No, she said she wanted to speak to me about a new venture. She didn't have an opportunity to bring it up because six women came into my shop looking for tea services and jewelry. She left while I was taking care of them, saying she'd be in touch."

"Any idea what the new venture is?" Luke asked.

Martha smiled at him. "Love your accent. But no, she didn't say anything to me about the new venture, just that it would be something worth my while." Martha snorted. "I doubt that very much. I learned a long time ago when someone says that, it usually means you get stuck with a lot of extra work and headaches. There's no such thing as a free ride. Whatever Barbara is involved with, I want nothing to do with it."

Gran shook her head. "I'm surprised she'd say that about Tim's will. Like Mia said, Tim left everything to Danielle. I hope she doesn't try to make trouble for Danielle."

"I know realtors have contacted Danielle about selling the store. I wonder if Barbara is trying to buy it since she didn't inherit it? And she mentioned someone was interested in the stock. She's told them both she doesn't know what she's going to do yet," Mia said.

Martha nodded. "Yes, Bev Matheson spoke with me yesterday. She asked if I knew if anyone else had put in an offer."

"I think everyone needs to just wait until Danielle's had a moment to breathe. She's smart and will decide what works best for her." Mia picked up her tea.

"Did you know Barbara before she moved away?" Luke asked.

"No, I didn't start my shop until fifteen years ago. I remember Tim telling me about the divorce. We'd been talking about my divorce. That's what got me into the business. We commiserated on failed marriages. He and Barbara's divorce had been rough. He had to buy her out because she had provided half of the start-up money. He told me the agreement they signed was tight. I met her a number of years ago. Like I said, she's been in Lakeview quite a bit over the last several years. She might even have a home here." Martha picked up a cupcake and set it on her plate. "When Tim started his shop, he was into furniture. It wasn't until later he started bringing in antiquities from Europe and Asia. I don't know how he managed to make money with those. They were very expensive to bring in. But he carried on and did well. There were always customers coming to his store, and he did a lot of business overseas as well."

"How so?" Mia asked.

Martha lowered her voice and looked around. "It's not common knowledge, but about seven or eight years ago, he told me he was getting into the antiquity auction market. I didn't know anything like it existed, but he needed money and lots of it. His wife was quite ill with MS and had taken a turn for the worse. There was an experimental treatment in California they wanted to try. Unfortunately, their insurance wouldn't cover the cost. He decided to sell a couple of items online at auction, and he did well with them. Enough that he was able to cover the cost of his wife's treatment and their travel expenses."

"Where did he get the items from?" Mia asked.

"He didn't say. I don't know if it was surplus he had in storage or if he just happened to find them."

"Where's his storage facility? Danielle wasn't sure where it was." Mia asked.

"It's out by the airport. Somewhere near Pearson, I'm not sure which facility. There are so many in that area. I remember he was going out there a couple of weeks ago."

"Is there anything else you can think of?" Mia asked.

"I don't know. I thought he was doing well. He'd had a few events that were by invitation only at the store, and they appeared to be well attended. During those events, he'd sell the stock he wanted to move. The prices were reduced, and the invitees would buy more than they normally would."

Gran nodded. "We were at his last one. I found a mirror I'd been looking for, and Mia found a painting. He had a large crowd that evening."

"He tried to keep them to about thirty people. More than that, he had a tough time managing them. His clerk, I think her name is Cheryl, would work those evenings as well. And I've seen his son-in-law, Steve, at the store more often lately."

"If Danielle keeps the store, do you think Cheryl would be suited to handle the business?" Mia asked.

"No. She doesn't have the knowledge required. It would be easy for someone to take advantage of her. If Danielle is going to keep the business, tell her to talk to me. I'll know people who can help her out." Martha nodded her head. "There she is."

Mia glanced in the direction Martha had indicated and saw Cheryl talking with Barbara. "Oh no! What is she doing here? Danielle can't see her. That will upset her."

Luke stood. "If you come with me, we'll see if we can escort her out."

Mia and Luke hurried toward Cheryl and Barbara.

"Hi. Cheryl, is it? I'm Mia Reid, a friend of Danielle's." Mia extended her hand.

"Ah, yes. I remember you from the event we had at the store last week. How are you?"

"I'm well. And you are?" Mia turned to Barbara.

"I'm Barbara Fraser. Tim's first wife."

"Right. Are you from the area? I thought someone told me you'd moved away."

"I'm not sure that's any of your business."

"It's my business because I was at the soirée on Wednesday evening, and I distinctly remember you bullying your way in. Danielle's a friend of mine, and I won't have her upset any further than she already is. So, what exactly are you doing here?" Mia's eyes narrowed as she focused on Barbara.

Barbara's eyebrows dipped, and she glared at Mia. "None of your business."

"We're making it our business. If you won't tell us what you're doing here, I'm sure Detective Martin, of the Lakeview Police Department, would be interested in speaking with you. You weren't welcomed at Mr. Fraser's soirée, and you were escorted out. That leads me to believe that you need to leave." Mia's voice was firm.

"If you must know, Tim and I had some unfinished business to deal with." Barbara spat the words out.

"Did you go back to see him that evening?" Luke asked.

Barbara glanced at Luke. "Who are you?"

"Luke Forbes, Interpol." Luke's voice was clipped.

Barbara's face blanched. "No, I didn't go back."

Cheryl turned toward Barbara. "You told me you'd be back when you left."

"That's good enough for me. Mia, I'll be right back." Luke turned around and walked out of the room.

"Where's he going?" Barbara asked.

Mia shrugged. "Don't know. Did you go back to see Mr. Fraser?"

Barbara didn't answer.

Luke returned with Detective Martin following him.

"Barbara Fraser, I'm Detective Martin with Lakeview Police. I need to ask you a few questions about last Wednesday evening."

"I have nothing to say to you." Barbara's face was pinched and her voice shrill.

"Well, you can come with me to the station. Luke, did you want to join us?"

"Gladly. Mia, I'll see you later."

"Come with us, Ms. Fraser. We're going to have a chat." Detective Martin took Barbara by the arm, and Luke followed closely behind them.

The people in the room watched as Barbara struggled to get out of Detective Martin's grasp. "Let me go. You have no right to do this."

Detective Martin shook his head. "We'll take this to the station. I'm sure we have a lot to talk about."

They left the room, and conversation slowly returned to normal.

"What's Interpol doing here?" Cheryl asked.

"Luke is working with AART. That's the Antiquities, Art, and Recovery Team. He's here for work with the Lakeview Police Department."

Cheryl shifted her feet.

Mia watched her carefully.

"Mr. Fraser wasn't doing anything illegal. His soirées at the store were for a select group of customers."

"I didn't say he was. I'm curious about how he conducted business. There's been talk of underground auctions in the city. Antiquities from around the world are finding their way to Lakeview and aren't staying here for long. The police are quite interested in his business, especially since he was poisoned."

"I don't know anything about that."

"Do you know Barbara?" Mia asked.

Cheryl bit her lip and nodded.

Chapter Fifteen

Cheryl nodded. "I started working with Tim eight years ago. She was coming around a few times a year then. He didn't say a lot about her at the beginning, but I learned she was his first wife. I remember mentioning to him that it was nice to see they still got along. He made it clear they weren't friends; she was someone he was doing business with."

"What kind of business?" Mia asked.

"He didn't elaborate then. I found out by accident that she was organizing auctions with him. Not the soirées he was doing with his valued customers, but auctions that were held off-site. I don't know where. He kept me separate from that area of the business. He told me it was for my safety, which was really weird. I didn't argue with him. He was always fair with me and paid me well. In the last few years, Barbara's been coming in the shop a lot more. I'd say it's closer to once a month, and these past few months, she's been in a few times a week. I think she's living here now." Cheryl pushed her hair back.

"Detective Martin may want to talk to you about this. Do you have a problem speaking with him?"

"No, of course not." Cheryl's eyes shifted to the left. "Please don't say anything to Danielle about this yet."

Before Mia had a chance to say anything, Danielle showed up.

"Mia, what were Luke and the detective doing with Barbara? And why was she here?"

Mia briefly filled her in on the situation.

"She said she was going into business with Dad. Is she crazy? There's no way Dad would have worked with her."

"I'm just telling you what she told us. Apparently, she's been to the shop several times in the last few months."

"Dad never mentioned her to me. Cheryl, do you know what they met about?"

"Mr. Fraser never gave me an explanation. And I didn't think it was my place to ask him for one. She did seem interested in the antique business. She asked a lot of questions about his auctions."

Danielle crossed her arms. "I need to ask you about the store's accounting program. I don't understand the system and need some help."

"What don't you understand? It should be straightforward." Cheryl tucked her hair behind her ear.

"The numbers don't add up, and they should. The math should be simple. He paid for antiques and sold them. But there's one file where the antiques just appear, and then they're sold."

Cheryl nodded. "Right. I think those were sold privately, not through the store."

"That doesn't make sense," Danielle said.

"I don't know what else to tell you. Maybe talk to the accountant?"

"I will. He's on my list for tomorrow." Danielle sighed. "There are a lot of things that aren't adding up. Do the police think Barbara had anything to do with Dad's death?"

"They had questions for her, but I'm not sure what exactly."

"Right, you said that. Sorry. My mind is all over the place. I'm tired."

Mia looked around and saw Steve. She waved him over. "Listen, you don't have to stay until the end here. No one expects that. Why don't you both go home and get some rest?"

Steve put his hand on Danielle's back. "That's a great suggestion. Danielle, I'll make a short announcement to let people know that they can stay until nine. We can leave. The funeral home staff will take care of getting everyone out. Okay?"

"Thanks. That sounds good. Mia, can I call you tomorrow?"

"Better to text me. I've got a new exhibit opening at the museum at noon, and I'll be busy until around four. We can meet after I'm done work if you want."

"Yes. I'm off for another week, but I want to get to the storage unit. I'll text you and let you know when."

"I'll chat with you later, get some rest."

"Have you decided about opening the store again?" Cheryl asked.

"It's going to stay closed until next week. There are too many things I need to look at right now."

"Did you want me to go in and clean up?" Cheryl asked.

"No, thanks. I'll make certain your wages are covered for this week. Take some time off. You need it too. We'll be busy soon enough with the store."

Steve made his announcement, and then he and Danielle left the building. Mia excused herself and found Gran.

She was still chatting with Martha. When Gran saw Mia, she said, "Is it time for us to leave?"

"I think so. Danielle and Steve have left. I'll take you home."

Martha stood and gathered her purse. "Marie, it was lovely to catch up with you. We'll have to do it again. I'd best get home as well. Good night, Mia."

"Drive safely." Mia watched as she headed out and then looked at Gran. "Are you all right? You look a little tired."

"You would be too if you'd had Martha talking your ear off. But I learned a few things about what's been happening in the antique world since I've been out of it." Gran picked up her purse. "Let's go. I'll tell you all about it on the drive home."

They were leaving the reception room when Gran asked about Luke.

Mia explained that he and Detective Martin had left with Barbara. "I'll go get the car. Can you wait in the lobby?" Gran agreed, and Mia hurried to get the Jeep, taking care to watch the surrounding area closely.

Mia pulled in front of the funeral home lobby, and Gran got in. Mia checked her mirrors and saw a white car similar to the one she'd seen yesterday. She frowned and decided to watch if the car followed her.

"What did Martha have to say?" Mia asked as she drove away.

"She told me that Tim had been receiving shipments of antiques every week. Now, that may not sound like a lot, but for a shop of his size, it is. And for what he sold. The trucks would come round the back alley and would stay parked there. Even overnight. And they would leave by seven the next morning."

"How does she know that?"

"Her apartment's over her shop. And she can see the back of his shop clearly."

"Oh, right. I forgot she mentioned that. Did she ever see what antiques they were unloading?"

"No. I asked her about the storage unit, and she says that he mentioned it once at a meeting of the shop owners' association. He didn't have enough storage at his shop and had to find an additional storage location. Someone at the meeting recommended a few places, including one out in Mississauga."

"But his store has a lot of space. And there's that basement section as well. Although if he was using that to make copies of antiquities, that would explain why he couldn't use it for storage." Mia stopped at a red light. "Danielle wants me to go with her to the storage unit tomorrow. I can't go until after work. She's willing to wait until then." Mia checked her side mirrors. No sign of the white car.

"Will Luke be going with you?"

"I think so. It's something he'd be interested in. I think Steve will be with us as well."

Mia turned into Gran's apartment building. She turned off the car. "I'll go up with you. I want to make sure you're okay."

Gran smiled. "I'll be fine. But come up anyway."

They walked into the building, and the security guard was at the desk. "Hi George. How are you tonight?" Gran asked.

"Mrs. Tremblay. I'm well. I see there's been some threats made. What's that all about?"

Gran rolled her eyes. "I don't think it's anything serious. A friend was killed last week, and Mia's been asking a few questions. Apparently, someone isn't happy with what she's doing."

"I'm glad to hear you're aware of the threats," Mia said.

"No one will get in who shouldn't be here. And if anyone wants to see you, they'll have to go through us. Don's patrolling the building outside, and one of us will be at the desk all night. If you need anything, don't hesitate to call us."

"Thanks. I will, but I should be fine." Gran and Mia headed to the elevator.

Gran pushed her floor button aggressively.

"Gran, are you all right?"

"I don't like being treated like a little old lady." Gran crossed her arms in front of her chest.

"No one's treating you like that. I'm glad security knows about the threats. I'll feel a lot better tonight about your safety."

The elevator doors opened onto Gran's floor, and they walked to her condo. Gran unlocked the door, and they went in. Cleo met them at the door, meowing in greeting.

"It's always so nice and cool here in the summer." Mia closed the door behind them and locked it.

Gran slipped off her shoes and picked up Cleo. "I'm going to put away my bag and change my clothes. I'd like a gin and tonic. Could you put that together?"

"Not a problem." Mia watched as Gran marched to her bedroom and shook her head. Gran wasn't happy. Oh well, she was glad the building security was taking the threat seriously. Gran would get over it. Mia walked across to the dining room and to the small bar that was set up. She filled the ice bucket with ice and took out some tonic water. She poured out a generous serving of gin and added ice and tonic water. Picking up another glass, she filled it with ice and added tonic water. Gran might have a drink, but Mia was driving.

Gran came out, dressed in silk leisure pants and a matching shirt. Cleo trotted ahead of her. "Let's go outside," she said.

Mia followed her out and set the drinks on the table. Gran sat on the love seat, and Cleo jumped up next to her.

Gran took a long swallow. "That's refreshing. Thank you." She peered at Mia over her glasses. "And I'm sorry I was cross earlier. I know you're just looking out for me."

Mia nodded. "I understand. I hate that someone would even think of going after you. I'll be careful with anything I learn, and the police will know about it immediately."

"Is the exhibit ready for tomorrow?"

"As ready as it will be. A lot of work was already done when I started at the museum. I just had to fill in a few areas. Making sure the text about the artifacts is clearly written and easy for people to understand was important. I think we got it right. The whole team's been great to work with."

"What's next for you?"

"I'm working on a project with remote schools up north. It's something the museum's done in the past, but with today's technology, we can do a lot more. We're sending some equipment up to the schools so they can make 3D images of the items we're discussing."

"That's exciting! How good are the models they'll be able to make?"

"Not an exact replica, which we don't want! But they'll be able to see how it applies in real life. We'll be meeting twice a week for forty-five minutes each time. We'll discuss the artifacts and what they were used for. I hope I can get them interested in looking in their communities for artifacts. We'll have to get outside soon because of the weather. Winter usually shows up by the middle of October for the northern communities."

"Will you be doing one-on-one with the schools, or are they all on together?"

"We've decided to combine two schools per session. I'll be doing six sessions a week."

"That's a lot of time dedicated to this project."

Mia nodded. "It is, but it's only for six weeks. It'll be intense for me, but hopefully a lot of fun for the students and their teachers."

They chatted for a little longer, and Mia left just after ten.

* * *

Mia sent Luke a text letting him know she was home.

Luke: Thanks, will be back in about an hour.

Mia: Will wait up.

Mia busied herself with some household chores that had been neglected. She threw a load of laundry in and then settled herself on the couch to scan through more of Mr. Fraser's documents.

She found a folder titled "Inventory" and opened it up. There were eight different documents, and the most recent one was dated last month. Mia opened it up and started reading through.

The first few pages showed an inventory of items in the store. There were photos, a short description, and each item was assigned a number. The list was extensive, and Mia found the mirror Gran had purchased and her painting as well.

The next folder was titled Storage Unit. Mia opened it, eager to see what was in the storage unit.

The file had been updated last week. Mia read through the documents. Notations on every item in the storage unit had been made.

Each item had a fact sheet. A color photo, description, and approximate age of the object, where it came from, and a price point were listed on the sheet. Mia scrolled through the first couple of items. They were definitely antiques. Furniture dating back to the early 1900s. Heavy and ornate.

The fifth page showed an artifact that looked as if it originated in Central America. It was a small jade statue, no more than six inches tall. But it was wide. The statue had the face of a snake on it and the body of a crocodile. *"Ugh!"* Mia thought. *"I wouldn't want to come up against that in a dig."* Mia didn't like snakes at all. They scared her, and unfortunately, they were part of life in Central America. She always made sure to check the area carefully when she worked a dig there.

Mia looked closely at the artifact. She'd read something about an artifact like this. She opened her internet and did a search. Yes. There it was. This artifact had been stolen from a museum in Belize. It had been on loan from the Mexico City Museum and very valuable. Mia's eyes widened at the amount it had been valued at. Close to six figures.

She went back to the document. The artifact's fact sheet showed that it would be listed at half a million dollars. It was valuable, but not that much. And if it was, why would it be in a storage unit? That wasn't the safest place for it.

Mia leaned back in her chair. That didn't make sense. What else was in that unit?

She looked through the document and found more artifacts from Central America and several from Indonesia as well. Mia sighed. This didn't look good. It wasn't proof that Mr. Fraser was dealing in stolen artifacts, but it was damning.

Mia heard Luke's key in the door and closed her computer.

"Hey, glad you're back." Mia walked to him and hugged him.

Luke held her close for a moment. "Glad to be back." He sighed. "What a piece of work that woman is."

Mia opened the fridge and pulled out a bottle of beer. "Drink?"

"Yes, please." Luke took a glass out of the cupboard and poured his drink.

They went into the living room. "Is there anything you can tell me, or is it top secret?"

"There isn't much to tell. She wouldn't talk to us until her attorney showed up, and when he did, he told her not to say anything. Then he proceeded to tell us we didn't have anything on her and couldn't hold her. We had no choice but to release her. But not until we had her fingerprinted and photographed." Luke took a drink. "We did that when we brought her in."

"Do you know who her lawyer is?"

Luke shook his head. "I don't remember the name. He's with some firm with offices across Canada. She had an attorney with them in Vancouver. When she called their office, they told her they'd send someone over from here. It didn't take him long to get to the police station."

"Nothing from her at all?"

"She did say that she hadn't had anything to do with Fraser's death. I suggested to Detective Martin that they should look through Fraser's computer and his email. I told him you'd found some email communications between the two of them. I couldn't remember what they were, though."

Mia nodded. "I do. The emails go back eight years. And the last email mentioned a Charles who wasn't happy. It also appears she was interested in his storage unit. And I might know why."

She filled him in on what she'd learned from the computer files and what Martha had told Gran about the shipments going to Timeless Treasures.

"The police may want to look through the storage unit. I'll talk to Detective Martin tomorrow. He might want to accompany us tomorrow evening."

"I agree. Danielle might find it difficult, but it's better she knows up front. I know the items I saw in the inventory were stolen. I've found the information online in various archaeology journals."

Luke took her hand. "I've no doubt you're right. I'll let Detective Martin know in the morning, and we'll make plans for tomorrow evening. How was the rest of your night?"

Mia leaned against him and filled him in. They sat for a while just talking. Mia loved this. She had missed having someone to share her life with. When they'd been together at grad school, there wasn't any topic she and Luke hadn't discussed. And they'd slipped right back into their relationship, even after ten years apart.

The laundry beeped, and Mia extricated herself from Luke's embrace. "That's the laundry. I'll be back in a few minutes. Just need to put things away."

"We should probably get to bed. You have a busy day at the museum, don't you?"

"Yes." Mia glanced at the clock, later than she'd wanted to be up. "You're right, I need some sleep so I can be fresh tomorrow. Fingers crossed nothing goes wrong." She smiled.

"I'm sure everything is ready. And if something needs to be fixed, your team will be able to help you."

Mia dealt with the laundry, and Luke put the living room and kitchen in order. Then they went off to bed.

Chapter Sixteen

Wednesday Morning

Mia woke up early the next morning. She'd slept well and felt rested. Luke was already up, and she could hear him in the shower. "Mmm, coffee first."

She slipped on her robe and padded down the hall to make some coffee. She was sipping her cup and watching traffic pick up along the waterfront when Luke appeared. He was dressed for work.

"Morning. I hope I didn't wake you," he said.

Mia shook her head. "Nope. It was time to get up. Are you having breakfast here?"

"Afraid not. Detective Martin texted that he'll pick me up, and then the team from the RCMP are with us today. We're having breakfast catered in less than twenty minutes."

"What time will you be through with work?"

"I should be clear by four-thirty. When are we meeting Danielle?"

"I told her I couldn't be there until six. I'm going to touch base with her again, just to make certain that works for her."

Luke nodded. "All right. I'll meet you here. How far away is this place?"

"Maybe twenty or thirty minutes."

"Good enough." Luke's phone buzzed with a text. "He'll be here in a couple of minutes."

Mia leaned in for a kiss. "Have a good one. And be safe."

"You too. Please be careful out there today."

Mia hurried through her shower and got dressed. She took time to straighten her hair. Some light makeup and jewelry finished the look. She slipped into a wrap dress and stepped into a pair of ballet flats. She grabbed a sweater from her closet, checked herself in the full-length mirror, and nodded. "You'll do. Thanks, Alex, for the help!"

Last month, Alex had taken her clothes shopping. Her wardrobe had received an upgrade, and she was confident in everything she wore. The clothes were comfortable and elevated her look.

She made herself a couple of eggs and toast. Turning on the television, she checked the morning program. They were talking about the exhibit at the museum. Bonus, she hadn't expected them to. They ran a short clip of yesterday's interview, and Mia smiled. Everything would work out. She wasn't going to let things get to her.

She tidied up the kitchen and then hurried to catch the subway. It would be the easiest way to get to the museum. She joined the rest of the commuters standing by the tracks. Mia was in the middle of the pack and felt someone push her forward. She bumped into the woman in front of her and quickly turned around. She couldn't see who had pushed her.

"You okay, miss?" the man standing next to her asked.

"Yes, but I thought I felt someone push me."

"It's crowded this morning, easy for someone to bump into you."

The train arrived, and Mia found a seat.

Arriving at the museum, she noticed there were signs everywhere directing patrons to the exhibit. She stopped at the front desk to check and make sure they had everything they needed.

"We're good, Dr. Reid. Marketing dropped off the information packages yesterday, and we have them ready for this afternoon. The gift shop received the shipment last week, and they're bringing everything out on the floor this morning."

"Thank you. I want everything to run smoothly. It's my first event here."

"Not a problem. We'll make sure everything goes well. You sit back and enjoy it."

Mia stopped in to check on the exhibits. Everything looked perfect. The signage was clear and legible, and the pedestals were gleaming. The display boxes were raised just enough to make it easy to look at the artifacts on display. She followed the arrows on the floor and made sure everything flowed well. There were no problems that she could see.

She saw Heather at the end of the hall with Christine Marks, the museum's CEO. Heather smiled, "It looks great!"

Mia walked to them. "It does. I'm pleased with it. I'll be curious to see how many patrons come through."

"One of the city day camps is bringing a group of eight-year-olds through," Christine said.

"Oh, that's good! They're the perfect age for this."

"How are you enjoying the work?" Christine asked.

"I'm happy with what I'm involved in. The exhibits that were started have come along well. The curators left excellent notes. I'm looking forward to working on the school project."

"I'm going to let you get to work. I have a few additional things to take care of this morning. We'll chat later today." Heather hurried off.

Christine walked with Mia to her office. "I've heard very good things about you from the rest of the staff. You've been an excellent addition to the museum."

"Thank you. The curators who had started working on this project left some excellent notes."

"We'll chat again soon. I'd better let you get to work." Christine headed up the stairs to her office.

Mia spent the morning getting work done on the school project. She'd sent a text to Danielle about going to the storage unit and had told her she and Luke could be there around six. No response from Danielle yet.

After lunch, Mia checked on the exhibit. There were the kids from day camp. Curious and eager to learn about the ancient Aztecs. Mia grinned as she overheard one of them say, "This is real gold!" Fortunately, all the exhibits were under lock and key. No one would be able to handle them or walk away with any of them.

She stood off to the side, watching as they ran from one exhibit to the other. Their excitement was contagious.

The teachers from the day camp gathered them together, and they asked them what they had liked the best. The answers ranged from the daggers with jewels in them to the crown that one of the high priests had worn. One girl asked if there had been any toys found. A docent who had been with the group answered the question.

Yes, there had been toys. They were in the last room under glass. Most of them were small dolls and weapons. The docent reminded the children that kids in those days went to school, helped out with chores, and contributed to the society of the village they lived in.

They'd been touring the exhibit for just over an hour, and they'd enjoyed it. There were several groups of adult patrons waiting to go through, so the teachers gathered the children and headed for the cafeteria for a snack.

Mia grinned. She felt the exhibit had weathered the toughest crowd. It had held their attention, and they hadn't wanted to leave. Good work.

She went back to her office and found a text from Danielle confirming meeting with them at the storage unit at six. She also indicated that Detective Martin would be there as well. Mia was glad he'd touched base with Danielle. An address for the storage unit was included in the text.

Mia finished up her day and hurried to catch the subway. She was pleased with the way the exhibit had been received, and there had been a steady stream of patrons all day. Friday night would be the Museum after Hours event for adults to go through the exhibit, and she would have to be there for that.

Arriving home, she changed out of her work clothes and slipped on a pair of capris and a T-shirt. She grabbed an apple and some cheese and cut them into pieces for a snack. While she ate, she looked through her fridge and decided to order some subs for dinner. There was a good sub shop in the lobby of her building, and that would take care of dinner.

Mia: Do you want a sub for supper?

Luke: Sure, and can you order one for Det Martin? A meatball sub for both of us with everything on it.

Mia: Sounds good.

Mia hurried out to go pick up the subs and snagged some soft drinks and chips.

Luke and Detective Martin arrived half an hour later.

"Mia, are you here?" Luke called as he entered her apartment.

Mia stepped into the living room. "I'm out on the balcony. I've picked up supper, so whenever you all want to eat, we can."

Detective Martin said, "Thanks. Traffic was busy. There's a baseball game tonight."

"That's right. I forgot about that. We should be okay to get to the storage unit for six, though?"

"Yes, we can take an alternate route."

They ate dinner, and Detective Martin and Luke discussed how their session had gone that day.

"Are you making any headway with the smuggling cartel?" Mia asked.

Luke shrugged. "Right now, we're in discovery mode, you might say. We have several individuals that are making presentations on how the artifacts are coming into the country. They seem to come by sea and by air. Once they're in the country, it's easy enough to put them on a transport truck or a train and transport them that way. The police can do checks across the country, but they can't stop everything. This is a big country."

Mia and Detective Martin both laughed when Luke said that.

"It's huge. And while we have one main highway that crosses the country, there are multiple routes that connect our provinces and territories. So, yes, for the police to stop every transport truck wouldn't work. But there's got to be a way to figure out which ones are coming out of suspect areas, isn't there?" Mia asked.

Detective Martin nodded. "There is. With the help of our counterparts and border agents across the country, we can monitor seaports and airports. The antiquities come in several smaller crates. They're not usually one huge shipment. And some items can be brought in by people returning from vacations or work."

"Depending on the items, that's true. Larger items, such as a sarcophagus, for example, would have to be shipped in a crate. But coins, jewelry, small paintings could easily be smuggled in. We need to get all the agencies working together. For the most part, they are. And we've been successful in stopping a number of antiquities from coming in. I'll be curious to see what we find in Mr. Fraser's storage unit," Luke said.

"I hope Danielle's up for this. I hate that she's learning about this side of her father." Mia took a drink of her Diet Pepsi. "What's your interest in the antiquity smuggling area?" Mia asked Detective Martin.

"I've been involved since my robbery investigation days. I remember when the Lakeview Museum discovered some of their artifacts were reproductions. That was about ten years ago. The museum came under a lot of scrutiny. That's when I learned about antiquity smuggling and reproductions. It took us almost a year before we solved the case."

Mia nodded. "I remember hearing about that. And Heather, one of the people I work with at the museum, told me it was someone who volunteered at the museum."

"It was. He'd been volunteering for a few years and helping himself to some beautiful artifacts. I was happy when we caught up to him. He's out of prison now and trying to make amends."

Luke set his drink down on the table. "Where are you with the two sets of books Danielle found?"

Detective Martin wiped his hands on his napkin. "Forensic accountants are examining Mr. Fraser's books. There may be a clue in there as to who he was working for and who were the individuals that purchased the antiquities." Detective Martin glanced at the clock. "We should get going. I don't want to be late."

Mia picked up their plates and put them in the dishwasher, Luke threw out the trash, and then they left.

They arrived at the storage facility at the same time as Danielle and Steve did. Detective Martin followed Mia's Jeep to the unit.

They parked their cars close to the unit and joined Steve and Danielle.

Steve had the keys and handed them over to Detective Martin. "I'll let you open it up."

Detective Martin opened the lock and pulled the large door up.

They stood in front of the unit, looking around. There were metal shelves along the two side walls. They reached the ceiling and were full of boxes. A couple of light bulbs hung from the ceiling, and Detective Martin walked over to the left side of the unit and turned on the lights.

"Can we go in?" Danielle asked.

"Yes. But if you're going to touch anything, please wear these gloves." He gave them all latex gloves.

Luke walked in and headed for the shelves on the right-hand side. He opened a box and whistled. "Look at these." He set the box down, and they saw that it was full of gold-colored statues. They appeared to be Asian.

"Are they real?" Steve asked.

Mia reached across and took one out. "It's heavy and crudely made." She turned the statue over several times. "I don't think these are real. They're all the same. They'd need to be tested, but I think these are copies."

"Why do you think they're copies?" Danielle asked.

"They're all the same. Real artifacts aren't mass-produced," Mia said.

Danielle looked at the statue. "I see what you mean. How many of these are there?"

Luke turned to the shelves to look at them again. "I think that's the only box of those statues. They may have decided to experiment with the equipment in the shop's basement and found that it didn't work. Instead of melting these down, they brought them here."

Detective Martin was on the other side of the unit. "I've found some items here. Could one of you look at them?"

Mia placed the statue back in the box and strode to him.

Detective Martin placed the box on a table in the middle of the room. Mia checked the contents. Her heart sank. These were artifacts that had been reported missing at the end of last winter. They'd been removed from a museum in Colombia, and there had been several reports about the thefts in the archaeology world.

"Luke, could you come here, please?"

Luke checked the box and looked at Mia. He nodded his head.

"Danielle, this box has artifacts that look like the ones that were reported missing in January. I'm sorry, but we're going to have to take them for testing to verify that they're the missing artifacts." Luke turned to Detective Martin. "We're going to have to go through everything in this unit. And I'd like us to have backup. We also need a secure location to examine them."

Mia interrupted. "Why not bring them to the museum? You'd have access to all the equipment you'd need to test the artifacts, and they'd be safe in the museum. We have round-the-clock security and vaults where items can be stored."

Detective Martin nodded in agreement. "I think that would be the wisest decision."

"Can you make that happen?" Luke asked Mia.

"Let me make a few calls." Mia stepped outside of the unit and made a call to Christine Marks.

After a brief discussion, Mia returned to the unit.

"We can bring everything into the museum. The CEO will make a couple of calls and get back to me shortly. She's arranging for transportation and for security to accompany us."

"Excellent," Luke said.

"Let's check the rest of the boxes and see what's here," Steve said.

"I can't believe Dad was involved with this. He never said anything about it. How would he have gotten mixed up with antiquity smuggling?" Danielle was wringing her hands.

Mia walked to her and put her arm around her shoulder. "This is something he kept from you for good reason. Smugglers rarely let family members know about their dealings. If they do, then their family members usually become involved as well. I think your dad was doing what he had to do for a long time and then had trouble getting out of it. He probably wanted to protect you."

Danielle's eyes filled with tears. "I feel like I don't know him at all."

"Let's check what's here," Mia said.

They quickly went through the remaining boxes. Out of thirty boxes, twenty had items that Mia and Luke deemed to be stolen. The rest of the items in the storage unit were large furniture pieces that ranged from bedroom suites to dining room furniture. Danielle recognized some of the pieces that her father had picked up at estate sales. Several boxes held files from the store, and Danielle looked through them quickly.

Mia's phone rang. It was Christine Marks confirming the museum would be sending a truck and two security guards. They were already on their way.

Mia thanked her and told the group what was happening.

They didn't have long to wait. Once the truck arrived, Luke, Detective Martin, and Steve loaded the boxes in question onto the truck. The security guard gave Danielle a receipt for the boxes, and they left.

Danielle and Steve left to go home. Mia, Luke, and Detective Martin followed the truck to the museum.

Mia glanced at her watch. It was getting close to nine.

They arrived at the museum, and security took charge of the boxes, and Mia followed them in. They placed the boxes in the vault they had been assigned and gave Mia the receipt.

She went out to speak with Luke and Detective Martin.

"What do we do now?" she asked.

Luke rubbed his face. "I'll need to work with the museum staff that are going to evaluate the items. Are you going to be part of that team?"

"I have no idea. I can ask, but my role here doesn't include that. And I can't ask anyone right now." Mia sighed. "I'll check tomorrow morning. Someone will be able to let me know the next steps."

Chapter Seventeen

The next morning, Danielle called Mia.

"Mia, I'm sorry to call so early, but I need to know who I can talk to about getting the stock in the store valued."

"Gran has offered to help you. If it's too much for her to do or if it's out of her area of expertise, she can recommend a good appraisal company."

"Thanks, I'll touch base with her. And I have another question. Am I under suspicion of being involved with the smuggling and reproduction of the antiquities? I didn't sleep much last night after what we discovered in the storage unit."

"I'm pretty sure you aren't under suspicion. Detective Martin and Luke were with you when we opened the storage unit. If you'd been involved with the thefts, I don't believe you would have allowed the unit to be opened. As for your dad being involved, well, it doesn't look good."

"And the items we found in the storage unit, are they at the museum?"

"Yes. They're safely stored. We have security twenty-four hours a day. I'll be speaking with Christine Marks today about who is going to be evaluating them. The museum has top-notch people working there who can do this. But this isn't a quick process. There are a number of tests that need to be done, and we'll have to cross-reference with reports on stolen artifacts. If they're found to be stolen property, then Luke and his team will take responsibility for getting them returned to their rightful owners."

"I thought so." Danielle paused for a moment. When she spoke again, her voice was firm. "I've made a decision about the store. I'm going to list it for sale. There are a couple of real estate agents who have expressed an interest in it."

"I'm not surprised. Running the store would be a full-time job. Don't let someone offer you a price for the stock without having some knowledge of the value of the items in the store."

"I'll call your grandmother and see if she can help. Thanks, Mia. I'll talk to you soon." Danielle disconnected the call.

Mia filled Luke in on what had transpired.

He nodded. "I don't blame her. She'd be under a tremendous pressure, and if the cartel is involved, they might push her to continue where Fraser left off."

"I never thought of that."

"In the meantime, the police are working to figure out who could have killed him."

"Can you tell me who they're looking at?"

"From what I understand, his first wife, Barbara, is under suspicion. Her behavior is questionable. Then there's the cartel. But that's a nebulous entity at this point. If they're involved, it would have been someone they hired."

Mia's phone pinged with a text. It was Christine Marks.

Christine Marks: I'd like to meet with you at 9:30 this morning. Does that work?

Mia: Of course. In your office?

Christine Marks: In the basement vaults.

Mia: Sounds good.

"Christine wants to meet with me in the basement vaults. She didn't say why, so I don't know what the temperature of the meeting will be."

"Don't worry about it. She may want you to take a hand in the evaluations."

"She might. I'd better get on my way. I'm going to bike to work. The bike lanes are pretty safe, and I'll be extra cautious. How are you getting to work?"

"Detective Martin is picking me up. He doesn't live far from here. I'll lock up when I leave."

"Sounds good, I need to head out. I'll see you after work."

A few minutes later, Mia left for the museum.

She headed for her office and checked numbers for the exhibit that had got underway yesterday. Mia was pleased with the numbers. A good number of patrons had come in, and more day camps were expected this week.

She spent a few minutes on the school project and then set it aside.

Her cell rang with Gran's ringtone.

"Morning, Gran. How are you?"

"I just heard from Danielle. She's going to sell the stock in the store and is wondering if I can give her the name of someone who can do an appraisal. Did you suggest she call me?"

"Yes. I know you know people. I didn't suggest you would do it, though."

"I don't mind helping her out, but there is a lot of stock. What happened with the storage unit?"

"Oh, I forgot to tell you." Mia filled her in. "Most of the stock in the storage unit is here at the museum."

"I feel bad for Danielle. No one knew Tim was involved in smuggling. I'll be spending some time today going through the stock at the store. Danielle and the clerk, Cheryl, are going to be there. Once I see what there is, I may tell Danielle that we need to bring some additional people in. I know some excellent appraisers, and that may be the way to go."

Mia glanced at the computer clock, "Gran, I need to get to my meeting. Can I call you later today?"

"Yes. Danielle is picking me up in an hour. She'll make sure to get me back home. If I need anything, I'll call you. Take care."

Mia hurried to the basement and to the vaults. The basement was also where the labs were located. The antiquities would be examined in the labs.

"Hello, Mia." Christine was outside the vault waiting.

"Hi. What can I help you with?"

Christine turned toward the vault and nodded to the security guard. He opened the vault and stood aside.

Christine motioned to Mia to follow her.

"What can you tell me about them?"

"Well, you know we found these in a storage unit in Mississauga last night. The unit belonged to Tim Fraser. He was an antique dealer with a shop on Queen Street. I'm friends with his daughter, Danielle. She asked me to go with her when she opened it up because she doesn't know anything about antiques. Luke Forbes, a good friend of mine, who's working for AART with Interpol, came with me, as did Detective Martin of the Lakeview Police."

"Are they stolen artifacts?"

"We believe they are. They look like artifacts that were reported stolen from South America in January. Danielle insisted she didn't know anything about them. And I believe her."

"I heard Mr. Fraser's death is being investigated as murder. Is that true?"

"It is. He was poisoned." Mia told her about the results of the autopsy.

Christine shook her head. "I don't have a problem with the antiquities being brought here. The police are aware of this?"

"Yes, Detective Martin didn't want them at the station because he didn't have anyone who would be able to examine them."

"I've looked over your qualifications. You're more than capable of examining the artifacts and providing confirmation if they are the ones that have been stolen. How's your current workload?"

"I have one exhibition that started yesterday. I'm working on a project for the beginning of the school year, and that one's almost complete. The next in-house exhibition won't be until just before Christmas. I have some time. But I wouldn't want to do this on my own."

"No, we'd have to bring someone in with you. Perhaps a couple of people so that you aren't working day and night." Christine smiled. "I have no intention of burning you out!" Christine looked at several of the artifacts. "And I suppose the police want answers immediately?"

"They and Luke Forbes think it's part of a smuggling cartel that's operating out of Canada. They've found some questionable items in Mr. Fraser's store, and it leads them to think he was involved in the smuggling."

Christine frowned. "I'm sorry to hear that. All right, when can you start on this?"

"Probably this afternoon. I need this morning to get some work finished before I can take this on. Did you want me to connect with someone here to help me out?"

"I'll find a few people to work with you. And this afternoon works well. It'll give me time to make sure we can reassign them."

They walked out of the vault and started back. The security guard locked up the vault.

"What do you think of working here?" Christine asked.

Mia smiled. "I'm enjoying it. I'd forgotten what it's like to work in a museum. It's been a while."

"Your interview with The Morning Show went very well. We've had a lot of calls and interest about your exhibit."

"That's good to hear." Mia stopped in the hall, "I'd better return to my office and get things sorted. I'll be in the lab by one this afternoon."

"Excellent, I'll have two experienced staff who'll be there to help you. Let them know what you'll need, and they'll take care of it."

Mia walked to her office, wondering about this change in responsibility. She knew she could do the work, but she also didn't want to not keep up with the work she was supposed to be doing.

She unlocked her office door and stepped on an envelope that was on the floor.

Frowning, she picked it up. Her name was on the outside in block letters. She opened it up and pulled out the single sheet of paper. STOP INVESTIGATING OR ELSE. There was a photo of her and Gran outside the funeral home, and Gran had a red X across her body.

Chapter Eighteen

Thursday

Her hands shaking, Mia set the paper on her desk and called Luke. His phone rang twice, and he answered.

"Mia, what's wrong?"

"I found another threatening note. I'm sending you a photo. It was slipped under my office door. Luke, whoever is doing this is threatening Gran again." Mia's voice broke.

"Hold on, I'm going to check the photo." Mia could hear him opening the text and heard him swear softly under his breath. "I'm going to go to you."

"No, you don't have to. I'm going to check with Gran. She's supposed to be going with Danielle today to help assess the stock at the store. I don't want her to go."

"I doubt Gran is going to take kindly to being told what to do."

"She has to listen. I don't want her in danger." Mia's voice snapped.

"Love, listen to me. I'll talk to her as well. I don't want her hurt either. Between the two of us, she'll listen to reason."

"All right. I'm calling her now."

"Text me when you've spoken with her and let me know how it went. I'll talk to you soon." Luke disconnected the call.

Mia sighed. *"Better get this done now."* She called Gran. Gran answered almost immediately.

"Gran, look, I have something to talk to you about, and it isn't easy."

"What's wrong, Mia?"

Mia explained about the threat and the photo she'd received that morning. When she was done, Gran sighed. "Well, that isn't good at all. The photo was taken at Tim's memorial?"

"Yes. It's when I'm helping you to the car."

"Well, I'm not going to go with Danielle. I'll put her off, and I'll give her a couple of contacts who can do the job for her. I'm sorry this is happening, but I know I'm safe in my building."

"Thanks, Gran. I was worried you'd still want to go."

"As much as I'd like to help Danielle, I want to be around for a few more years. Let me call Danielle and let her know I can't make it. I'll talk to you later today."

Gran disconnected, and Mia blew a sigh out in relief. She sent Luke a quick message.

Mia: Gran staying home today. Will send Danielle a couple of names for appraisers.

Luke: Wonderful news. You stay safe. I'll pick you up after work.

Work always helped Mia steady herself, and she turned her attention on the remote school project. A few hours later, the last of the images had been selected, they'd been uploaded, and the technicians would make sure everything was ready for two weeks from now. Information packages were being completed for the schools, the teachers, and the school boards.

Her phone buzzed with a text from Alex.

Alex: Lunch at Noodles?

Mia: I need to be back before 1

Alex: No problem. I do too.

Mia: 10 minutes?

Alex: Yes

* * *

Mia and Alex arrived at Noodles at the same time.

"Hey, what's up?" Mia asked.

"Not much. Just haven't talked to you in a couple of days."

They walked in, and the hostess seated them in a booth next to the window.

The server arrived, and they gave her their orders. Mia chose a large salad, and Alex picked a lunch size serving of spaghetti Bolognese.

"What have you been up to?" Alex asked.

Mia filled her in on what they'd discovered in Tim's storage unit. She watched Alex as she spoke. Alex's eyes widened when Mia told her about the stolen antiquities.

"I can't believe this. Why would Uncle Tim do this?"

Mia took a sip of Diet Pepsi. "From what we can tell, it started when his wife got sick. There were treatments he wanted her to have, and they cost a lot of money. They had to go to the States for them."

Alex nodded. "I remember that. We started a GoFundMe for them. I know the amount raised was significant, but it wasn't enough to cover all the costs. And he didn't stop after she passed away?"

"No. It may have been a situation where he couldn't get out of it."

"What happens to the antiquities you found?"

Mia looked around the restaurant and lowered her voice. "We brought them to the museum. I'm going to be working with some of our staff to verify the artifacts and locate where they were taken from. I spoke with Christine Marks last night about it, and she agreed the museum would be a good place to do this. We'll begin working on them this afternoon."

"That makes sense. Are the police aware of this?"

"They are. Detective Martin was with us last night. And Luke has connected with his people at Interpol, so they're aware of the situation as well."

"I don't have to be concerned about Danielle, do I?"

Mia shook her head. "From all indications, she didn't have anything to do with the running of the store. The police have questioned her and are satisfied she knew nothing. And so's Luke." Mia paused. "And I need to tell you about the latest threat Gran and I've received."

"What threat? What's happening?"

Mia explained the notes she'd received.

"Why did you come with me for lunch? You're putting yourself in danger!" Alex's voice shook.

"I came because the restaurant isn't far, and it's broad daylight. I don't think anyone will harm me."

"Well, I'll be escorting you back to work."

The server came by with their bills, and they wrapped up their lunch.

"Come on, I'll walk you back," Alex said, grabbing her purse.

"I thought you had to prep for a meeting?"

"I do, and I can do that when I get back."

They walked the short distance to the museum, and Alex's head kept swiveling the entire time they were walking, looking for someone who was following Mia.

"Thanks for walking me back. Be careful going back to work. I'll see you Friday night for certain."

"No problem. I'm going to take a cab back to the office. Let me know if anything else comes up."

"I will." Mia watched as Alex hurried to get a cab.

Mia dropped off her purse in her office and then headed to the labs. Arriving in the basement, she spoke to security and asked them to bring the artifacts to the second lab. She turned on the lights in the lab, moved a few chairs around, and then heard a knock on the door.

"Hi, Dr. Reid? I'm Peter Michaels, and this is Nancy Doucet. Ms. Marks asked us to give you a hand."

"Hi, thanks for coming, and please, call me Mia. I've got the security team bringing the artifacts in. What did Ms. Marks tell you?"

"Not a lot. Just that you had some artifacts that you would need help identifying," Nancy said.

The security team arrived with the artifacts. "This is the lot. Let us know when you want them returned to the vault. One of us will always be outside the door."

"Thanks, I'll let you know when we're done."

They left, and Mia saw one of them stay by the door. She pointed to the boxes. "We found these boxes in a storage unit last night. The police and an Interpol agent were with me. I recognized one of the artifacts; it was reported stolen in January. I'm hoping you can help me identify the remaining artifacts and where they would have been stolen from."

"Who's aware of this?" Peter asked.

"From the police, Detective Martin was with me when they were discovered, and Luke Forbes from AART of Interpol. From the museum, Christine Marks and yourselves. Two other people were with us when we discovered the boxes. They're the owners of the storage unit. You need to be aware that this project cannot be discussed outside this group."

"That's not a problem," Nancy said. "Can we open the boxes?"

"Yes, let's get started."

They covered the long tables with cloths to protect the tables and the artifacts. They removed the artifacts from two of the boxes and began to catalogue them. It was slow work, and the artifacts they removed were beautiful pieces.

Ceramics from Asia, gold statues from India, jeweled pieces from Central America, jade statuettes from the Orient, coins from Italy.

"There's so much from everywhere!" Nancy said.

"Yes, and it's a sign that the items were probably stolen. Unless they're from another antique dealer, which I doubt." Mia looked through the box they'd emptied. "If they came from another dealer, there'd be a paper trail. And there isn't one here."

They each took an artifact and began working on it. Each artifact was photographed, weighed, measured. The features of the artifact were noted, any damage was listed. Mia worked alongside Peter and Nancy. While looking at some of the artifacts, Peter said, "This looks like the statue that was reported stolen in December. It was taken from a museum in Honduras. I remember the report that came out." He held up the statue he was speaking about.

Mia leaned forward to get a better look. "You're right. They'll be happy to have it returned."

They continued sorting the artifacts in silence.

Nancy broke the silence. "These coins may have been in a private collection.

I don't remember seeing anything about coins being stolen."

"I don't either," Peter said.

"If they were part of a private collection, it's possible they were illegally obtained, and the owner wouldn't want to report them stolen," Mia said.

They worked steadily until four. Someone knocked on the door, and Mia went to answer it.

"Ms. Marks, come on in."

"I'm just coming to see if you've discovered anything."

"We have. Almost everything we've examined has been reported as stolen. We've verified them with the reports. I'm astounded by the value of the items," Peter said.

"Did you want me to report this to the police, or do you want to take care of that?" Mia asked Christine.

"I'll let you deal with your contacts and let them know what you've found."

"I'll call Detective Martin and Luke Forbes and advise them."

"Do you want us back here tomorrow?" Nancy asked.

"Yes. We'll need to put in a full day tomorrow. We have a lot to get through. Are you both available?"

They nodded.

Christine cleared her throat. "I'll contact the Board of Directors and let them know what's happening. I don't want any of this out in the public. The last thing we need is for interest to shift to the museum being involved with smuggled artifacts. Peter and Nancy, I think you need to plan on being here for the next few weeks."

"Not to worry, we can do that," Peter said.

Mia hurried to her office. The afternoon had been productive, but had eaten away at her schedule. She sent Luke and Detective Martin a text letting them know what had been discovered with the antiquities. It would be up to Luke and the AART team to make sure they were returned to the rightful owners.

She looked through her agenda to see what she needed to do before the end of the week. The event on Friday evening was the most pressing one. She composed an email to the front desk that handled ticket sales to see what the numbers were like for tomorrow night. That sent, she checked in with Heather to see if she'd heard if any media would be attending. Heather responded almost immediately with an email advising there would be several reporters at the event, and they wanted to speak with her. Mia rolled her eyes. That was a new development. She'd have to make certain they kept the questions to the exhibit on display. She didn't want to let anything slip about the recovered antiquities. Mia sent Heather an email confirming she'd speak with them at the event.

Luke responded to her text.

Luke: Our suspicions were correct then. Will pick you up at work in twenty minutes.

Mia: See you then.

Detective Martin responded a few minutes later.

Detective Martin: Will confer with Luke on next steps.

Mia: He's aware of the findings.

Mia completed the few tasks left for the day and waited for Luke. She'd taken her bike to work and would need to walk it back home with him. She took her bike from the employee room and then locked her office. She walked her bike to the front reception, where she waited for Luke.

He walked into the museum a few minutes after she got there and smiled when he saw her.

"Let me help you with the bike," he said.

Mia smiled. "It's all right. I can handle it. We'll just need to be careful not to bump into too many people."

They left the museum and started toward Mia's condo. Pedestrian traffic was high. It was the start of rush hour traffic. People were done for the day and walking home or meeting friends for a drink after work. There was a lot of congestion along parts of the path going home. Mia paid attention to where her bike was and felt unnerved by all the people. "I really don't like this. There's too many people," she said to Luke.

"We'll be home shortly. We can slow down a bit if you'd like."

Mia and Luke stood at a stoplight, waiting for it to change. "No, I want to get home as soon as we can. I don't feel comfortable at all." The words were barely out of her mouth when she felt a strong push that propelled her in the path of a city bus. She stumbled over the curb, hit her hip on the pavement, and felt the heat of the bus's engine. She heard the squeal of the bus's brakes and Luke's voice yelling her name. Then she was being dragged out of the way.

Chapter Nineteen

Thursday Afternoon and Evening

Luke wrapped his arms around her and held her close. His head was whipping back and forth as he looked around. The bus driver opened the doors and yelled out, "Lady, you okay?"

Mia nodded and winced. "Thanks. I'll be fine."

The driver leaned forward, "I saw you being pushed. It was a woman, wearing a black ball cap and a black t-shirt. I couldn't make out her face, but it was deliberate."

Luke let go of Mia. "Hang on. I need to speak to you."

"Buddy, I can't be late." The bus driver started to close the doors.

"Wait!" Luke scrambled to the bus and gave the driver his business card. "Call me, please."

The driver nodded, and Luke jumped out.

A small crowd gathered, and Mia noticed a few people had their phones out and were probably recording the accident.

"Did anyone here see anything?" Mia asked.

The woman standing next to her said, "I saw a woman's arm. That's all. Are you all right? You're lucky you weren't run over."

Mia nodded. "I'm okay."

The man who'd been behind her said, "The woman was about your height, slender. She was Caucasian, and dressed like the bus driver said."

"Did you see any distinguishing features?" Luke asked.

The woman shook her head and then said, "It happened pretty fast."

The man said, "I didn't see anything else. I didn't see her face." He looked at Mia, "You were lucky. If he hadn't pulled you away, you'd be dead."

Mia knew he was right. And the description they'd given didn't provide enough information to point the finger at anyone.

Luke thanked the man and the woman for their help.

A police officer showed up. "Is there a problem here?"

Luke turned to the officer and showed him his identification from Interpol. He explained the situation.

"Are you all right, ma'am?"

"I will be. I'm sore and bruised, but I'm alive. You need to know I received a threatening message today. Let me explain." Mia filled him in on what had transpired.

"I'll put a report together, and we'll have it on file. Unfortunately, there isn't much more we can do. We'll check footage of the CCTV cameras in the area, and I'll make certain Detective Martin gets a copy of the report. Do you have any idea who would be threatening you?"

"I'm not sure. I've been staying out of the police's business with Mr. Fraser's death. And there isn't anything else in my life that would be dangerous."

The officer finished his report. "All right, you can go. Do you need help getting home?"

Luke shook his head. "Thanks, officer. We're just around the corner. I'll make sure we get home safely."

Mia watched the officer leave. "Who could have done this? Do you think Barbara did this?"

"Could be. She's blond. But we didn't get a good look, neither did anyone else. And she could have paid someone else to do that. I don't know that she'd be strong enough to push you that hard."

"Let's go home. I'm sore and dirty."

Luke nodded. "Almost there, love."

They made it to her condo without any other incident.

The concierge at the front desk gasped when he saw Mia coming in. "Dr.

Reid, what happened?"

"Almost had a run-in with a city bus. I'm okay."

"Please let us know if there's anything we can do."

"Actually, have you seen the person who dropped off that envelope for me the other day?"

The concierge shook his head. "No, we haven't. And since that happened, we've stepped up our security around accepting packages and envelopes. If we see anyone matching that description, we'll let you know and will contact the police."

"Thank you." Luke and Mia headed for the elevator.

When they arrived, Luke took Mia's bike and hung it in the utility room.

"I'm going to soak in the tub for a bit. My whole body's sore."

"I'll bring you a glass of wine to take the edge off. But first, I'm going to call Detective Martin and let him know what happened."

Mia walked into her bathroom and started filling up the claw-foot tub with warm water, and generously poured in Epsom salts and bubble bath. She pulled off her clothes and shook her head at the holes in the knees of her pants. "Another pair ruined."

She put her hair up in a knot on top of her head and slid into the tub. The water was the perfect temperature, and the tub was almost full. Leaning forward, she turned off the taps. "Siri, play Andre Gagnon." The soft piano music filled the bathroom, and Mia leaned against the bath pillow and sighed.

A few minutes later, Luke came in with a large glass of red wine. There was a small round table by the tub, and he put the glass on it. He sat on the floor next to the tub.

"I spoke with Detective Martin and told him about your accident. He believes, as I do, that it was intentional. He'll get the report from the officer, and he'll speak with the bus driver. The bus should have had a dash camera, and that may have caught the incident."

"That would be great. Did he say if the city has any street cams operating nearby?"

"He did. They'll check those as well. But he isn't hopeful we'll be able to identify the person who pushed you. He suggested driving to work until they can catch whoever is threatening you."

Mia frowned. "And how long will that take? I don't like having other people tell me what to do." She picked up her wine glass and took a long swallow. "I know that sounds ungrateful. And I know I need to be careful. So, yes. I'll drive to work. At least for the next few days."

Luke leaned forward and kissed her gently. "Please be careful. I just got you back in my life, and I don't want to lose you again."

Mia closed her eyes and nodded. "I promise."

They sat quietly listening to the music for a while. Then Luke stirred. "I'm going to order something in for dinner. Any preferences?"

"Pizza would be good."

"I'll order it in and let you know when it arrives."

"Thanks, I'll be out soon."

They watched a bit of the news with dinner, and Mia's accident had made the news. Someone had recorded the event, and there was a clear image of Mia being pushed onto the street. Mia's phone rang with Gram's ringtone.

"Oh, oh. It's Gran."

Mia answered the call, and Gran didn't waste any time.

"Mia, are you all right? Where are you?"

"Gran, I'm fine. I was rattled, and my knees are sore, but I'm okay. The police are on it. The bus driver might have a dash cam that would show who pushed me."

"Was Luke with you?"

"Yes, he was. If you'd watched the whole recording, you'd have seen him pulling me off the street."

"I don't like this one bit. Not at all. Leave the investigating to the police. They are equipped to handle it; you aren't. You're a very good archaeologist, but you are not the police."

Mia knew Gran was upset when her voice was clipped, as it was now. "Gran, I'm not looking into anything really."

"Good. Do the police know who did this?"

"Detective Martin said they'd be looking at all available cameras. But I haven't heard anything from him. I'm sure it's going to take some time for them to figure it out."

Mia's phone pinged with a text from Alex.

"Gran, I have to go. I'll be careful, please don't worry."

Mia disconnected the call.

"How upset is she?"

Mia turned to Luke. "Pretty upset. Part of it is that I didn't tell her anything about it. And she found out on the news. I just got a text from Alex, and I'll bet she's ticked off too."

Alex: Are you okay?

Mia: Fine, a bit bruised, but Luke pulled me away.

Alex: Are the police looking into this?

Mia: Yes.

Alex: Please be safe!

Mia: I will. I'll see you tomorrow at the museum.

Alex: Yes.

Mia sighed as she put her phone down. "Okay, everyone should be fine for a while."

Chapter Twenty

Friday

The next morning, Mia drove herself to work. She took her time to find parking close to the entrance of the museum.

Peter and Nancy arrived at the lab at the same time as Mia. "Let's get the boxes out and start on them. I have a few things I need to deal with later this morning."

"You have that event this evening. Are you ready for it?" Nancy asked.

"That's what I need to look at. I may have a few items to wrap up. You guys are all right doing the assessments, right?"

Nancy nodded. "We're good. We've done these a lot in the last couple of years."

"The museum's been called to do this type of assessment from different organizations. We have a good system," Peter said.

"That's great. I'll go back to my office and come down before lunch to see how you're getting on."

Mia left the lab confident the work would be done. She opened her file on her computer for tonight's event and checked her master list. Everything was in order. The museum's events team, though small, was excellent. She'd go to the exhibit and check to see that everything was in place.

Mia strolled down to the exhibit. The cases would need to be buffed up, but since the exhibit was open until four today, it would have to wait until the museum closed its doors to the public.

There was another day camp going through this morning. They'd enlisted one of the docents to provide additional information, and they were a lively group. When they were through the exhibit, they would be able to go for lunch in the cafeteria. It was all part of the admittance fee for the day camps.

Mia returned to the lab to see what progress had been made.

Peter smiled when she came in. "Wait until you see what we found!"

Mia hurried to the table. There were several artifacts of Aztec origin grouped together. She noted the artifacts were stone sculptures. One of them was of a kneeling woman, another was a snake sculpture with snakes entwined with each other. The most eye-catching one was a small jade jaguar.

"These are beautiful." Mia pulled on a pair of gloves and picked up the kneeling woman sculpture. She examined it carefully, taking note that the woman's feet were turned inward. The figure was dressed simply in a plain dress that had a rope around it. Her shoulders and head were bare. The woman's hands were resting on her legs.

"Have you seen one like this before?" Nancy asked.

Mia nodded. "It was similar, not exactly like this. The one I saw had a necklace carved on her neck." Mia put the sculpture down and examined the other two pieces. "These are excellent pieces. The jaguar is very small. But the attention to detail is exquisite."

"These don't show up on any of the reports we have. It's possible they were taken from a private collector," Peter said.

"I agree. Especially the jade jaguar. There is a larger one, but that's in the museum in Mexico. This one looks as if it might have been a practice piece for a sculpture." Mia put the jaguar down. "When they're photographed and documented, send me the information, and I'll forward it to Luke. He'll know what to do with them."

"Will do."

Mia turned her attention to the other artifacts on the table. There were gold pieces, rings, and a few necklaces. "There's a wide variety of artifacts here. Do you think they all came from the same location?"

Nancy sighed. "It's difficult to tell. With the statues, we know the era they came from. The rings and necklaces are a bit harder to determine. We will, though. We have tests to complete on them, and they should give us additional information."

"We'll finish up as much as we can this afternoon. We won't get everything done, but we'll have enough information that the police and Interpol can start to sift through their databases."

"Thanks very much. Let me know if you need anything from me."

Mia went back to her office. Danielle wouldn't be happy with the information Mia and her team had uncovered. It appeared Tim was very involved in the antiquity smuggling trade. What would that mean for Danielle? Would the people Tim had been working with expect Danielle to keep up with the deal her father had made? What would they do now that those artifacts weren't in Danielle's possession anymore? Whoever was in charge was out money and would want to get it back.

Mia's cell phone rang. It was Luke.

"Hi, I have a few minutes between sessions, and I'm curious what you and your team have learned about the artifacts."

Mia quickly filled him in.

"Thanks for that information. I'll be sharing it with the officers here. Detective Martin was asking for news."

"What does this mean for Danielle? Is she in danger from whoever is running this?"

"I don't know. I would suspect the smuggling cartel is involved in this. They won't be pleased to lose the artifacts, but I doubt they'll go after Danielle. The police are keeping a tight lid on this, but I think a press release about finding the artifacts may be in order. It would come from my department. The press release would let the smugglers know Danielle doesn't have access to the artifacts."

"Well, not if you say where they were found."

"We wouldn't have to elaborate on where the artifacts are. We can simply say acting on a tip, we located missing artifacts. Trust me on this. I've done this before, and it does protect the innocent involved. It also sends a flag to the smuggling cartel that we're on to them."

"Okay. Do you want me to talk to Danielle?"

"I'll do it. She needs to know what's happening, and with the information you've provided me, I can explain the situation to her. I'll stress that she needs to make certain the store's security is working and to take additional precautions if she goes there."

"Thanks. Are you still coming with me to tonight's event?"

"Yes. Is there a dress code?"

"Business casual will work. You don't need to rent a tux or anything."

"I've got to run. I'll let you know how things go with Danielle."

Mia's next call was to Christine Marks to let her know what they'd discovered in the lab.

"Mia, how are things going?"

"I was speaking with Peter and Nancy. They believe all the artifacts they're going through have been stolen. I spoke with Luke Forbes, and he's going to be in communication with Danielle Fraser to let her know."

"That's going to be tough for her. Is there anything we can do to help her?"

"I don't know. Danielle may need a good lawyer to help her get through this."

"I agree. Please let her know if she needs help finding one. I know of several that may be able to help her."

"Thanks, I will. I'm going back to the lab and help them wrap things up. I'll be back here around six tonight."

"I'll see you then." Christine disconnected the call.

Mia shook her head. Danielle's day was going to get more difficult.

In the lab, Peter and Nancy were beginning to put the artifacts away. Mia helped them finish up.

"How long will it take before all the reports are done?" she asked.

"We can get the reports on this first set of boxes by the middle of next week. Why?" Nancy answered.

"There are a lot of moving parts to this investigation, and I want to make sure we have everything we need from the artifacts."

"Are they going to take the artifacts out of here?" Peter asked.

"I'm not sure where they'll be stored until they get repatriated," Mia said.

"Are you excited about tonight's event?" Nancy asked.

"I'm looking forward to it. The tickets have sold well." Mia glanced at her watch. "And I'd better get home so I can come back in a short while. Thank you both so much for your help. I'll let you know as soon as I know what's going to happen with the artifacts."

They left, and Mia made sure the artifacts were stored in the vault before she hurried upstairs.

Chapter Twenty-One

Friday Evening

At home, Mia took a quick shower before Luke got in. She had planned her wardrobe for tonight. A nice summer dress with blue, white, and gold colors running through it. It showed off her tan well. She'd bow to fashion and wear heeled sandals and a clutch purse that would work. She'd be able to store anything she didn't need in her office. Mia was looking forward to this evening. Alex would be there with Gran. With Luke by her side, she felt happy. She still didn't know where their relationship was going to go, but for now, it worked.

Luke arrived just as she finished dressing. "You look stunning."

Mia smiled. "Thanks! Are the heels too much?"

"Not at all. Let me grab a quick shower, and I'll change into something more appropriate. When do we have to leave?"

"I have a car coming to pick us up in forty minutes. I want to be at the museum by six."

"Plenty of time. You relax while I clean up."

When they arrived at the museum, Mia was happy with the transformation of the exhibit space. At the back was a raised platform where a string quartet was getting their instruments ready. A long buffet table of finger foods, snacks, and desserts was being set up along the far wall. Non-alcoholic drinks were on offer on a separate table. In the middle of the room, there was a circular bar with alcoholic drinks. Patrons had two complementary drink tickets with their entry and could purchase additional drink tickets if they wanted. There were mini lights drapped around the buffet and the bar area. The lighting in the exhibit area was dimmed, and the exhibits themselves were well-lit. Mia noted the glass cases had been buffed and shined so that everything gleamed.

"Happy with the way it looks?" Luke asked.

"Yes. They've done great work in a very short amount of time. They only had an hour and a half to do all this." Mia smiled.

The doors opened at seven o'clock, and the patrons were excited to see the exhibit. Mia stood on a raised platform and took the microphone.

"Welcome, ladies and gentlemen, to our Lakeview Museum Walk Through Time with The Aztecs. My name is Dr. Mia Reid, and I'm the curator of this exhibition. You'll be able to see the different pieces the Aztec people used in everyday life and for specific ceremonies. There are information cards all around. If you prefer to listen to the information, there's a QR code that will allow you to do so with your phones. If you have questions, please ask me or any of the museum staff. You can identify us by our name tags. Enjoy the exhibition, the food, drinks, and music!"

Mia stepped down and joined Luke, Gran, and Alex.

"Well done, Mia. I'm proud of you, dear." Gran wrapped Mia in a hug.

"Thanks, Gran."

Luke put his arm around Mia's waist. "What do we do first?"

"I'm going to have a glass of wine. I have to circulate and talk to people."

Alex burst out laughing. "Talking to people isn't that bad. You do it very well. We'll take care of Luke; you go do your thing!"

"Well, no one really needs to take care of me, but I'd like to escort Alex and Gran around if that's all right?"

"I'd love that." Gran put her arm through Luke's. "Go on, Mia. We'll be fine. Do what you have to do, and we'll reconnect."

"See you all later." Mia hurried to the bar and got a glass of white wine. Then she started mingling with the patrons.

There were a lot of people, and Mia was quickly encircled by curious patrons about the exhibit. She watched as people walked through. Some of them were using their phones, others were reading the information cards. If she was going to see the exhibit, she'd prefer the information cards, they'd give her more of an opportunity to examine the exhibits closely.

Mia had been circulating for forty-five minutes when Christine Marks arrived by her side. "Well done, Mia. This exhibition is drawing in a lot of new people to the museum."

Mia smiled. "Thanks, but all I did was execute the plan that was made earlier. It was well organized."

"That's true. But you've also managed to put your stamp on things. There have been a few subtle changes, and they work well." Christine paused to take a drink of wine. "What's the word from the police on the artifacts?"

Mia looked around before she answered. She didn't want anyone overhearing. She dropped her voice. "Interpol is sending another agent to work with Luke Forbes. They'll be dealing with the artifacts and eventually repatriating them to the rightful owners. Luke thought they'd work out of the police station."

Christine nodded. "They could do that. Or they could work from the museum. I'd give them the space and equipment they need." She looked around the room. "Is Luke here?"

"Yes. Do you want to meet him?"

"Please. I'll speak with him about the possibility of working here instead. If we can get it set up tonight, I'll make sure they have access when they need it."

"Follow me." Mia led Christine to Luke. She made the introductions and then left them. The rush of patrons had slowed down, and most people were enjoying food and drink. Mia noticed a couple who were still looking at the exhibit. They were stopped at one of the pedestals that featured a necklace with gold and jade in it.

Mia walked closer to them.

The woman said to the man, "How long is the exhibit here for?"

The man shrugged. "It doesn't say. We'd need to be careful, though."

Mia cleared her throat. "Hi. Did you have some questions about the artifacts? I'm Dr. Mia Reid, and I'm responsible for the exhibit."

The woman turned to face Mia. She had fair skin and short black hair. Her eyes were dark brown. Mia noticed that her clothes were expensive and stylish. Her jewelry was understated but stunning. A gold necklace with a teardrop emerald and matching earrings. She had a large emerald and diamond ring on her ring finger.

"Dr. Reid. My husband and I were admiring the antiquities and wondering how they had come to the museum. Could you tell us?"

"Of course. This exhibit is on loan from the Mexico City Museum. The artifacts are from a collection that was acquired over the course of several years. Some came directly from digs. Others were purchased through collectors. We were fortunate to be able to work out an agreement that was mutually beneficial to both museums. They will showcase some of our collections."

The man had turned toward Mia. "And how were they delivered?"

Mia frowned. "I beg your pardon?"

"How did the artifacts arrive here? Were they shipped by air?"

"Are you in the shipping business?"

The man tilted his head to the side. "Just curious."

Mia didn't like people who played games, and she didn't like people who were sneaky about asking questions. What was this guy up to?

His wife smiled. "And if we wanted to purchase any of the artifacts, how would we go about doing that?"

"I'm afraid none of the artifacts are for sale. If they were, you'd need to speak with the Mexico City Museum directly. We do have reproductions in our gift shop. They're good, but not good enough to fool an expert."

"Perhaps we'll take a look in the gift shop, although I don't think we'll find what we're looking for." The woman slipped her arm through her husband's.

"I can always provide you with the Museum's contact information if you'd like."

The man smiled. "Sure, and if you can give us your contact information as well. My name is Josh Humphries. I'm in real estate. My wife and I are here for a long weekend; we're from Montreal."

Mia's eyes widened at his name. She remembered seeing it in Tim Fraser's email. "Let me get a card, and I'll be back soon. In the meantime, please, help yourself to some food and drink." Mia pointed toward the buffet and the bar.

"Thanks, we'll look for you shortly."

Mia looked for Luke. He needed to be told about Josh Humphries. She saw him chatting with Gran and Alex and hurried to his side. "Sorry, I need to borrow Luke for a minute. Do you mind?"

Alex chuckled. "No, go ahead. We'll have another glass of wine while we wait."

"What's up?" Luke asked.

"Follow me." Mia headed toward her office and filled him in on Josh Humphries. "I know I saw his name in Tim's emails. There was a series of emails with him. I think it's suspicious that he's here and asking questions about how the artifacts were shipped and if they were for sale."

"He said that?"

"Yes." They'd arrived at Mia's office, and she unlocked her door, grabbed a handful of business cards. "He wants my card to stay in touch."

"What do you want me to do?" Luke asked.

"Can you get a photo of him without him noticing?"

"Of course. You think he has something to do with the smuggling cartel. Please be careful with him."

"I will. There's security everywhere, so I'm not worried. Let's go." Mia locked her office, and they returned to the event.

Mia found Josh and his wife at the bar. Luke stood back. Mia hoped he'd be able to snap a good photo.

"Josh, here's my card. As I said, none of the artifacts are for sale. But if you're interested in purchasing artifacts through a reputable source, please contact me."

Josh took the card. "Thanks. Do you know what's happening with the antique store, Timeless Treasures? I had an appointment to meet the owner, Tim Fraser, but when I went to the store, it was closed."

Mia watched his face carefully as she spoke. "I'm afraid Mr. Fraser passed away last week. He was the father of a friend of mine. She hasn't decided what to do with the store yet. Was there something in particular you were looking for?"

"We had discussed an Aztec statue that he was sourcing for me. I was expecting a call from him last week, but never heard back from him. Was he ill?" Josh took a drink of wine.

"No, he wasn't. His death was sudden, and the police believe he was murdered," Mia said bluntly.

Josh's eyes widened. "That's terrible. Would you have his daughter's contact information? I'd like to know if he found the statue we had spoken about."

"I'll touch base with her and give her your card."

Josh reached in his inside jacket pocket and handed Mia a business card.

"Please let her know I'm still interested in the statue."

"I will. And if she knows anything about it, she'll contact you." Mia placed the card in her bag. "I'd better chat with a few other people. You know how to reach me if you have any other questions."

Mia left the bar and strolled toward the exhibit. Luke joined her. "Did you get his photo?" she asked.

"I did. Several good ones of both of them. I've forwarded them to my supervisor and asked that they be run through our database. How did you leave things with him?"

Mia told him about the conversation.

"You didn't give him Danielle's contact information?"

"No. I don't want him reaching out to her."

"Good. His asking about Timeless Treasures is a bit off-putting. We'll keep an eye on him and his wife as well. Are you going to talk to Danielle about him?"

"I'll bring it up, but I'm also going to talk to Cheryl about it. She might have information or have seen him if he came to the store. His email correspondence with Tim proves that he knew him."

Mia saw Gran and Alex sitting at a table. "Let's check in on Gran and Alex."

They started walking toward them, but Christine Marks stopped Mia.

Luke continued toward Gran.

"Who was that man you were speaking with at the bar?" Christine asked.

Mia explained who he was and what he wanted.

Christine scoffed. "Unbelievable. How did he react when you told him it didn't work that way?"

"He switched subjects quickly and asked about Timeless Treasures being closed. I explained what had happened. He's not from the area, so he may not have heard about it."

Christine nodded. "I doubt the death of an antique dealer would make national news. What are you going to do about his request?"

Mia shrugged. "I'll talk to Danielle to see if she knows anything about the statue he was asking about, but I didn't see anything in the inventory that would suggest it was there. I didn't give him Danielle's contact information. He seems to be the kind of guy who won't take no for an answer."

"Smart decision. I'll let you go, I see someone I need to speak with. Mia, this exhibit is going very well. You've done great work in a short time." Christine smiled and then left.

Mia walked to Gran, Alex, and Luke, determined not to get waylaid again. "How are you doing?" she asked as she arrived.

"I'm just about ready to go home. I'm waiting for Tom and Fran Esly to finish up their drinks, and I'll go home with them," Gran said.

"I can drive you back," Alex said.

"Nonsense. Tom's a good driver, and he's drinking tonic water. Fran told me they were leaving in about ten minutes. The exhibition has brought out a lot of people. It looks as if it's sold out."

Mia nodded. "For tonight's event, it is. There's lots of opportunities for people to come in and see it. We've been getting day camps coming in during the morning, and the reports I've seen say the kids are really enjoying the exhibit. There were a few comments about not enough swords and knives, but it depends on the age group."

Luke chuckled. "Certain ages would want to have a lot of blood and gore, wouldn't they?"

"Yes. I felt like telling them to come back in November. We'll have an exhibit on the world wars then."

Fran Esly walked up to Gran. "Marie, are you ready to head home? I think Tom's done talking golf with his buddies."

Gran stood. "I am. Mia, this exhibit was very well done. I'm proud of the work you did to pull it all together." She leaned closer to Mia and gave her a hug. "I'll call you tomorrow, and we'll chat. Alex, Luke, thank you both for escorting me around this evening."

"It was my pleasure. We'll chat again soon." Luke smiled.

Watching Gran leave, Mia sighed. "Are you wishing you could leave, too?" Alex asked.

Mia snorted. "Yes. I have another hour to go before this is done, and then I'll need a few minutes to check on everything."

"If you're okay, then I'm going to head home. This was a nice evening," Alex said.

"Thanks for coming and being with Gran. It made it easier for me knowing you were with her."

"Not a problem. We'll chat soon." Alex placed her glass on a table and gave Mia a hug.

"Want to walk around with me? I still have to be available if anyone has questions." Mia asked Luke.

"Of course." Luke held out an elbow, and Mia slipped her arm through his.

The next hour went by quickly. Museum patrons had questions for Mia, and she was able to provide them with the information they were looking for. At the end of the evening, there were only a few stragglers, and Mia made the announcement that the museum would be closing in a few minutes. Everyone made their way to the exits, and Mia breathed a sigh of relief.

"Done. Let me go check the artifacts. I'll be back in a few minutes."

Luke nodded. "I'll wait for you by the exit."

Mia hurried through the exhibit, checking the cases. There were a few that had some spills on them, but the cleaning crew would be coming through in an hour, and they'd ensure everything was spotless for the next day. She saw something shining on the floor next to one of the pedestals. Bending down, she picked up a strange-looking button. She didn't think it was a button from a piece of clothing. It looked like it was a tracker of some kind. She'd drop it off at security on the way out.

She walked back to Luke. "I want to go to my office and pick up my phone. Come with me."

"Certainly."

"What do you make of this?" Mia showed him the button.

Luke checked it out and then turned on his flashlight app on his phone. "Where did you find this?"

"Next to one of the pedestals."

"It's a monitoring device. We've seen them in museums where there have been thefts. Show me exactly where you found it."

Mia retraced her steps and showed Luke.

Using his flashlight app, he scanned the area to see if he could find any other buttons.

"I need to check the entire exhibit before we leave. It's possible someone was here earlier and left it behind."

Mia shook her head. "The cleaning crew was in before catering showed up and vacuumed the floors thoroughly. There wasn't anything on the floors."

"Okay, so that tells us it was dropped this evening."

They walked through the complete exhibit. In the last room, Luke found another button.

"Yes. Definitely a monitoring device. I'm going to take them both with me and disable them."

They walked to Mia's office and ran into Christine Marks. "Christine, I need to show you something." Mia stopped her.

Luke pulled out the monitoring devices and explained the situation to her.

Christine's face paled. "And you say these were found in museums where there'd been thefts?"

"Yes. We don't know how long the monitoring devices were in place. But here, we do. Mia believes they were dropped tonight."

"What do we do about it?" Christine asked.

"I'll take them with me and see what we can learn from them. But you need to know that once whoever dropped these in place realizes they aren't operational, they'll send someone in to install more. And we probably won't be able to find them."

Christine sighed. "Okay. I'll alert security, and we'll have them monitor the exhibit closely. Do you think someone is planning to steal the artifacts?"

Luke nodded. "I think this is the first step. They'd monitor to see when the museum is busy, when security passes through in the off hours, and to gather as much information as they can. I'm not sure what your resources are like, but is it possible to have security physically in the rooms?"

"We can. I'll contact the head of security this evening and speak with him. We'll work something out right away."

"It would also be a good idea to monitor who's coming in. If the same person comes in several times over a few days, they might be someone to follow up on," Mia added.

"Good point. I'll follow up with security, and I'll touch base with you tomorrow morning. Luke, could I have your contact information?"

Luke and Christine exchanged business cards. "I'll look forward to chatting with you in the morning."

"Thanks for bringing this to my attention. We'll be better prepared to prevent someone from stealing anything. Good night." Christine left to go to her office.

Mia and Luke gathered her things from her office and went back to Mia's condo.

Chapter Twenty-Two

The next morning, Luke connected with Detective Martin and told him what they'd found at the museum the night before. Mia listened to Luke's side of the conversation and got up to make herself more coffee. It appeared the detective would be coming over.

"He'll be here shortly," Luke said after hanging up.

"How is he still involved with all this? Do you think this has anything to do with Mr. Fraser's death?"

"He's my contact with the police, and he's also part of the artifact recovery training that I'm doing. I was told by the chief of police to deal directly with him in any matters that I worked on." Luke took a sip of coffee. "As for this having to do with Mr. Fraser's death, I'm not sure. But I know he was involved in smuggling artifacts."

"I need to call Danielle about Josh Humphries. I'm going to let her know he set off my weird guy alert system. And that if she decides to work with him, he's probably trouble."

"That's smart. She needs to know that."

Mia walked into the kitchen and pulled out some croissants and jam. Her phone rang; it was Christine.

"Mia, I spoke with the head of security last night. He's going to have a guard posted in each room of the exhibit and two in the hallway. He's concerned about the monitoring devices you found. Is there any way Luke could share exactly what they are with him?"

"Let me ask Luke." Mia muted her phone and relayed Christine's request.

"The police are going to be taking them. I'll send the photos to Christine now." Luke snapped some photos while Mia explained to Christine what was going to happen.

"Thanks, Mia. I'll forward the photos to security. They'll know what they're looking for. Have a good weekend. We'll talk on Monday."

Mia disconnected the call. And watched as Luke sent the photos to Christine.

The apartment intercom rang, and Mia answered. Detective Martin had arrived.

Luke greeted him at the door, and Mia offered coffee.

They sat in the living room, and Luke filled Detective Martin in on what had happened the previous evening.

Detective Martin picked up one of the monitors and examined it. "I've seen these before. They're small but very effective. The battery life is seventy-two hours, and the signal can be tracked. The trouble we've had is that the signal disappears before we can finish tracking it."

"Mia is certain it wasn't in the exhibits until last night. So, we should be able to track it. How do we set that up?"

"Let me talk to our IT department. They'll be able to tell me."

Detective Martin made a quick call. "I'll need to bring this in. The tech lab will check it out and will run a trace on it. They don't know how long it'll take. Did you want to come with me?"

Luke looked at Mia. "Do you mind if I go?"

"Not at all. I need to touch base with Danielle. We'll catch up later today."

Mia called Danielle a few minutes later. She got her voicemail and left a detailed message asking Danielle to call her back. That done, she hurried to take a shower.

Twenty minutes later, Danielle called her back.

Mia explained the conversation she'd had with Josh at the museum.

"I haven't come across anything in Dad's files with his name. And I haven't seen anything about an Aztec statue." Danielle sighed. "Are you available to come to the store this morning?"

"Of course. What did you need?"

"Steve can't come with me, and I don't feel comfortable going there by myself. I need to go through some of the files in Dad's office."

"When did you want to go?"

"Maybe twenty minutes?"

"Sure, did you want me to pick you up?"

"No, I'll meet you there. I need to run some errands after I leave the store. Thanks, Mia. I'll see you soon."

Mia gathered her purse and grabbed a protein bar and a water. She sent Luke a text.

Mia: Going to meet Danielle at the shop. Checking stuff in files.

Luke: Good. Will be working with the tech lab for a bit. And then a video call with the people in Vancouver. Will let you know when I'm through.

Mia: Sounds good.

Mia drove to the antique store and found parking just down the street from it. She was early. Danielle's car wasn't around, so she strolled down the sidewalk and waited in front of the store.

Danielle arrived a few minutes later. She pulled into a parking spot and hurried to meet Mia.

"Thanks again. I didn't feel comfortable coming by myself, and I didn't want to ask Cheryl to come in either."

"Not a problem." Mia watched as Danielle unlocked the front door and then entered the alarm code. "How did things go yesterday with the estate appraisers?"

Danielle closed the door and locked it. "I'm not sure. I had two different ones come in. Both of them were in the same ballpark as far as the value of the stock in the store. And I can always check their amount with the information Dad had in his files. That's part of what I want to check." Danielle wrinkled her nose. "Ugh. What's that smell? It smells like bad meat."

Mia put her hand out. "Just wait. Who was in the shop yesterday?"

"Why?"

"Was Cheryl here?"

"Yes, but she left when I did. I closed up the shop and set the alarm."

Mia glanced around the store. There wasn't any sign of anyone else being in the store, but the smell Danielle alluded to indicated someone or something was in the store. "Did you have any food while you were working here yesterday?"

"Yes, pizza."

They walked to the office. And opened the door. Danielle turned the light on and screamed.

Chapter Twenty-Three

Saturday

Mia grabbed Danielle's arm and led her out of the office. She pushed her into a chair and called 911.

When the operator answered, Mia calmly said, "I'm at Timeless Treasures at 1200 Queen Street. We walked into the office, and a woman's been shot."

"Is she still alive?" the operator asked.

"No. She's dead."

"Is there anyone else in the building?"

"No. The door was locked when we came in."

"I'd like you to leave the premises and wait for the officers at the front door. I'll stay on the line until they arrive."

Mia urged Danielle to get up, and they left the store. Danielle leaned against the storefront, and Mia stood next to her. The operator stayed on the line until officers showed up.

The operator hung up the call, and one of the officers went into the store; the other one spoke with Mia and Danielle.

"Can you tell me what happened?" she asked.

Danielle explained what they'd found.

Mia looked around and saw that a crowd was gathering. She noticed Martha Jones, the antique dealer from down the street. Martha pushed her way to Danielle.

Crouching down, she put her arm around Danielle's shoulders. "Honey, what's wrong? Can I help?"

Danielle turned to her and burst into tears.

The officer looked frustrated at the interruption.

"Officer, could you contact Detective Martin? He's been working on Mr. Fraser's murder, and I think this one is related to his," Mia said.

"I'll do that. He'd be the one to catch this case, too."

The officer stepped away, and Mia watched as she asked to be connected with Detective Martin.

A short conversation later, the officer returned to Mia and Danielle. "Detective Martin will be here shortly. He asked if you were both okay. I told him neither of you were injured."

Mia watched the crowd of people gathering on the sidewalk. She didn't see anyone she recognized. Glancing to her left, she saw Martha comforting Danielle. Martha had been on the spot when all this started. Granted, she had a store just a few feet away, and she lived on the top floor. Mia wondered if she'd seen anything last night. She shuddered at the image of Cheryl in the office. Why had she been there?

The paramedics arrived on scene and hurried into the store. A few moments later, one of the paramedics came out and spoke with the officer who was standing next to Mia. She overheard the paramedic say, "Nothing we can do. Victim is dead of a gunshot wound to the head. It appears to have happened last night sometime. We'll need to get the coroner here."

The officer moved to the side and called in to dispatch to advise the coroner would be required.

Mia sagged against the building. It was difficult to process. Another violent death.

Detective Martin arrived and hurried out of his car. Mia wasn't surprised to see Luke with him, although he had no jurisdiction in a murder. She was glad he was here.

Detective Martin stopped in front of Mia. "Dr. Reid, are you and Ms. Fraser all right?"

"We're not hurt. Danielle's quite upset. We didn't know Cheryl was in the office, and when we turned on the lights, well, it was awful."

"Right. We're going to want to speak with both of you. Do you want to wait in my car?"

"My vehicle is right across the street; we could go there."

"We'll need to separate you. If you can go to your car, I'll have Danielle wait in mine. I'll be as quick as possible."

"No problem."

"Mia, I'm going in with Detective Martin. Are you going to be all right?" Luke asked.

"I will. I'm concerned about Danielle."

"I'll get her in Detective Martin's car, and one of the officers will stay with her." Luke pulled Mia into a hug. "Hang in there."

Mia nodded. "I'll be fine. It wasn't a pleasant sight." Mia walked to her car and sat in the driver's seat. She opened her windows to let the air circulate and took a drink of water. She watched as Luke assisted Danielle to Detective Martin's car, and an officer stood next to her.

She watched the scene across the street roll out. The officers were in and out of the shop. There were a few people looking on. Martha Jones was still there. Mia wondered if she'd seen anything the night before and made a mental note to ask her. The coroner arrived, and so did a forensics team. She watched them cover their shoes, hair, pull on a white jumpsuit over their clothes, and glove their hands. Luke and Detective Martin did the same. They entered the store. Mia leaned her head against the seat's headrest and closed her eyes. This wasn't how she had planned to spend her day off. But she needed to focus on what she'd seen.

Cheryl had been sitting in the desk chair. The filing cabinets in the desk were open, and papers were strewn about the floor. The overhead lights had been turned off. Danielle had turned them on when they entered the office. But the desk lamp was on. One of the bookcases had had books removed, and they were on the floor in front of the bookcase. The front of the store hadn't been touched. Did Cheryl open the door to the person who killed her? Were they already in the building?

Mia sighed. So many questions and no answers. Mia opened her eyes and recognized a news van. She slipped further down her seat. She didn't want to have to answer any questions from reporters. The news van door opened, and a reporter and videographer jumped out. The reporter set himself up in front of the store, and Mia could see him talking. She was too far away to hear what he said, but she imagined it was about another victim at Timeless Treasures.

Detective Martin came out of the store and walked toward his car and Danielle. Mia watched him sit in the front seat with Danielle, and they spoke for about ten minutes. He exited the car and strode across the street to Mia.

He stopped next to Mia's open window. "Dr. Reid, can I ask you a few questions?"

"Of course, the passenger door is open."

He walked around the front of her Jeep and sat in the passenger seat.

"Can you tell me what happened when you arrived at the store?"

"I was a few minutes early, and I waited for Danielle to show up. She had the keys. When she arrived, she unlocked the door and disarmed the security system. She turned on the lights in the main part of the store. We chatted a bit about our day and started walking toward the office. We both smelled something that, well, it reminded me of rotten chicken. It smelled pretty bad. We walked to the office and turned on the light. And that's when we saw Cheryl. She was slumped over the desk and sitting in the chair. She wasn't moving." Mia paused and closed her eyes. "She was facing the door." Mia stopped and swallowed some water.

Detective Martin waited for a moment and didn't say anything.

Mia continued. "I noticed the file drawers in the desk had been opened, and there were papers strewn all over the desk and the floor. One bookcase had books that had been pulled out and thrown on the floor, too. I could hear a high-pitched tone, like when a telephone is off the hook. And I remember seeing the landline phone's receiver dangling off the side of the desk."

"You didn't see anyone else?"

"No. When I realized what had happened, I got us out of there fast. I called 911 as soon as we were outside."

"You did great. You remembered different things than Danielle did, and that gives me a clearer picture." Detective Martin made some notes in his phone. "Anything else?"

Mia shook her head. "Not that stands out."

"That's fine. If you remember anything else, let me know."

Mia watched as the officers dispersed people from the sidewalk, telling them to keep moving. Cheryl's body was moved to the coroner's van. There were a few people still out on the street. Mia watched as a man wandered closer. She gasped. He looked like the man at the museum last night. Josh Humphries.

Detective Martin heard her gasp. "What did you see?" he asked.

Mia pointed out Josh. "He was at the museum last night asking to buy artifacts. He said he had an appointment with Tim Fraser, but couldn't get a hold of him. I told him the store was going to be closed for a while. Why would he show up here?"

"Where is he from?" Detective Martin asked.

"He's a real estate developer from Montreal. I had a weird feeling about him. He didn't seem to be a regular collector. Luke was going to check him out. I don't know if he's heard anything back yet."

"It's not a crime wanting to buy artifacts, at least legal ones. And maybe he thought he'd try the store one more time."

"I don't like coincidences and seeing him last night and then again today just seems like that." Mia sighed. "And now he's leaving." She watched as Josh turned around sharply and walked away quickly. "What happens now?"

"We'll work this case. It will be a separate investigation from Mr. Fraser's. We'll follow the evidence, and there's evidence there. You and Danielle should get home. Are you okay to drive?"

"I am. But I'd like to check in with Danielle first if that's all right."

"Sure. I'll send Luke on his way with you. There isn't much he can do for us here."

Mia got out of her Jeep and crossed the road to see Danielle.

"Danielle, wait up!" Mia called out as she saw Danielle opening her car door.

Danielle held her door open and turned toward Mia.

"I'm going home. The police have said I don't have to stay."

"I know, I am too. How are you?"

Danielle sighed. "Upset and angry. I don't understand why Cheryl was in the store. She left with me and didn't say anything about going back. Why would she do that? Was she meeting with someone? And what was she doing at Dad's desk?"

Mia frowned. "Those are all good questions. I'm sure the police will find the answers. Are you okay to drive home?"

"I don't have a choice. I can't get hold of Steve; his phone goes straight to voicemail. He could be meeting with a client."

"I can drive you home. When Steve gets back, he can come pick up your car."

"You don't mind? I'd appreciate it."

"Not at all. Lock up your car, and I'll get you home."

Martha Jones came up to them. "Danielle, I'm just checking on you. Are you all right?"

"I will be. Mia's going to drive me home."

"Martha, could I ask you something?" Mia asked.

"Yes, of course. How can I help?" Martha stood a little taller.

"I wondered if you happened to see or hear anything last night? Something that was unusual?"

Martha paused for a moment. "Well, my shop closes at six. And then I do some cleaning up. After that, I go upstairs to my apartment."

"I'm thinking of anything that might have happened later, say after eight or nine."

"Well, I was sitting on my balcony having a glass of wine. I noticed Danielle, Steve, and Cheryl leaving the shop. I stayed out on the balcony until about ten. It was a lovely evening. Not humid like it had been all day. I was getting ready to turn in when I saw Cheryl walking down the street and then going into the shop. I was surprised. I had never seen her do that before." Martha cleared her throat. "A short time later, a man walked up to the shop and banged on the door. I heard that clearly. The door opened. I was curious what was happening, so I stayed on the balcony a little longer. I didn't know if Cheryl had Danielle's permission to be in the store, but I assumed she did. And I thought the man was someone interested in buying an item from the shop. About fifteen minutes later, the man left the store. He had something in his hands, but I couldn't make out what it was. I waited about fifteen minutes, but Cheryl didn't come out the front. I can't see the back door from my balcony, and I thought she might have left through the back."

Mia drew a breath. It was possible that Martha had seen Cheryl's killer. "Have you spoken to the police?"

Martha shook her head. "No one's asked me anything."

"Please wait here. I'll get Detective Martin." Mia hurried to the front of the store. The officer standing there stopped her.

"I need to speak with Detective Martin. There's a woman who may have seen something last night."

"Let me connect with him." The officer made a call and spoke with Detective Martin. "He'll be right out."

Mia watched Martha to make sure she didn't leave as she waited for Detective Martin. Once he arrived, she told him what Martha had said.

"Thanks, Mia. I'll get one of the officers to take her statement and information." He called out to one of the officers, who hurried to him. "Please follow Dr. Reid. There's a possible witness I'd like you to speak with."

"Yes, sir."

Mia escorted the officer to Martha.

"Thank you, Dr. Reid. I'll take it from here," the officer said.

"Danielle, I'll take you home." She and Danielle walked back to her Jeep, where Luke was waiting.

Luke opened the passenger door for Danielle, and he slid into the back seat.

"I have to drop Luke off first, and then I'll take you home."

"That's fine. Thanks."

Luke gave Mia the address where he was working, and she plugged it into the Jeep's navigation system.

"Danielle, can I ask you a few questions?" Luke asked.

"Of course."

"How involved was Cheryl in the day-to-day operations of the store?"

Danielle took a drink of water from the bottle Mia had given her. "From what I understand, Dad had her doing most of the sales in the store. I remember he told me she had great customer service skills and could sell anything. She moved some pieces Dad had in the store for a year without difficulty. She was starting to learn more about the buying process, but Dad wasn't confident in her abilities in that area yet."

"Did she know about the basement room?" Luke asked.

Danielle frowned. "I don't know. Dad didn't share that part of the business with me. It's possible."

"Who did the books for the store?" Mia asked.

"Dad had a friend who was the business's accountant. His name is Howard Banks, and he's been working for Dad for the last ten years. I gave the police all this information."

"Does anyone else have the alarm code for the store?" Luke asked.

"Just Steve and I."

"And Cheryl didn't say anything about going to the store last night?"

Danielle shook her head. "She wasn't supposed to be in the store. I knew she had keys and the alarm code, but I didn't think she'd go there after hours. We'd been in the store earlier in the day, going over the stock that was there. We had appraisers in for that. And today we were supposed to have a real estate broker in to give me an estimate on the value of the store. I need to get a hold of her and let her know not to come today."

"Were the security cameras on last night?" Mia asked.

"Yes. The police have asked for the recording, and I've sent them the link. Do you want it as well?"

"If you don't mind. I'm wondering if whoever did this is the same person who killed your father."

Danielle pulled out her phone and pressed a few buttons. "I just sent you the link. And that's always a possibility. But there wasn't anything on the recording when Dad died. For some reason, the front door camera didn't show anyone coming in."

They'd arrived at the police station where Luke was working for the day.

"When are you done today?" Mia asked.

"I'll be done by three-thirty. I'll text you when I've wrapped things up. What are you going to do today?"

"I'm not sure. I'll check to see if Alex is available. But I'll be home when you get there."

Luke dropped a kiss on Mia and hurried inside.

Danielle had watched the interaction with interest. "He's a nice guy. How long have the two of you been dating?"

As Mia made her way to Danielle's house, she explained her and Luke's history together. "We knew each other in grad school, we dated exclusively. We had planned to stay together after we graduated. He went back to England for the summer and wound up marrying a former girlfriend. I was in South America on a dig and couldn't be reached. When I finally did get access to the Internet, it was too late."

"No bad feelings over what happened?"

"Oh yes, there were bad feelings for a while, but I've moved past it. We connected this summer in Scotland on the dig I was on." Mia pulled up to Danielle and Steve's house.

There was a car in their driveway. "Whose car is that?" Mia asked.

"Steve's. He must have just got home. We'll go back and get my car in a little while. Mia, thanks for the drive. I'm so glad you were with me this morning."

"No problem. You take care."

"I will." Danielle closed the Jeep's door and went into the house.

* * *

Mia drove home and then texted Alex.

Mia: You busy today?

Alex: At the cottage with Zack, sorry.

Mia: No problem.

Alex's parents had a cottage on the same lake as Gran's cottage, and Alex was a frequent visitor there.

"Time for some yoga." Mia changed her clothes, rolled out her yoga mat, and found a practice online that she enjoyed. Going through the asanas, she felt her body relax, and her mind slow down. It had been a stressful morning, and she needed the break. Forty-five minutes later, she felt much better. Her mind was clear, and her body was loose. She headed for the shower and then got dressed.

She walked into the kitchen and poured herself a tall glass of lemonade and added ice cubes. Mia grabbed a notepad and pen and sat at her patio table on her balcony. There was a warm breeze blowing, and the air felt nice.

She wrote down everything she had learned about Tim Fraser, the stolen artifacts, the reproductions of antiquities, the people who worked with him. There were several pages of notes.

As she read through her notes, she highlighted sections that she thought needed a closer look. The auctions Tim had done for the past eight years. The list of people who'd died recently, the emails from Barbara, and the fact that she was in Lakeview far more often than she'd let anyone know. What was behind that? Did she lose her business? The mention of 'Charles' in her emails to Tim. Was he Charles Gordon? Mia tossed the pen aside and groaned. She didn't have any answers, just more questions. Ugh.

Then she remembered Danielle had sent her the video surveillance of the store. She opened up the file and watched it.

She saw Steve, Danielle, and Cheryl go into the store just after six, and then they all left about an hour later. At around nine-thirty, Cheryl arrived at the store. She was wearing all black clothing and entered the code. Approximately ten minutes later, a person arrived at the store. It could have been a small man or a woman. They wore a ball cap on their head, a black hoodie with the hood up, and black jeans. They had a pair of black driving gloves on their hands. They knocked on the door, and Mia saw Cheryl opening the door. Ten minutes later, the person left the store. Cheryl was nowhere to be seen. Mia sped through the remaining hours until she and Danielle arrived. No one else approached the store.

Her phone rang with Gran's ringtone.

"Mia, I just saw the news, and it seems there was another death at Timeless

Treasures. Do you know anything about that?"

"Yes. It's Cheryl, Tim's clerk. Danielle and I found her earlier this morning when we went to the store. Danielle wanted to check something in the office files."

"Oh, no! What happened?"

Mia gave Gran as much information as she could about Cheryl's death.

"Do the police have any idea who might have done this?"

"No. Danielle shared the surveillance video with them and with me, but they haven't said anything yet."

"Did you see anything on the video?"

Mia described what she'd seen.

"You didn't get a clear view of the person's face?"

"No, it could have been a man or a woman. And I couldn't hear what they said either. But Cheryl was expecting them. Otherwise, she wouldn't have opened the door."

"That's true. Could it be the man from the museum looking for his statue?"

"I don't think so. He was almost as tall as Luke and heavier set than the person on the video. And he showed up at the store this morning when the police were there. So I doubt it was him."

"Who is the detective in charge?"

"Detective Martin, the one who's working Tim's murder."

"Makes sense. I hope he can discover who did it. Is Luke working today?"

"Yes, he should be done soon, though."

"Why don't you both come over for dinner? We can do take-out. I'll order from down the street. Is there anything Luke can't eat?"

Mia chuckled in spite of the day she'd had. "No, Luke will eat just about anything."

"Fine, both of you come over after five. Just text me when you leave."

"Thanks, Gran. We'll see you later."

Luke texted her at three-thirty.

Luke: Done with work, will be back shortly.

Mia: Great. Can't wait to see you.

Luke arrived within ten minutes. He'd taken a cab from the police station.

"How was your afternoon? Did you get together with Alex?"

"No, she's away at the cottage. I did some review of what I know about Tim and Cheryl."

"I wish you'd take your mind off this."

"It's hard to. Have you spoken with Detective Martin?"

"I saw him as I was leaving. He's got his hands full with this investigation. He mentioned Danielle had shared the surveillance video, but it doesn't show the person clearly. Did you look at it?"

"I did. Let me show you."

Mia opened the video file, and Luke looked at it closely.

"I was thinking this Josh fellow you met last night might have been involved. But this person isn't big enough to be him."

"That's what I thought too." Mia closed the video. "Gran called and invited us for dinner. Take-out, her treat. Anytime after five tonight."

"That sounds good." Luke frowned. "You saw this Josh fellow this morning at the store, didn't you?"

"I did. And I told Detective Martin. I don't know if he learned anything from him."

"No, he didn't. He told me he hadn't been able to get to him. But he has officers looking for him. He has a few questions for him."

"He's from Montreal. Could he be part of the Montreal connection with the smuggling ring?"

"Perhaps. But it's a leap to think like that without any evidence. We have to be able to connect everything together. He may have been the person responsible for dropping those monitoring devices in the museum."

Mia snorted. "I think it's bold that he would attend the event last night. And that he mentioned Tim Fraser. I think he's the same Josh Humphries as the one in Tim's emails."

Luke smiled and pulled her closer to him. "You're probably right. I think he was there to check on some of the artifacts. Did you notice if he took any photos?"

"I didn't. But there's signage saying no photography allowed." Mia leaned into him.

"Using a cell phone is pretty easy. We're so used to seeing people with them that it doesn't register with us when someone uses one. Tim had a 3-D printer in his basement. I would think that anyone involved with smuggling artifacts would have one, and it's not a stretch to believe they're making copies."

"Tim had a lot of wealthy people on his email list. How would he have gotten their information?"

"As part of the smuggling cartel, he would have been given specific clientele to work with. The people who were killed in other countries had similar lists. As they were eliminated, their lists were distributed to others."

"That sounds cold. And you're certain Mr. Gordon is the head of this cartel?"

"Yes. We don't have any doubts about that. He's escaped us for now, but we'll find him. He can't stay under the grid forever."

Chapter Twenty-Four

Saturday Evening

Mia and Luke arrived at Gran's just before five. Mitch, the doorman, greeted Mia.

"Dr. Reid. Your Gran's waiting for you. She called down to let us know you were coming."

"Thanks, Mitch."

They rode the elevator to Gran's floor, and she was waiting for them at the door.

She pulled Mia into a hug. "I'm so sorry you're dealing with all this. How are you?"

"It wasn't pleasant at all. But I'm okay. Danielle was upset. You know she's going to sell the stock and the store, too. I think she's worried that having two murders in the store will affect the sale of the building." Mia bent down to stroke Cleo, who was circling her feet. Cleo purred loudly and then moved on to Luke.

"It might. But you never know with people." Gran ushered them into her apartment. "I've ordered plenty of Chinese food. I know we all like it, and it seemed to be the easiest thing to get."

"Sounds wonderful," Luke said as he picked up Cleo.

"Well, she's taken a liking to you, Luke. Mia, would you mind pouring us drinks?" Gran asked. "I've got wine, gin, and whiskey."

"Not at all. What'll you all have?"

They gave her their drink orders, and she complied with white wine for Gran and herself, and poured Luke a whiskey.

"Gran, what do you know about Martha Jones?"

"She's been in the business for about fifteen years. Her store has been doing well enough, I guess, because she's still selling. I don't know much more other than what I've already told you."

"Was she in business when you were?" Mia asked.

"She was just starting out. I remember thinking it would be interesting to see how she did coming from her background."

"Which was what?" Luke asked.

"She and her husband lived in Washington, D.C. He was some sort of government appointee and worked there. They divorced, and she moved back to Canada. I'm not sure where he is. But she'd spent a lot of her time in D.C. learning about antiques, and their home was well decorated. It looked like a showroom."

"Did you see their home?" Mia asked.

"No, but I saw photos in a magazine about D.C. Their home was in the write-up. Beautiful pieces. If she got them as part of the settlement, she would have done well to sell them."

Gran's landline rang, and it was Mitch at the desk letting her know the food was on its way up.

"I'll get it," Mia said.

"Here's my card. I'm paying for dinner." Gran held out her credit card, and Mia had no choice.

They set the food up on the dining room table and sat down to eat.

Mia asked Gran, "So is Martha part of the antique dealers' guild?"

"I think she still is. It's a good networking group."

"Was Mr. Fraser?" Luke asked as he passed the rice to Mia.

"He was as well, since the beginning." Gran put a small amount of gingered beef on her plate.

"Is there a list of members?" Luke asked.

"Yes. I can get a copy for you. Remind me after dinner." Gran cut into her eggroll and added some sauce.

They spent the next twenty minutes engaged in dinner and chatting about nothing important. Luke and Gran seemed determined to keep the conversation away from the murders at Timeless Treasures and to keep Mia focused on more pleasant subjects.

Luke and Mia cleaned up after dinner, and Gran put together some tea and a small dessert tray.

"Gran, those desserts look so good! Where did you get them?"

"Butter tarts from Amy's Pastries; cheesecake from Matt's Cakes; chocolate truffles from David's; and the lemon puffs from Syd's. Tom and Fran Esly went out this afternoon, and they picked them up for me."

Mia sighed. "The butter tarts are the best. You have to taste them, Luke."

While Mia and Luke were sampling the desserts, Gran went to her desk and opened a filing cabinet. A few seconds later, she pulled out a file and brought it to Luke.

"Here's the information on the guild members. It hasn't changed a lot in twenty-five years."

Luke took the folder and began looking through it. Mia was sitting next to him and read the file as he did. There were names, addresses, phone numbers, and email addresses. A brief description of the store the members were associated with. Gran was right, there wasn't a lot of change in the membership. In the last ten years, only one or two stores had changed hands, and there was only one new shop that had opened.

"Does this include dealers who would work from home without a storefront?" Luke asked.

"You mean online only?"

Luke nodded.

"I think there are a couple who do. They would be the ones who have recently retired and have some pieces they're selling. When COVID shut down so many businesses, three or four members closed their shops and went online. But they didn't sell large pieces. They dealt mostly in jewelry or personal items."

"May I keep this?" Luke asked.

"Of course. Just return it to me when you're done."

"I'll make a copy of it and return the original to you." Luke put the folder on the end table next to his chair.

"The association has been active for a long time. I remember as a kid going to a couple of the meetings with Gran, and there were lively discussions about some of the sales that were being made."

Gran chuckled. "I know which ones you're talking about. That was when we had several new businesses coming in. The old crowd was worried they would take all their customers. That never happened. There are always plenty of customers to go around."

"What about sellers who go to fairs and markets? Are they listed in here?" Luke asked.

"Some are. It's not mandatory to join our association. Anyone can buy a business license and say they're selling antiques. It's very much buyer beware."

Luke nodded. "I understand that."

"Do you think Martha is going to buy the Timeless Treasures stock?" Mia asked.

"I don't think she has the space for the full inventory. She'd have to put a lot in storage. And what's happening with the items you found in Tim's storage?"

"We've taken everything out, and we're going through it all. There are a lot of items that were stolen. I'm working with two other museum staff to assess the artifacts," Mia said.

"What about the stock in the shop?"

"We didn't find anything stolen there. We found some things that made us question what exactly he was using the shop for. Like in the basement."

"What was in the basement?"

Luke filled Gran in on what they had found in the basement. Mia also told Gran about the delivery area for the larger trucks and the belief that stolen artifacts first came to the basement and copies were made, then the artifacts were shipped to the storage unit.

"And how did he sell those?"

"We think those artifacts made up the bulk of the underground auctions.

The items were photographed, a detailed description would accompany the photographs, and they'd go in a package to potential buyers. For the in-person auctions, the artifacts would be moved to the auction location for display."

Gran sat back. "I'm sorry to hear he was involved. I never knew he needed money that badly."

"Mrs. Fraser had experimental treatments for her MS. I remember Danielle telling us about them. She had to travel to the States for them, and it wasn't covered under their health insurance."

Gran nodded. "They were gone several months at a time. And the treatments were done three times a year. They had to maintain a residence here and have a place to stay where they were going for the treatments. It was costly. And in the end, it didn't give her much time."

"I'm curious about Martha. I don't think she's involved with any crimes, but she seems to be on the spot all the time," Mia said.

"It might be because she's close by. It would be hard to miss the police activity at the shop. It's less than a hundred meters from her place. And she's very nosy," Gran said.

"Gran!"

"Well, it's true. She has to know everything about everybody on that street. She's always been like that."

"Did you know Barbara? Tim's first wife?" Luke asked.

"Yes, I did. I was surprised she showed up like she did. What happened when you and the detective questioned her?"

"She had a lawyer present, so we didn't get much information from her. And we can't place her at the store at the time of death."

"When did the coroner say it was?" Gran asked.

"Between ten and two."

"And we all saw her being escorted out shortly after she arrived."

"Do you remember when they divorced?" Mia asked

"It was nasty. He hired a private investigator. The investigator was able to prove that she was cheating on him with a man from Vancouver who would come to Lakeview every two weeks. He was an engineer and had started a construction company. He was establishing himself in British Columbia and in Ontario. He would come in for meetings with the provincial government and meet with Barbara. She fought to keep the store, and the judge didn't side with her at all. The judge agreed with Tim and told Barbara to cut her losses."

"How long after did he marry Danielle's mom?"

"I guess it was a year later. We were all surprised, but Rita was so nice. A lovely woman who worked hard with Tim to build their business."

They finished their tea, and then Mia and Luke left shortly afterward.

Chapter Twenty-Five

Sunday

Mia and Luke were having breakfast when Mia's phone rang. She picked it up and heard Danielle's voice.

"Mia, the police want me go down to the station. They have questions about Cheryl's death, and they seem to think I had something to do with it." Danielle's voice cracked.

"Do you have a lawyer?"

"No, should I?"

"Yes. Even if it's just the lawyer for your dad's estate. He'll be able to at least make sure that the police don't badger you. Don't go until you've contacted the lawyer. And don't go unless you have one with you. Do you understand?"

"Uh, yes. But I didn't do anything."

"It doesn't matter. If the police are asking you to go speak with them, you need someone who can protect your rights."

"All right. I'll call him now."

"If he can't go, tell him to recommend another lawyer. And if you can't find another one, call me back. I'll find someone for you. But don't go until you have a lawyer who'll meet you at the station."

"Okay."

Mia hung up.

"Problem?" Luke asked.

Mia told him what Danielle had said. "Why are they looking at her? Danielle doesn't like guns, and she wouldn't have taken me with her to find Cheryl."

Luke shrugged. "Maybe they just have questions. Although I agree, it's a good idea for Danielle to have representation."

Mia picked up her coffee mug and took a drink. Setting her mug down, she said, "Has Detective Martin said anything about who they think killed Cheryl?"

"I don't think they have enough information yet. She wasn't supposed to be at the store. Detective Martin thinks she may have been meeting Mr. Fraser's killer and blackmailing them."

"Why?"

"Some of the texts they found in her phone indicated a meeting at the store and that she knew what they had done."

"That's not very smart."

Luke shook his head. "People don't always do smart things. And in this case, if Cheryl thought she knew who killed Mr. Fraser and was accusing them, they reacted in a manner that was predictable. Maybe she left something behind at the store that would give information on who she spoke to."

"Do they know who the texts were sent to?"

"Yes. And they've tried calling the number, and it's no longer in service."

Mia frowned. "Who does that?"

"Someone who doesn't want to get caught. But I have faith in Detective Martin. He's working hard on finding the killer or killers. I think it's all part of the smuggling ring, and that's where we should focus our attention."

"What does Detective Martin say about that?"

"He doesn't agree. He thinks it could be someone who's trying to steal valuable antiquities from the store. And got caught."

Mia snorted. "I don't think so. I agree that it's to do with the smuggling ring. I'd like to take a closer look at Barbara. I think it's convenient that she showed up and shortly after Mr. Fraser was killed. I think she knows more than she's telling people."

Mia's phone pinged with a message.

Danielle: Lawyer is coming with me so is Steve.

Mia: Good, let me know how things work out.

"Danielle has a lawyer, and Steve will be with her too. Now, how do we find Barbara?"

"Let me see if I can get her information from Detective Martin." Luke sent a text, and shortly after, his phone rang. He spoke with the person briefly and explained why he wanted to connect with Barbara. He motioned to Mia for a pen and paper, and she quickly got him a notepad and a pen. He scribbled a phone number and then hung up.

"Right. He isn't thrilled with me talking to Barbara, but he did give me her phone number. I'll give her a call and see if we can set up a meeting with her, maybe for lunch?"

"That would work."

Luke made the call and spoke with Barbara. Mia could only hear his side of the conversation, and it appeared as if he was successful. He hung up and said, "Lunch at eleven-thirty at a restaurant close to her location. At least that's what she said."

Mia looked at the address. "That's not far from Timeless Treasures. We won't have to leave for another hour or so."

They spent the next hour putting together a list of questions for Barbara. Mia hoped they didn't scare her off.

Mia showered and got dressed. The restaurant they were going to was casual, and a sundress, sweater, and sandals would be appropriate. It was cloudy and humid outside with thunderstorms predicted for later in the day. Luke wore lightweight pants and a shirt.

They drove to the restaurant, and Mia found a parking lot behind the restaurant.

Entering the restaurant, Mia's eyes adjusted to the darkened room. She was glad she had a sweater on because the air conditioning was running, and the restaurant was almost frigid.

The hostess asked if they were meeting anyone. Luke gave her Barbara's name, and she led them to her table.

Barbara was seated at a booth in the back, away from other diners.

Luke and Mia took their seats, and the hostess gave them menus.

Barbara took a drink of her Caesar and watched them. "What's happened that you need to speak to me?" she asked.

"Cheryl's dead. She was killed on Friday evening. It just seems a little strange that she was in the shop that night. Danielle and I went to the shop on Saturday morning and found her. It wasn't pleasant."

Barbara raised an eyebrow. "And this matters to me why?"

"I'm curious why you're here. According to Mr. Fraser's lawyer, he paid you out for your share in the store when you divorced. Almost forty years ago. Why did you come back now?"

"Maybe I think I'm owed more than what he gave me."

Mia shook her head. "The value of the store and the stock is a result of the work Mr. Fraser put in all those years. Nothing to do with you at all. I find it strange that you show up, and he dies. And then his store clerk dies shortly afterward."

"Maybe it was their time." Barbara took a drink.

"Can you tell me what you've been doing in British Columbia? Were you involved in antiques?" Luke asked.

Barbara smiled. "I had a lovely shop. I sold a variety of antiques. Mostly small items. And it did well. Until it didn't. The last few years have been difficult for small businesses like mine. I came back to Lakeview a few months ago to talk to Tim. I wanted to see if he was interested in a partnership. I'd heard his wife had passed away and hoped we could mend fences."

"You planned to move back here?" Mia asked.

The server arrived to take their orders, and they all ordered the lunch special.

"I had to sell my shop in Kelowna. I wasn't sure if I wanted to go it alone again." Barbara took a drink. "I'd been speaking with him for a few months. I knew about his little soirées and wanted to attend one so I could see how he operated. I thought it would be something I could work with him on. He wasn't forthcoming. Cheryl was working when I went in the last time, and she's the one who told me about the one he was doing the night he died.

I didn't think there'd be any harm going or trying to go. I didn't know he would throw me out like he did."

"Did you go back that evening?"

Barbara smiled. "Aren't you clever. When I was booted out so rudely, Cheryl told me to come back around nine-thirty. I did. She was leaving, and I slipped in. Tim was in the office having a glass of whiskey. It must have been a successful event because he was in a better mood. We spoke for about thirty minutes, and he explained how his soirées got started. It was a way to bring people together and make sales while having fun. No pressure on the sales staff or the clients."

Mia was silent for a moment. Then she asked, "Did you see anyone when you left?"

"No. I didn't see anyone else." Barbara finished her Caesar and rattled the ice in her glass. The server showed up. "Another drink, ma'am?"

Barbara nodded. The server left.

"What time did you leave?" Luke asked.

Barbara sighed. "What's with all the questions? I didn't answer them with the police, and I'm not giving you anymore information."

"I'm trying to figure out a few things. Danielle's worried the store won't sell." Mia sipped her water.

"Well, yes, that's a problem. I can't think too many people will want to buy a shop where two murders took place."

The server arrived with their food and set the plates down. She asked if they needed anything else.

"My drink." Barbara snapped.

The girl returned promptly with her Caesar and then left them alone.

Mia took a bite of her sandwich and then set it down.

"Something doesn't make sense. If you've been here for a few months, why did you wait until the soirée before contacting Mr. Fraser?"

"I didn't. I told you, I met with him when I first got here a few months ago. Then I met with Martha, her shop is just down the road. I was trying to see if she was interested in selling her store."

"And is she?" Mia asked.

"No. No one on that street is. It's a great street with shops that work well together. It's like a strip mall without the fees."

"The real estate in that area is expensive. Would you be able to afford it?" Mia asked.

"True. But if I had the right backer, it could work."

"Have you been in antiques all your life?" Luke asked.

"Most of it. When I went out to Kelowna, I wasn't sure what I was going to do. They didn't have a lot of antique shops, and I saw a need. I did some research and found a good location. I had to start from scratch. Tim wouldn't give me stock."

"That's not true. I know he sent you stock from his shop." Mia glared at her.

"Oh, please. He sent me a few items. Nothing that set me up. I had to scrounge up money to buy my stock. And in British Columbia, it's very different than here. People were looking for completely different stock."

"You'd do well to remember that people around here know what happened when you left. There are still people who are involved in the business. I'd be careful about trying to slander Mr. Fraser." Mia's temper was short. She felt Luke put a hand on her thigh. A signal for her to stay calm.

Mia sat back and waited to see if Barbara would respond.

"It's not slander if it's true. And in spite of what you might think, Tim wasn't Mr. Clean. He didn't care where the antiques or artifacts came from. All he cared about was that he could sell them and make a good profit."

Luke raised an eyebrow. "Do you know that for a fact?"

Barbara nodded. "He was involved with a Charles. His last name escapes me. That started when his wife got sick. I remember because I'd heard about it. The antique world is a small one. I heard about all of this in Kelowna. This Charles guy was bringing in antiquities from around the world, and no one knew how he was getting them. Tim got involved with him because he needed to make money, a lot of money quickly. That's when the auctions started in Montreal, here, and in Vancouver."

"Nothing in Kelowna?" Luke asked.

"No. It's too small. Plus, Vancouver is easier to get to." Barbara played with her fork. "I tried to get the auctions going in Kelowna. I wrangled an invitation to one auction in Vancouver, and the people who showed up were extremely wealthy. They flew in on private jets, had security with them, and tons of money to throw around."

"I heard you lost your shop because of gambling debts. How would you have managed to get auctions going in Kelowna?" Mia asked.

"I spoke with this Charles guy. He laughed at me. Told me I was small potatoes and to keep my nose out of his business or else." Barbara shrugged. "I didn't need to be told twice. And as for losing my store, there were a lot of factors. I managed to keep working."

Luke pulled his phone out and found a photo of Charles Gordon. "Is this the Charles you spoke to?"

Barbara looked closely at the phone. "Yeah. That's him. He was younger but still looks the same."

"This man is wanted by Interpol. He's involved in an antiquity smuggling ring. If you see him again, please contact me." Luke gave her a business card. "There's a reward out for his capture."

Barbara raised an eyebrow. "How much?"

Mia hid a smile. Barbara was showing her cards.

"Two-hundred-fifty thousand U.S. dollars. If the information leads to his capture." Luke tucked his phone in his pocket. "Have you seen him recently?"

"Unfortunately, no. I could use that reward. I'll keep an eye out in case I do see him."

"I'd be careful if I was you. He's dangerous and involved in a lot of different facets of smuggling. We believe he's head of a cartel and has connections around the world." Luke picked up his fork.

Mia was watching Barbara. She saw her eyes widen at Luke's words.

Mia pushed her plate away. "Can you explain exactly what you're doing here? I'm a bit confused. Are you looking to open an antique shop in Lakeview, go back to Kelowna, or start a new venture?"

Barbara focused her attention on Mia. "I don't know why it's a concern to you."

"It will help me understand what you were doing with Mr. Fraser after the soirée. You being there places you under suspicion."

Barbara chuckled. "That's ridiculous. I had nothing to gain from his death. And if you tell the police, I'll deny it. No one's around who can say differently."

Mia raised an eyebrow. "How handy for you."

"Isn't it?" Barbara smiled. "I wouldn't have known that Danielle would inherit it or that she was going to sell. And I didn't want to buy it. I wanted to be in a partnership with Tim."

"Were you planning on moving here permanently?" Mia probed.

Barbara frowned. "I don't know why that's your concern."

Mia sighed. Barbara was good at blocking questions she didn't want to answer, and she couldn't force her to answer them.

The server arrived with their bills, and they settled up.

"If there's nothing else, I'll be on my way. Let Danielle know I'm interested in the store. You have my contact information; she can call me." Barbara picked up her purse and left the restaurant before Mia and Luke got out of their seats.

Chapter Twenty-Six

Sunday Afternoon

Mia and Luke left the restaurant and walked to Mia's car. "I'm not sure we got anything that helps us figure out who killed Mr. Fraser." Mia unlocked the Jeep.

Luke waited for Mia to get in. "I think we did. We know she's lying to us. She sold her shop in Kelowna a long time ago. And according to the emails you found, she's been working with Charles for quite a while. She was corresponding with Tim for eight years. And she told us she'd been at the shop after the soirée on Wednesday evening. That's a lot of information."

"Do we tell Detective Martin what we learned?"

"We need to. I'll send him a message and tell him what Barbara shared with us." Luke pulled out his phone and started composing his message. A few minutes later, Mia heard the swoosh of the message being sent.

They drove to Mia's, and Mia pulled the car into the underground parking. "We have a couple of hours before we need to be at Gran's. Is there anything you'd like to see?"

"Is there something close by?"

Mia nodded. "Lots, do you want to go to the CN Tower or the aquarium?"

"Let's go to the Tower. I'd like to see the city views from there."

Mia checked on her phone and booked tickets. "We're booked to go up in about thirty minutes. Plenty of time to get there."

Luke took her hand, and they strolled down the street toward the CN

Tower. "Let's give our minds a break from murder and smuggling. There isn't anything else we can do right now. Detective Martin will message me when he has time."

"A break is a good idea. Something might come to us while we're busy doing other things."

They queued up for the elevator to get to the observation deck of the CN Tower. Mia showed their tickets on her phone, and they crowded on.

"Good thing I'm not claustrophobic." She muttered to Luke.

He grinned, "That would make your choice of careers a poor one." He squeezed her hand. "We'll be there soon enough."

The elevator stopped at the main observation level, and everyone hurried off. The walls of windows offered breathtaking views of the city, the lake, and the surrounding area. Mia and Luke explored the level, taking in the sights. They walked one level down out to the lower observation level. The floor of this level was a clear acrylic type of glass, allowing people to see the street view below the tower. Mia noticed kids lying on the floor and their parents snapping photos of them. She chuckled. One of the boys had his arms and legs splayed out and had an expression on his face as if he was screaming. That would make a great keepsake.

Mia glanced at her watch, "We should start heading back. I'd like to change before we go to Gran's."

"Sure. This has been fun!" Luke took her hand as they headed toward the elevator.

"I'd like to stop and pick up some wine for dinner tonight. There's a shop on our way home."

Mia's phone rang as they were walking back to her place. It was Alex.

"Hey, what's up?"

"Gran invited Zack and me for dinner, too. What time are you going?"

"Probably in an hour or so. Did you want me to pick you up?"

"No. Zack's on call, so he might have to go back to work. We're going in his car. We'll meet you there soon. I was just checking on the time. We're bringing dessert."

"I just picked up some wine. I've got a couple of bottles of Peller Estates newest offering."

"We should take Luke to Niagara-on-the-Lake and tour some wineries and distilleries. When does he have to go back?"

"Oh, that's a good idea. I'm not sure when he's leaving. It kind of depends on a few things."

Mia and Luke had arrived at her condo. "We're going to get changed. We've been doing the tourist thing, and I need to get out of these sweaty clothes. I'll see you at Gran's."

"Why was Alex asking when I'm leaving?"

Mia explained about the wine and distillery tours Alex had mentioned.

"Sounds like fun. And you're right. I'm not sure yet when I'm leaving. I may have to stay a bit longer than expected. Especially since we've found that small factory in Mr. Fraser's store and the stolen artifacts in his storage unit."

"I don't have a problem with you staying longer." Mia smiled.

"We're going to have to discuss where we're going in this relationship soon. I've enjoyed my time here with you a lot."

"And I've loved having you here. You're right. We are going to have to talk. Can it wait until after dinner tonight?"

"Of course. It's not something we can resolve in one conversation."

They hurried off to shower and change. Mia didn't want to be late, and she hoped Gran wouldn't mind answering some questions about Timeless Treasures.

At Gran's, Luke and Mia arrived before Alex and Zack.

"What have you two been up to today?" Gran asked.

Mia filled her in on their lunch with Barbara. When she finished, she asked Gran, "Did you know her when they started the store?" Cleo walked up to Mia and jumped up on her lap. Mia smiled and rubbed Cleo's neck.

Gran put her water glass down. "I did. They were very much in love, and I wondered if their marriage would take being together twenty-four hours a day. Not every marriage can." She sighed. "I wasn't really surprised when we heard they were divorcing, and she was leaving for British Columbia. What did surprise me is that Tim bought her out. They hadn't been in business that long. He must have taken out a loan to do that."

"Was that common practice?" Luke asked.

"It depends on the situation. He and Barbara's relationship didn't end well at all. They were both bitter."

Mia snorted. "She told us they were 'friendly,'" Mia added the air quotes. Cleo jumped down and ran to the French doors that were open to the balcony. Mia watched as she curled up on her bed in a sunbeam.

"No, they weren't. You could hear her yelling at him from down the street. Always arguing after the first six months. I don't think either of them were happy."

"Do you believe her when she says they'd been talking the past few years?" Luke asked.

Gran shrugged. "It's hard to say. Why would she lie?"

"All kinds of reasons. I think she had something to do with his death. She was there that night. And she wanted more from him."

"Well, it's hard to get something from someone who's dead. I don't think she killed him," Gran said.

"He was poisoned, and it was in his whiskey. She might have had a drink with him, and while he was getting her glass, she could have dumped the poison in his drink." Mia walked to the French doors.

"That's true. She could have. But why would she?" Gran puzzled.

"I don't know," Mia admitted. "The only thing I can think of is that she wanted the shop. And if he was dead, Danielle might sell. I also think she might have wanted to take over his role in the auctions."

"There's no telling if she could have taken over the auctions. And Danielle might not have sold. So that would be a big gamble." Luke sat next to Gran. "I don't see her killing him. I think she would try her hand at changing his mind and working with her. And then she'd take advantage of him."

Gran's apartment phone line rang. "Send them up, please." Gran hung up. "Alex and Zack are here."

"I'm glad the front desk is taking care who comes up." Mia walked to the front door.

"They're not taking the threats lightly."

Alex and Zack arrived. Cleo hurried over to check them out. Alex made all the right noises for Cleo, and then Cleo lifted her tail and turned her back on them. She went back out on the balcony.

Mia poured drinks for everyone, and they sat around talking about places Luke should see before he left for England.

"It would be great to take you out fishing for an afternoon. Are you working the entire time you're here?" Zack asked.

"I'll be spending most of the next week working. I may have some time off next weekend. And I'm going to see if I can take a few days off before leaving."

"Well, let me know how things work out. I have a boat, and we can get out quickly." Zack and Luke exchanged numbers.

Dinner was served: lasagna, one of Mia's favorites. Gran kept everyone entertained with news from around the retirement community. Dinner and dessert were a hit. Mia and Alex cleared the dishes and the dining room while Gran chatted with Luke and Zack.

They spent some time out on the balcony with their dessert and tea.

When it was time to leave, Gran held Mia back for a minute. "Be careful when you're asking questions. I don't like that you and Luke met with Barbara. She sounds as if she has an agenda."

Mia nodded. "I'm careful, Gran. But Barbara's on my list. Luke's looking into her background. It seems strange that she would come back to Lakeview. Does she have family in the area?"

"I don't think so. But she may have friends in town. Just watch yourself around her."

Mia hugged Gran. "I will. Don't worry."

She and Luke left.

On their way home, Luke's phone rang. "It's Detective Martin. I'll put it on speaker phone. Hello Detective, I have you on speaker. Mia's in the car with me."

"Thanks for the message about Barbara. I'm not happy that you interviewed her without me being there, but I think you were able to get more information out of her than I would have."

"Are you going to bring her in for questioning?" Mia asked.

"Yes. I have officers looking for her, but she isn't responding to her phone or answering her door. We'll find her. And when we do, she'll have to answer our questions."

"Right, I'll see you in the morning. I wanted you to know what we'd learned from her before tomorrow."

"Yes, we'll talk in the morning. In the meantime, I'd advise you to stay away from Barbara. I think she's dangerous." Detective Martin disconnected the call.

"Well, that went better than I thought. I assumed he'd be upset with us." Mia pulled into her parking spot and turned off the Jeep.

"He could have been. I think the fact I was present may have helped the situation."

* * *

Monday

The next morning, Mia was in a hurry to get to work. Luke had left earlier, and they'd promised they would spend this evening talking about the future. She wasn't sure how things were going to work out, but she knew she wanted Luke in her life.

She drove her Jeep to the museum, using back streets to navigate the early morning traffic. She had a meeting with Christine Marks later this morning, and she needed to check some information before meeting with her.

A cup of coffee and a granola bar would have to suffice for breakfast. She scrolled through her email, checking to see if the box office had sent the reports for the weekend on the exhibit. Clicking it open, she saw that they'd broken the previous attendance record. That was great news! The marketing they'd done was working. When asked, a number of respondents indicated they'd learned about the exhibit through Mia's segment on The Morning Show. That was gratifying. All the stress and preparation that had gone into it was worth it.

She clicked on another email, and in this case, the message wasn't so great. STAY OUT OF TIMELESS TREASURES OR ELSE UR NEXT.

Mia sat back in her chair. Was this from the same person who'd sent the message through her mail? Mia looked closely at the sender. It was a generic email with an email program anyone could get an address with. Nothing to identify the name of the person. The sender's name was Lilanon. Mia's cell phone rang. Glancing at the caller id, she saw Danielle's name pop up.

"Hey, how are you?" Mia asked.

"Not so good. I just got a nasty email about the store. It's telling me to sell it fast."

"What exactly does it say and who's it from?"

"It's from an anonymous account, and it says: 'Sell the store now and you'll be okay. Don't, and you'll wind up like your father.'" Danielle's voice shook.

Mia drew a deep breath. "Okay, you need to contact the police immediately. Call Detective Martin and let him know what it says. Did it go to your personal email or your work email?"

"My personal account. Not a lot of people have that."

"Make sure to tell the Detective that. And have you shown it to Steve?"

"Not yet. He's at work, and I can't reach him right now."

"Call the detective and then call me back. I'll wait for your call." Mia waited until Danielle had hung up.

She sent Luke a quick text with the information from her email and let him know Danielle had received a similar one.

A few moments later, her phone rang; it was Luke.

"Are you all right?" he asked.

"I'm fine. This came in on my work email, which is easy for anyone to find."

"I'll alert Detective Martin. What are you doing at work today?"

"I'm on site at the museum. Mostly in my office, but I'll probably go through the exhibit at least once to make sure there aren't any questions or problems."

"Did you drive to work?"

"Yes. No troubles getting here."

"I'll make certain Detective Martin contacts you today. Please be careful."

They disconnected the call. She settled into work.

A short time later, her cell phone rang.

"Luke just informed me that you received a threatening email. Can you read it to me, please?" Detective Martin asked.

After Mia complied, he said, "Please forward me the email. Our IT guys are going to work on this and the one Ms. Fraser received. It's likely from the same person, and we may be able to figure out where they were sent from."

Mia sent the email and then said, "What are you going to do about the threat to Danielle?"

Detective Martin sighed. "There isn't much we can do about her threat or yours. I've told her to be cautious and not go out on her own for now. And Dr. Reid, I'm the police officer here. You need to step away from investigating. I don't do your job, please don't try to do mine. Or I'll have to bring you in on obstruction charges."

Mia was silent for a moment. "Can you really do that?"

"Ah, yeah, I can. Step away from this investigation before something happens to you. I wouldn't want anything to happen to you."

"I understand. I won't keep digging into this."

"I'll let you know if IT finds anything out about where the email came from." Detective Martin hung up.

The rest of the morning was spent doing administrative tasks. She had reports to complete and more work to do on the school program. At lunchtime, she walked to the cafeteria and grabbed a salad, some fruit, and a water. She made her way to a table away from patrons and ate her lunch.

Heather arrived shortly after and asked, "Do you mind if I sit with you?"

"Of course not. How have you been?"

Heather set her tray down. "I'm good. Did you have a nice weekend?"

"Yes, it was. We had dinner with my Gran, and I showed Luke around a bit. How was your weekend?"

"Good! We took in a play. It was fun."

They chatted a few more minutes, and then Mia's phone rang. It was Detective Martin.

"Excuse me, I need to take this." Mia moved away from the table and answered the call.

"Dr. Reid, I can tell you that your email and Ms. Fraser's both came from the same IP address. We believe the same person sent them. Are you aware if Ms. Fraser spoke with Barbara over the weekend?"

"I don't know. Luke and I spoke with Barbara on Sunday. She didn't say anything about speaking to Danielle."

"I want you to be careful and on your guard. I don't trust Barbara at all. I have a BOLO out for her."

"Have you spoken with Danielle?"

"Yes. And she's been told to be careful as well. If you see anything that seems off, contact me immediately."

"I will. Thanks."

"We'll get to the bottom of it. Just be cautious."

Mia disconnected and went back to her table. Heather looked up from her salad. "Everything okay?"

Mia shrugged. "The police are still investigating Tim Fraser's death. The detective in charge had a few questions for me."

"It was murder, wasn't it?"

"Yes. He was poisoned."

Heather gasped. "I didn't know that. His daughter must be upset."

"She is. It was tough enough when she thought he'd died from natural causes, but to learn he was poisoned made it that much harder."

"Do the police have any leads?"

"Not that they've shared with me. They had a few persons of interest, but that just means they're looking into different people."

"What's she doing with the store?"

"I think she's going to sell it. There have been a few real estate brokers speaking to her about the shop."

They talked for a few minutes longer, and then Mia returned to her office. She was puzzling over the BOLO for Barbara. She shouldn't be that hard to find. And did the police have any leads on Cheryl's death? There was no mistaking that one for anything but a murder.

Mia shook her head. She needed to focus on her work. She opened the file for the remote school program and reviewed the first two weeks. All the materials were ready, nothing to be added. She sent an email to the school board advising them that the materials the students would need for the labs were going out in the mail later that week. School was scheduled to start in two weeks, and the materials were required for the first class.

At four o'clock, her phone pinged with a text.

Luke: I'll be back at your place in twenty minutes. When are you leaving work?

Mia: In a few minutes. I'll meet you there.

* * *

Monday Evening

Mia met Luke in her condo. He reached for her and gave her a hug. "Well, this shows that you've made someone upset. Enough that they're threatened by you. The only person I can think of is Barbara. We saw her yesterday, and now this happens."

"She'd be showing her hand too quickly. I don't think she sent the messages. And I don't think she killed Tim or Cheryl." Mia put her keys in the bowl in the hall and walked into the kitchen. She opened her wine fridge. "Do you want a glass of wine?"

"Yes, please. If not Barbara, then who do you think is responsible?"

"I don't know. Who benefits from Tim and Cheryl's deaths?" Mia poured them each a generous glass of the Australian Shiraz.

"Danielle benefits from Tim's death. She inherits the store, stock, and his house. I don't know who benefits from Cheryl's death. Her next of kin is a cousin." Luke picked up his glass and followed Mia into the living room.

"Isn't it usually the person who benefits that police look at?" Mia put her wine glass on the side table. "I can't see Danielle killing her father, and there's no way she killed Cheryl, not with her reaction when we found her."

Luke's phone pinged with a text. He looked at his phone.

"Detective Martin says they've found the general location of the IP address that sent the email to you and Danielle. It's a downtown office building on a city block that has several large office buildings."

Mia rolled her eyes. "Is there any way to get closer than that?"

Luke chuckled. "Patience, my dear. They're going to look closely and see what they can find."

"What's the name of the building or the address?"

Luke sent a text.

"It's a group of buildings on Bay Street. That's all he can provide for now."

"Danielle works at a bank in that general area. I'm not sure if it's on Bay Street or not."

Luke messaged Detective Martin with the information.

"He says he knew this. And Steve, Danielle's husband, also works in that area."

Mia shrugged. "I didn't know that. I wonder if the two messages were sent at the same time. Is there any way to find out?"

A moment later, Detective Martin responded to Luke's question. "He says they appear to have been sent at the same time. He'll stay on top of this and will let us know what they discover."

Mia sighed. "How was your day?"

"Not bad. I may have some good news on the work front. The RCMP have contacted my supervisor. They're impressed by the training I've been doing and want to know if there's a way I can work with them on a contract. Nothing has been decided yet; they just contacted my supervisor today."

Mia's face lit up. "This is great! Would you be here or would you have to travel around?"

"I didn't know anything about this until late this afternoon. And I haven't heard anything from my supervisor about it. Just from the RCMP officer I've been liaising with. There would probably be some travel involved, but I'd be based out of Lakeview."

"We need to celebrate this good news! Let's see what we can cook up for a meal. I'd rather not go out."

"I agree. I can help in the kitchen."
Mia grinned. "Sure thing."

Chapter Twenty-Seven

Monday Evening

Mia looked through the fridge and pantry and decided she could cook up a steak and a salad. Luke washed and chopped the vegetables for the salad, while Mia set up the sous vide machine to cook the steaks. In short order, supper was ready.

They ate dinner, making plans for the next few days.

"I'll be working the rest of the week at the police station. I would like to bring the officers in to see the cache of artifacts we discovered in the storage unit. Do you think that would be possible?"

"I can ask Christine. She'd have to okay it. I don't think it would be a problem. Peter and Nancy are very knowledgeable about the artifacts, and they can answer any questions the officers would have."

They cleaned up after dinner, and then Mia called Danielle.

"I wanted to see how you were doing. Have you had any other messages?" Mia asked.

"No. I spoke with Detective Martin about the email. He said they were able to narrow down an IP address, but they haven't been able to identify who the person could be yet. I'm okay. Just tired of all this drama."

"Have you made any decisions about the store or the stock?"

"I'm going to sell everything. I don't think the store will sell quickly, given what's happened there. I'm meeting with two real estate agents on Tuesday. They reached out to me about the store."

"That's a good idea. Have you heard anything about a service for Cheryl?"

"She left specific instructions, and she didn't want any kind of service. Her cousin is honoring her wishes. I'd better go; Steve just came home. I'll talk to you later."

Mia relayed the information she'd learned to Luke.

"I think she's smart to sell the store. Managing it with her career and a new baby coming would be challenging," Luke said. "I just received a text from D.I. Anderson about the ring you found at the dig this summer. He says it's been in the museum on the Isle of Skye and hasn't left. He was away on vacation last week, that's why he didn't get back to me."

"Oh, that's good. So, the ring in Mr. Fraser's study isn't the original. But it could be a copy, right?"

"Yes, that's right. He could have worked from a photograph of the ring and used the 3D printer in his basement to make it."

* * *

Tuesday

The next morning, Luke insisted on driving Mia to work. "I'll pick you up at the end of the day. I don't want you taking any chances. The police still haven't caught the person responsible. We need to be smart about this."

The drive to work was uneventful. Luke pulled up in front of the museum. Mia leaned across and kissed him. "Thanks. I'll see you later this afternoon."

"Take care today. I'll text you before I leave."

Mia hustled into the museum, smiling to herself. It was a little strange to have Luke here and being so careful with her, she didn't mind it as much as she thought she would.

Mia walked through the exhibition. It was a popular attraction. She paused next to a necklace on display. It had a gold breastplate decorated with emeralds. It wasn't a large necklace, and the archaeologists who had discovered it had determined it was probably worn by children of royal blood. The necklace next to it was similar but sized for adults.

A short distance away were daily utensils used for cooking and eating. They were made of wood and pottery.

Mia was pleased with the exhibit. The curator who'd worked on it before Mia arrived had done excellent work. She'd tweaked a few of the exhibits, written the scripts for the narrators, and the exhibition labels for each artifact on display. This exhibition was close to her heart. She'd travelled to Central America many times to take part in or lead digs in the region. The people of the area were friendly and enjoyed helping her when she worked with them.

She walked to her office, and her phone buzzed with a text.

Danielle: When you have a minute please call

Mia closed her office door and called her.

"Mia, thanks for calling so quickly. Um, I have a couple of questions about something I found in Dad's file." Danielle paused a moment.

"I'm here. What do you need?"

Danielle sighed. "I'm not clear on a few things. Dad had the space in the basement, and apparently, that's where copies of artifacts were made. And then it looks like he stored them in the storage unit. He has notes about the different people that were involved." Danielle's voice broke. "Mia, I think Steve was involved in this."

Mia gasped. "Why do you think that?"

"There's a couple of notes about who was helping him transport the copies to the storage unit. Steve's name and phone number are part of the notes."

"Can you send me those notes? I don't remember seeing them."

"I will. I just don't understand why Steve would do that."

Mia's phone pinged with the receipt of the text. She put Danielle on speaker phone and opened her text. She looked at the note Danielle had sent. It clearly showed Steve's name and phone number, the date of the message to Steve, and the instructions. The next text showed Steve's response, saying he'd take care of it later that day. The dates were two weeks before Tim had been killed.

"Do you think Steve had anything to do with your father's death?"

"I'm not sure anymore. He's been acting strange the last few days."

"How?"

"Really distracted and not talking to me about what's happening. He's pretty much left me to figure things out on my own. I've asked him for help, and he's snapped that he's busy at work. But I know he hasn't been at work since Dad died. I called there this morning, and he's not there."

"Have you said anything to him about your suspicions?"

"No. I wouldn't do that, I'm not sure of anything anymore."

Mia thought for a moment. "Are you alone right now?"

"Yes. Why?"

"I'm not sure what to think about this. I want you to have your phone with you all the time. If anything happens that seems off, call the police immediately."

They disconnected, and Mia thought about what Danielle had told her. Danielle was safe at home, but what if Steve had killed Tim and Cheryl? Why would he do that? Money was one reason, and Danielle would inherit everything. Was Steve involved with the antiquity smuggling? Mia groaned. So many questions were swirling in her head.

She needed to figure this out. She wished she had her notepad that she'd written information down, but it was at home. She pulled one out of her desk and started to make notes.

Tim Fraser had been involved with the antiquity smuggling ring and was selling them at auction. He'd been doing that for eight years.

Cheryl had been working for Tim for eight years. It was possible she knew about the auctions and the antiquity smuggling. Could she have talked to the wrong people about what Tim had been doing? Did she threaten someone with exposure, and instead of having her work with them, they decided to get rid of her?

How did Steve fit into this? What was his role in this? If he was making deliveries for Tim, he had to know about the smuggling ring and the fakes. Did he want more money for his involvement? Was he tired of playing second fiddle to Tim? Did he think he could take over the Lakeview operation? Why was he involved? Did he kill Tim and Cheryl? Why would he kill them?

Was Charles Gordon still involved with the smuggling ring? Was he the person Tim reported to?

"Ugh. All I have are questions. None of this makes sense." Mia tapped her pen on the desk. Maybe Gran could help her with this.

She grabbed her cell and called Gran.

"Gran, do you have a few minutes? I need to talk something out with you."

"Of course, what do you need?"

Mia outlined what she knew about Tim and Cheryl's death. And what she had on the smuggling ring. She went through everything she knew, what she thought might have happened and why. When she was done, Gran waited a moment before speaking.

"You think Steve was involved with Tim and the smuggling, right?"

"Yes. But then why would Danielle sell the store and the stock?"

"I don't think Danielle's aware of his involvement with the store or with Tim. Do you know where he works?"

"I think Danielle said some kind of investment firm, but I'm not sure."

"I wonder if he's still working. Is there any way you can find out?"

"Danielle said she'd called him at work, but there was no answer. Let me see if I can get a number for him."

"If you do reach him, what are you going to say?"

"I guess I'll ask him if he helped Tim at the shop. I'll see how he answers, and I'll take it from there."

"Just be careful. You're smart. Make sure you have some questions prepped before you speak to him. I wouldn't want him to get suspicious of anything you say."

"I'll be careful. I don't want him to do anything that would endanger anyone."

"Let me know what you find out."

Mia disconnected the call and checked her contact information for Steve. She found a work number and a cell phone. Before calling either number, she thought out her options. She was going to ask him if he knew anything about Tim's business and how he knew Cheryl.

Mia called his work number, and a brief recording came on saying to leave a message. It didn't identify Steve as the person at the number. Mia disconnected without leaving a message. The message had given her the name of the company. She located the company's main number. She called it and asked for Steve.

"Steve hasn't worked here in four weeks. He was let go as part of a downsize. Can someone else help you?"

Mia was surprised. Danielle didn't know about this.

"When exactly was he let go?"

"I'll transfer you to our HR department. Someone there can answer your questions."

"How can I help you?"

"I was looking to speak with Steve Hardy, but apparently, he's no longer working with your company. Can you tell me when he was let go?"

"I can only tell you that on July 15th, we had a reorganizational downsize in our company. A number of people were involved in that event. I can't tell you any specifics about who was let go."

"Thank you." Mia disconnected the call. The HR department wouldn't give out names of individuals, but it made sense that Steve had been let go at that time. She wondered if he'd been given a severance package. That would have been customary. She tapped her pen on her desk. Nothing left to do except call Steve's cell. She'd ask him about helping Tim and see what he said.

She called, and it went to voicemail. Mia disconnected before leaving a message. She wasn't concerned that he'd know she'd called him, as she'd blocked her number.

Mia's cell rang. It was Luke.

"Just checking in on your morning."

"I have something to tell you." Mia filled him in on what she'd learned over the last hour and a half.

"I don't think the police have looked at Steve as a suspect. Let me talk to Detective Martin and tell him what you've learned. Are you available to talk to him?"

"Of course. I'm a bit concerned that we don't know where he is right now. Danielle isn't aware that he's been let go from work."

"I don't think he'll do anything to Danielle. I'll speak to Detective Martin now and get back to you."

Mia disconnected the call. She got up from her desk and paced the floor. "Ugh! I don't like this. Danielle could be in danger."

She called Danielle. "I haven't been able to reach Steve either. He might just be tied up in a meeting. Do you have plans for the rest of the day?"

"I'm meeting with the lawyer to sort out some things with the estate."

"What time are you meeting with your lawyer?"

"In about forty-five minutes. I have to leave here soon."

"Was Steve supposed to go with you?"

"No. He's back at work. He could only take last week off."

"Do you mind if I go to the store and check something out?"

"No. That's all right. What are you looking for?"

"I want to check the storage in the loft."

"Are you at work? Because I can drop the key off in a few minutes. The museum is on my way to my lawyer's office."

"That would be great. Have you changed the alarm code?"

"No, I haven't. I'll see you soon."

Mia made up her mind. She'd go to the store and check to see that everything was in order. Danielle was selling everything, and they'd had a chance to go through the stock. She doubted that Steve would be there.

She changed her voicemail to out of office, grabbed her bag, and hurried out the front. She waited a few minutes, and Danielle pulled up. Mia walked to her car.

Danielle rolled down her window. "Here you go. I don't need it today, but I will tomorrow afternoon."

"Thanks, I'll drop it off tonight."

Danielle left for her appointment, and Mia flagged a cab down.

She gave the driver the store address and sent Luke a text.

Mia: Going to Timeless Treasures to check something out.

Luke: Rather you waited until I can go with you.

Mia: I'll be fine. Danielle at a meeting, Steve isn't around.

Luke: I'll meet you there as soon as my session is over.

The cab stopped in front of the store. Mia paid the driver and decided to check the back of the store first. If there was no one parked there, she'd be comfortable going in the store. However, if someone was there, she'd have to wait until they left. She didn't want to go inside if anyone else was there.

Hurrying around the corner, she stopped suddenly. There was a moving truck parked behind the store. The garage door was open, and Mia could hear two men talking. But she couldn't make out what they were saying. She crept closer to the open door.

"I've got to get these out of here today. Danielle has someone coming in tomorrow, and they'll be going through this place carefully. Anything that's here is going to raise a red flag. I told her I'd taken everything out." Steve's voice was loud.

"I understand. But I need to talk to you today. After all, if you're going to take on Tim's role in this venture, you need to be briefed completely."

Mia frowned. Who was that man? His voice was familiar.

"Listen, Charles, I don't have a lot of time. What do we need to talk about?"

Mia gasped. That's who it was, Charles Gordon. He was back in Canada! Mia needed to let Luke know before Charles slipped through their fingers again.

Chapter Twenty-Eight

Tuesday

Mia backed away from the open door and hurried around the corner. She texted Luke.

Mia: At Timeless Treasures. Charles Gordon is here with Steve. I'm at the back in the alley and listening to them.

Luke: Leave immediately. Alerting the police.

Mia silenced her phone. Luke would get the police here. In the meantime, she was going to see if she could listen and learn more about Mr. Gordon's operation.

She crept back to the open garage.

Mr. Gordon was still speaking.

"We have several people working for us at the airport. They're told when a shipment is coming in, and they're well paid to look the other way. Tim was responsible for picking up the shipments. No one thought twice about an older guy making pick-ups. Lots of retirees do that type of work. Once you arrive, you'll show id, and we'll make certain it will pass any test they give it, then you'll pick up the items and leave. Your new identification will be sent to you by courier, and we'll communicate using burner phones. I don't have to tell you not to talk about this. You've seen what happened to Tim."

"Why did you kill him?" Steve asked.

"He knew too much and wanted out. Remember that. There is no out. Once you've started working for me, you don't ever leave."

"I thought Cheryl would be working with us."

"She's gone because she got greedy. She worked with Tim and was getting a cut. She thought she could take over and wanted more than what Tim was getting. Remember that in the future."

Mia glanced at her watch. Where were the police? What was taking so long? She saw a car pull in next to the truck. Who was that? Mia watched the car door open and bit back a gasp. What was Barbara doing here?

"Charles! Are you here? I need to speak with you."

Mia moved quietly behind a dumpster. She didn't want to get caught, but she had to hear what was happening. She peered around the corner and could see Barbara, Charles, and Steve.

Charles walked out of the storage room and stood in the open garage door. "Barbara, what do you need?"

Barbara stomped her way to him. "I just spoke with Danielle. She's meeting with the lawyer. What's the hold up? I need this stock so I can move it."

"What do you mean you need the stock? Charles told me it's mine to sell." Steve came out of the basement.

"As if. Do you honestly think you're getting this? You have zero experience doing these auctions. I'll be taking these on from now on." Barbara glared at Mr. Gordon. "Didn't you tell him?"

Mr. Gordon shrugged. "I knew you'd be here soon. If you want the business, you're going to have to deal with him. The same way you dealt with Tim."

Steve's face blanched.

Gordon laughed. "Barbara's been working for me for a long time. She's been instrumental in keeping everyone in line for the last eight years. Tim didn't realize she was working for me until it was too late. And Cheryl didn't know who she was up against."

Barbara pulled a gun out of her purse and aimed it at Steve. "Come on. Get this truck loaded now. I don't have all day."

Steve didn't move. Barbara waved the gun. "Move it."

Steve rubbed his face and then turned to the basement. Mia could hear him moving equipment around, then he started putting boxes in the back of the truck. Mia counted twenty-five in all. Steve pulled down the door of the truck, locking it in place.

Barbara smiled. "Well done. Now, you're going to take it to my storage unit. I'll follow you. Any wrong move, and I'll call the police and tell them you have stolen merchandise in your truck. You'll be in jail and then dead within a week. Charles, I'll touch base with you tomorrow. Are you going to be in town?"

Just then, Mia heard several police sirens as the police cars came up the back alley.

Charles heard them too. "I'd best get away while I can. If you get caught, use our lawyer. I'll be in touch."

Mia watched as Charles hurried toward the other side of the building.

Police came out and called. "Hands in the air, and down on your knees." The police came from everywhere, including the front. Steve dropped to his knees. Barbara raised her hands.

Mia saw Detective Martin and Luke come around the corner. Mia hurried to Luke and saw her Jeep on the street. "Charles is gone. He left around the other side. I'm going after him." Mia raced toward her Jeep.

"Mia, wait!" Luke called out as he ran after her.

Luke reached the Jeep a few seconds after Mia. He yanked the door open.

"I'm going after him. I think I know where he's going."

"Right with you." Luke buckled in.

Mia scanned the street, looking for a car that had Charles in it. She spotted a black town car driving away down the street. "That's him. I'm certain."

Mia pressed hard on the gas and caught up to the car. "Can you read the licence plate?"

"Yes, I'll send it to Detective Martin." Luke texted the license plate, and Detective Martin answered.

"He's telling me we need to back away and let the police take this."

"No way. I don't want to lose him. And the police aren't anywhere near us." Mia stayed on the town car as the driver sped up. "He knows I'm after him, and he'll get away."

Mia followed the car through the busy city streets. Traffic was heavy, construction had closed several streets, and there were detours across two major intersections. Mia swerved to miss a bus, and Luke sucked in his breath. "Careful, love. Won't do us any good to get flattened."

Mia squeezed in behind a truck, giving her a bit of space behind the town car. "Maybe they'll think they lost us. Can you keep an eye out to see where they are?"

Luke opened his window and leaned out. "I see them. There are two vehicles ahead of us, stopped at a red light."

"Good. We'll catch up with them."

The light changed, and Mia saw the town car surge ahead. The truck in front of Mia was slow to move forward, and two other cars slipped behind the town car. "No, no, no! I can't lose them." Taking a breath, Mia judged whether she could overtake the truck. It would be tight. She accelerated and passed the truck on the inside lane, just clearing the truck before a pedestrian attempted to cross the road. Mia leaned on her horn, and the pedestrian jumped out of the way.

Mia saw the town car ahead. They had cleared the construction zone and were moving swiftly. Mia was almost caught up to them when the town car ran a red light, and she had to stop.

She banged her hand on the steering wheel. "Oh, that makes me mad! He's headed to the Island Airport. That's the only place that makes sense. Can you let Detective Martin know?" Mia watched as the town car drove away.

"Will do." Luke sent the text. "He says they have officers at the airport. If he's going there, they'll capture him."

Mia nodded. "I wonder if there's another way for him to get there. He wouldn't have to park his car. But to get to the airport, you either go through the tunnel on foot or you take the ferry. Could he have a boat waiting? That would be faster."

The light changed, and Mia drove as fast as she could. She knew the area and remembered that parking at the airport would be a headache. It was a very small lot. Racing down a side street, she parked her Jeep in the first empty spot. She and Luke ran down to the waterfront.

"Where are we going?" Luke asked.

"I need to see if he has access to a boat. If he does, he can skip the ferry and the tunnel." Mia stopped as she saw a small powerboat pull away. "That's him." She pointed to a tall, grey-haired man. As if he knew Mia was pointing him out, he turned in her direction and sent her a salute.

"Ugh! The arrogant jerk! He's getting away."

Luke was on the phone with Detective Martin, explaining the situation.

"What did he say?"

"He'll get the Harbor Police out and watch for him. I didn't catch the boat's name, did you?"

Mia shook her head. "I can't believe he's going to get away again."

Luke put his arm around her shoulders. "Come on. Let's go to the shop. I want to see what was in those boxes."

Mia drove them back to the store, fuming that she'd missed catching Charles Gordon. Traffic was still heavy, and it took them almost thirty minutes to get back to the store.

Detective Martin had his officers loading the boxes in squad cars. Mia noticed that Steve and Barbara weren't around.

"Where are Steve and Barbara?"

"They're on their way to the station. They'll wait in a holding room until I'm ready to talk to them. We'll keep them locked up."

"Did the Harbor Police get Charles Gordon?" Mia asked.

"No. I think he slipped through. There was a private jet that left about fifteen minutes ago. It could have been him," Detective Martin said.

Mia frowned. "How are we going to get him? What happens next?"

"Interpol will issue an alert for him." Luke shook his head. "We'll get him. Sometimes it just takes a bit longer."

Mia looked in the back of the moving truck. "What are you going to do with the boxes?"

"We'll take them to the station and hold them there. I don't suppose you'd like to consult with the Lakeview Police to identify the artifacts?"

"I could, but it's something I'd have to do after hours from the museum."

"We can work around that."

Mia's phone rang. Danielle.

"Mia, have you heard what happened?" Danielle's voice shook.

"I have. I'm so sorry, Danielle. Anything I can do to help, you know I will."

"Thanks. I'm furious! Steve called me from the police station. I can't believe he was involved with this. I just got off the phone with my lawyer. I'm starting divorce proceedings. I don't care if Steve claims he's innocent. I can't have him in my life."

They spoke for a few more minutes and then disconnected.

"How is she doing?" Luke asked.

"Better than I thought she would." Mia filled him in on the call.

"Good for her, moving forward. She'll have a tough go of it."

"Yes. But we're here for her, and she knows that. Sometimes, it's easier to deal with things when you have people who stand with you. I need to let Alex know what's happening."

Mia sent a short text to Alex, telling her to get in touch with Danielle. Alex replied with a thumbs-up.

"Could you follow me to the station? I'd like to get your statement while everything is still fresh in your mind." Detective Martin asked.

Chapter Twenty-Nine

Tuesday Afternoon

Mia and Luke followed Detective Martin to the police station. When they pulled into the parking lot, Detective Martin was waiting for them.

"Dr. Reid, I'll need you to come with me. We're going to bring Barbara Fraser and Steve Hardy in separate interview rooms. They'll wait to be interviewed. I'm hoping Steve will spill everything he knows, and that will make it easier for all of us."

"Where are you going to be?" Mia asked Luke.

"I'll be connecting with my superior to advise him of what's happened. There are more antiquities that will need to be processed. I'll be waiting for you when you're through. Chin up. This should be a piece of cake for you." Luke pulled her into a quick hug. "I'll see you soon."

Mia and Detective Martin walked into an interview room.

Detective Martin asked Mia, "Do you want some water or coffee?"

"Water would be good, thanks."

He hurried out and came back with two bottles of water. "I'm going to record your statement, and then tomorrow you can come in and review it and then sign off on it."

Mia nodded. "I don't have a problem with that."

"Okay, why don't we start at the beginning. Why were you at Timeless Treasures today?"

Mia explained why she'd gone and what she'd done when she'd arrived and realized someone was there. She kept her statement factual and didn't add any information that wasn't pertinent to Detective Martin's questions.

They went through her statement twice, and then Detective Martin said, "Excellent. A lot of good information. I wish all our witnesses could be as factual as you are." He turned off the recording.

"It's my training. We have to be precise when we find something in the field." Mia finished her water. "What do you think is going to happen to Barbara and Steve?"

"They won't get off easy." Detective Martin listed off the offences. "Murder, theft of antiquities, forgery of antiquities, selling stolen property. They're looking at serious time in prison."

Mia stood. "Do you think I'll have to testify?"

"You might have to. But that won't happen for some time." Detective Martin escorted her out of the interview room and to the waiting area, where Luke was finishing up a phone call. "Thank you for your statement. But please, please, don't get involved in anything like this again."

"You're welcome. And trust me, I don't want to have to get involved again!"

Luke stood. "Do I have your word on that?" he asked with a grin.

"Well, I'll try. I've had my fill of stolen antiquities and murder." Mia shook Detective Martin's hand. "Thanks, I'm glad this is over."

"Let's get home." Luke took Mia's hand.

Back at Mia's condo, Luke poured them each a glass of wine. Mia glanced at the clock and shook her head. It was past seven in the evening, and she was starving. "Pizza?" she asked.

Luke nodded.

Mia placed the order online. "I need to touch base with Gran. I'm pretty sure this has been on the news."

"You'd better make that call. The agent my supervisor sent arrived this afternoon. I'll go in your office to make that call."

Mia called Gran.

"Mia, were you involved in what went on at Timeless Treasures today? I just got off the phone with Martha Jones. She says the police were there and there was a high-speed chase too!"

Mia sighed. Of course, Gran knew about this. "Let me tell you what happened." For the next ten minutes, Mia filled Gran in.

"Oh, my goodness! You're sure you're all right? You didn't get hurt?"

"No, I'm fine, Gran. Charles, Barbara, and Steve didn't see me when I was behind the store. I hid by a dumpster. I'm not happy we didn't get Charles, but the police and Interpol are on the lookout for him."

"And how's Danielle?"

"Upset and rightly so. She told me she's going to divorce Steve. I let Alex know to get in touch with her, and I'm pretty sure she's with her."

"Alex and her mother will make sure Danielle will be all right. She's had a very rough two weeks."

"She has. And Alex's mom has a list of good lawyers that Danielle can work with. Danielle's stronger than she thinks."

"If my hair wasn't already white, I'm sure it would be after this latest escapade of yours. Can you promise me you'll not get involved in police matters again? I truly don't want to lose you." Gran's voice broke.

Mia sighed, "I'm sorry, Gran. I don't purposely try to get involved with the police. I promise I'll be more careful in the future. But I can't let wrongs go by. You know that. I have to try to make things right."

"I guess I'll have to be okay with that."

"I'd better go, we've ordered food in, and it should be here soon. I'll call you tomorrow."

The pizza arrived, and Mia took the delivery into the kitchen. She set the pizza on the counter and went looking for Luke.

He was just coming out of the office.

"Pizza's here if you're ready to eat. Did you get your call done?"

"I did. I spoke with our agent, and we're going to meet tomorrow morning at the police station. How's Gran?"

Mia led him back to the kitchen and started plating the pizza. "She was upset. She'd heard from Martha Jones about the activity on the street and at Timeless Treasures. She did calm down when I explained what happened."

"I can imagine." Luke picked up the bottle of wine, and Mia took the plates.

They sat in the living room and ate their pizza.

"Are you okay?" Luke asked.

Mia took a deep drink of wine. "I am. I feel bad for Danielle. In less than two weeks, she's lost her father and her husband. I don't think she's going to have an easy time of this."

"Is she going to divorce Steve?"

"That's what she said. And I don't blame her. You think you know someone until you realize you don't."

Mia's phone rang with Alex's ringtone. "Hey. What's up?" Mia asked.

"I just wanted to say thanks for the heads up. I'm with Danielle, and I've called my mom. She's on her way to the city. We're going to get Danielle through this. Mom has some excellent contacts for divorce lawyers and to get Danielle the support she's going to need in the next while. And I wanted to check in to see how you are?"

"I'm glad your mom's coming. She has good connections. I'm okay. Luke's with me, and we're going to have a quiet night. I wasn't hurt, just got scared. And I'm angry we didn't get Charles Gordon. He slipped away again. I've spoken to Gran, and she's glad this is over."

"He'll get caught. I'm going to take some time off work to be with Danielle."

"I'll talk to you soon." Mia disconnected the call.

"Is everything well?" Luke asked.

Mia told him what Alex had said.

"Danielle's fortunate to have Alex and her mother on her side."

"Mrs. Bennett can be formidable when needed. She'll make sure Danielle makes out well." Mia took a bite of pizza. "What happened with the antique dealers we found in Tim's contacts? The ones who died."

Luke swallowed his wine. "Interpol's been working with the local law enforcement agencies. It appears we were right. They were all part of the smuggling ring. They all had ties to Charles Gordon. In some cases, autopsies were done. Interpol is asking for those reports. The first few that have come in show the individuals were poisoned, and that's opened the door for more investigation. It's going to take time to go through all of them, but I think we'll be able to prove that they were murdered. Tying it all back to the smuggling ring may be difficult, but we aren't going to quit."

"It would be good if Charles Gordon were captured. I'd like to see him pay for everything he's done." Mia picked up her wine glass. "We'll just have to be patient."

* * *

Wednesday

The next morning, Mia and Luke hurried to work. Luke dropped her off at the museum, promising to pick her up no later than four.

Mia had received a text from Christine Marks asking to see her when she got in. She dropped off her bag in her office and went upstairs to Christine's office.

The secretary nodded to Mia. "Knock on the door. She's waiting for you."

Mia grimaced. That didn't sound good. She knocked on the door and opened it when she heard Christine's voice.

"Hi, you wanted to see me?" Mia closed the door behind her.

"Yes. Are you all right after what happened yesterday?"

"I am. I'm sorry about what happened and not letting you know about it. Things moved very quickly."

"That's not a problem. I was more concerned for your health and safety than anything else. Are you certain it was Charles Gordon who was behind this?"

"I am. I've met him; I worked for him in June. There was no mistaking him. Do you know him?"

"Yes, he was on our board of directors. That's a stain on our reputation, and we're working hard to disassociate ourselves from him. It's not easy. I'm in communication with our lawyers and drafting a memo to go out if necessary. Have a seat, please."

Mia took the chair in front of the desk, wondering what was going on.

"I wanted to let you know we've had excellent feedback on the exhibit.

And I just spoke with one of the principals from the schools up north that you're working with, and they're very impressed with the program you've lined up."

"That's great news. I'm happy to hear that."

"There's more. The Mexico City Museum is sending two of their curators to work with us in the next month, and they've asked if you would work with them. They're also bringing with them a statue of a jade jaguar that will be loaned out to the museum."

"Wonderful! I'm happy to work with them."

"You're doing well with us, Mia. You're an excellent asset to the museum. I'll let you get back to work."

"Thanks very much."

The morning sped by with Mia working with Peter and Nancy on the antiquities they'd brought in from Tim's storage unit.

"These artifacts will need to be cleaned before we return them. Are we responsible for doing that?" Peter asked.

"I don't know that we're responsible, but it would be a good idea," Mia said. "We have to clean them to be able to examine them, so we may as well do it properly."

After lunch, Mia returned to her office to deal with paperwork.

Detective Martin called Mia at three-thirty. "Could you come by the station and check your statement?"

"Yes, I forgot to go there this morning. I'll be there shortly." Before leaving, Mia sent Luke a text that she was going to the police station and would see him there.

Mia grabbed a cab and hurried to the police station.

Detective Martin came out to meet her. "If you'll follow me."

He took Mia to an interview room and laid a file down on the table. "Can you read the statement and, if it's correct, sign it?"

Mia read through the document. The information was accurate, and she signed off on it.

She sat back and looked at Detective Martin, "Did you have any other questions?"

"No, your statement is very good."

Mia wondered if he'd answer any of her questions. Couldn't hurt to try. "Are they going to be released?"

"There will be a bail hearing. And it will be set high. So, I'm not sure they'll be out."

"Can you tell me what happens next?"

"We're going to continue to build the case against each of them. We aren't going to let them walk away with this."

"Who killed Tim?"

"Steve's saying it was Barbara. He admits to killing Cheryl; he says he was forced to. But that it was Barbara who poisoned Tim. She's not talking."

"How would she get cyanide? Isn't it a controlled substance?"

"Steve says she knew people who worked with it and was able to get it from them. She told Steve she mixed it in his whiskey. He complained of the taste, but she was drinking with him and told him it was excellent. He drank his glass quickly."

"I thought it took time to die of cyanide poisoning."

"She stayed with him. He lost consciousness, and she wanted to make sure he didn't regain it."

There was a knock on the door, and Detective Martin called out, "Come in."

Luke entered the room. "Everything all right?"

Detective Martin nodded. "Just getting Mia's signature on her statement and answering a few of her questions."

"Who was behind the threats I received?" Mia asked.

"Steve. He hired a courier to take the envelope to your condo and to your office. The photos were taken by a private investigator. And the threat you and Danielle received, he sent them both."

Mia shook her head. "Unbelievable. At least I know who did it."

"Ready to go?" Luke asked her.

"Yes. Thanks, Detective Martin, I appreciate you taking the time to talk with me."

"No problem."

Detective Martin walked them out to the back entrance. "Luke, I'll see you tomorrow. Mia, I hope we don't see each other again professionally."

Mia grinned. "Me too."

They arrived at Mia's and had walked in the door when Luke's phone rang. "I need to take this, it's my supervisor."

"I'll figure something out for dinner, okay?"

Luke nodded and headed for the office in Mia's second bedroom.

She was still looking through the fridge to figure out what to make for dinner when she heard Luke opening the bedroom door and finishing up his call. "That's excellent. Thanks. I appreciate the opportunity."

Mia looked up as he came into the kitchen. "What's up?"

Luke reached for her hand. "I have some news to share."

Mia's hand stiffened, and she took a deep breath. "Okay, what is it?"

"The head of AART has agreed to second me to work with the RCMP here in Canada. They're working on getting the paperwork sorted and are going to meet with the Commissioner and his executive team to hammer out the details. And the term they are looking at is for a year."

"Oh, my goodness! That's amazing news!" Mia threw her arms around Luke. "When will everything be finalized?"

"I'm not sure how long it'll take, but I know both AART and the RCMP want to get this done soon. I don't have a lot of details about the workload, but I know I'll be around for the next year. They've offered me a generous living allowance to find a place of my own, but I told them I'd let them know."

"You can turn that down. Unless you don't want to live here with me?" Mia wondered if he would want his own space.

"I can't think of anywhere else I'd rather be."

"This calls for a celebration!"

Acknowledgments

Thanks go to Patricia Middleton, beta reader extraordinaire. Thank you, my friend, for reading and providing such great feedback.

To my friends at Murder, They Write. Thanks for all the support!

To my family: Gary, Stephanie, Jay, Greg, Claire, and Mom, Thank You for being there for me. Stephanie, thanks for helping out with the behind-the-scenes communication teams and morning shows!

To the team at Level Best Books, Shawn Reilly Simmons and Deb Well. Thank you for all you do for us authors. You are much appreciated.

About the Author

Retired in Southern Ontario with her husband, Rose spends her days crafting mysteries featuring strong, smart women who use their resourcefulness to solve crimes. When she's not writing, she enjoys discovering the hidden gems of the region and indulging her lifelong curiosity.

AUTHOR WEBSITE:
  https://rosekerr.com/

SOCIAL MEDIA HANDLES:
  Facebook: https://www.facebook.com/RoseKerrAuthor
  Instagram: https://www.instagram.com/r.m.kerr/?hl=en
  Pinterest: https://ca.pinterest.com/RoseKerrauthor/

Also by Rose Kerr

Death at the Scottish Broch, A Mia Reid, Archaeologist, Mystery

Death on the Set, A Brenna Flynn Mystery

The Secret Ingredient: The Mystery Writers' Cookbook